AF264645

BORN TO LOSE

A Novel by

JOE VAN RHYN

Published by El Cid Publishing, Las Vegas, Nevada
7/26/2020

Paperback ISBN# 978-0-9986798-2-2
e-book ISBN# 978-0-9986798-3-5

The author may be contacted at joevanrhyn@cox.net

Additional information about the author can be found on his website: www.joevanrhyn.com or on Facebook @Joe Van Rhyn, Author.

I dedicate this book to my Mom and
Dad. Mom, for giving me an appreciation
for family and friends, and Dad for
teaching me that honesty and hard
work would take me a long way in life.

CHAPTER ONE
Graduation

Graduating from high school should be one of the happiest days in a young person's life, but losing a friend—your best friend, two days before will change that. Sarah Jean leaned against her locker. She adjusted the wooden crutches and found a new position for the ankle encased in yards of elastic bandage. "Just a bad sprain," the doctor said. "Best to keep your weight off of it until the swelling goes down.

The crowded hallway was quiet. Most of her classmates stood motionless, failing to raise their eyes to meet hers. She couldn't shake her paranoia. Did they blame her? Did those bewildered looks mask a collective feeling that she could have done more to prevent Deloris' death? *My God, I would have given anything if I could have been the one to die.* No one said a word. Most had their heads bowed, perhaps hoping anything they might say would be written on the floor. A few girls fiddled with the buttons on their gowns. Others primped their hair. Several boys stroked the tassels attached to their flat board caps. Everyone seemed lost.

Robbie, class president, football captain and the guy everyone looked up to, put a hand against the locker above Sarah's head. "How did this happen? I can't believe she's gone." His voice cracked mid-sentence.

"You, too?" Sarah slapped the metal door. The noise turned heads. "It was an accident. I couldn't stop it." She swiped tears off her cheeks. "I feel as bad as everyone."

Robbie drew back. "No one is blaming you. We all know how close the two of you were."

Her word *sorry* was barely audible.

"I just wanted to know if you're doing okay," he said.

Sarah drew a thin smile. A nod her only reply.

Noisy chatter filtered in from the gym through the double doors at the end of the hall.

"I think the whole town is out there," Sarah said.

Robbie cracked open one of the doors. "The bleachers are full. So are the chairs on the floor."

The crowd fell silent as the band teacher tapped his baton on the music stand. Heavy on horns and drums, a slow rendition of Pomp and Circumstance started unevenly with no two musicians on the same note.

"This is it guys. Let's line up." It was natural for Robbie to take charge. "Girls, remember, you move up one spot in line."

Sarah knew all his bravado was an effort to conceal an aching heart.

"I know this is tough," he said. "But let's smile, be strong, and do this for Deloris." Everyone shuffled into place. A couple of boys stepped forward and opened the doors.

The gym lights dimmed. The spotlight's brilliant blast illuminated the doorway. Robbie stiffened. He covered his mouth. His eyes glazed as his fingers twisted his lips.

Sarah tapped Robbie's leg with her crutch. "If you break down none of us will get through this," she said. "Come on, let's go. Remember. We're doing this for Deloris." Sarah extended the crutches and swung her bound foot into motion.

Robbie jumped to catch up. A short stutter-step put him in unison with her.

Everyone in the gym stood. Dozens of flash bulbs popped as Robbie and Sarah led the way. Applause erupted in a tremendous show of support and emotion. Sarah looked straight ahead. She felt her heart in her throat. *Focus on the music. Step to the beat.* Before making the turn and starting up the center aisle, Sarah glanced ahead. The stage seemed farther than she remembered from practice. Her underarms ached from muscling the wooden supports. Stealing a peek at the crowd revealed nothing but sad faces.

The gym had a festive look. Green and white crepe paper streamers decorated the walls, windows, and basketball hoops. She and Deloris spent days making the bows that hung above the doors. They also painted the large congratulatory paper banner that hung above the stage. Most of their efforts went unnoticed.

Halfway down the aisle, Robbie leaned her way. "Are you doing okay?"

"No," she whispered. "It feels like every eye in the building is glued on me."

"I know," he said. "They should have cancelled this thing and mailed us our diplomas."

"They can have mine—it'll just be a horrible reminder." Sarah paused when reaching the steps to the stage, unsure if she could navigate her way up.

In what must have looked like a carefully planned move. Robbie bent, hoisted her in his arms and proceeded up the stairs, crutches, and all.

Sarah gasped. She ran the gamut from surprise, to anger, to relief, as he eased her down, first to her good leg and then onto a chair. His unexpected chivalry brought a few chuckles as the rest of the graduates came up on stage.

Principal Chester Davis stepped to the podium and motioned for everyone to be seated. "Welcome to the 1947 Ely High School Graduation. "Before we begin, let's take a moment to remember the young lady who should have been here with us this evening—to celebrate this occasion. Many suggested we postpone graduation. We left the decision up to these young people assembled on the stage. They voted to proceed as scheduled, feeling Deloris would have wanted it that way. It was a tragic accident that took Deloris Johnson from us. Her loss will be felt for a long time. It's up to us…each in our own way…to bridge across our sorrow and move on." He then introduced the faculty and members of the school board.

"Move on?" Sarah whispered. *How do I move on when my heart has been ripped from my chest? How do I get past the anger—the guilt—of wondering if there was anything more I could have done—or didn't do?* She closed her eyes, hoping by some miracle, this was all a bad dream and when she opened them, her friend would be sitting on the stage next to her—just like at rehearsal. The disappointment hurt. Her lips quivered as she fought to hold back tears. Pulling a hanky from her sleeve, the tassel of black string fell and swung past her face. The silky strands reminded her how much Deloris had looked forward to graduating.

Sarah wiped her cheeks and straightened the black robe that covered her knees. She looked at the scuffed loafer on her one good foot and the ugly bandage on the other, instead of the new two-inch heels her mom bought for the occasion. The tan elastic windings covered her limb from toes to just below her knee. *How is it fair that she dies, and I get nothing more than a few scratches and a sprained ankle?*

When Chester finished introducing the local dignitaries, he began enumerating the many accomplishments of the class. Most were things that happened before Sarah arrived. She'd only been in Ely for two years. Her mind drifted to the events of the past two days.

Wednesday had begun like any other. Well, not quite, the entire student body struggled to contain its excitement. The decibel level of noise and chatter in the hallways far exceeded anything resembling normal. With graduation looming on Friday, seniors were being turned loose after second period. Sarah and Dee planned to stay for one last meal in the school cafeteria. The menu included their favorites, Spanish hamburgers, Cole slaw and rabbit food. They'd eat, grab the early school bus to Dee's place, saddle the horses, and ride into Bristlecone Canyon. Neither could think of a better way to spend the day.

It felt strange, but Sarah could recall every word and visualized every facial expression, and every gesture her friend made. It was like seeing the entire day replayed in her mind…in living color.

At lunch, Dee shared her fears that Robbie would tire of waiting for her to complete college in Reno. "He'll probably latch onto someone else," she lamented. "Maybe take up with Lucy Barry."

"What makes you say that?" Sarah asked.

"He's not going to wait four years to pop my cherry, when he can get all he wants from 'Loosey-Goosey Lucille.'"

"Dee!" Sarah gasped. "You shouldn't say things like that. You don't know…"

"Sarah Jean, you're such a ninny," Dee said, as she stabbed her fork into her friend's cole slaw. "It's all over school. The last time Lucy said 'no' to a guy was in eighth grade."

Sarah put her cup of slaw on Dee's tray. "I prefer to give her the benefit of the doubt."

Dee threw down her fork. "Robbie could be jabbing Lucy right here on this table, and you'd want a signed affidavit from both parties, attesting to the event."

"I wish you wouldn't talk that way," Sarah whispered. "I certainly wouldn't want people saying things like that about you—or me, for heaven's sake."

"I'm sorry." Dee buried her face in her hands. "I've been so looking forward to graduating, getting out of this town, and now that it's here…" she took a deep breath, "I'm just so—all mixed up."

Sarah pushed her tray to the center of the table. "Maybe you should give Robbie a chance to make up his own mind on whether he'll wait for you."

"It doesn't matter, my dream is to get my degree in criminal justice, move to Washington D.C. and work for the FBI. I won't let anything—or anyone get in my way."

Sarah laughed. "Who knows, you may find someone to take Robbie's place."

Her friend waved off the thought. "Regardless, college is my ticket out of this town. I want to travel. See the world. Make a big splash with my life."

Dee stole a celery stick from Sarah's tray. "How about you and Freddy Stone? You still got the hots for him?"

Sarah's red face clashed with her chestnut hair. "We only had the one date…for homecoming."

"They say he's a good kisser," Dee teased. Then dancing her fingers in Sarah's face, "Did you have trouble with his, you know, Roman hands and Russian fingers?"

Sarah threw her carrot stick, hitting her friend in the chest. "Dee Johnson, I can't believe you said that."

Sticking the carrot in her mouth like a pretend cigar, Dee mimicked an interrogating officer. Speaking in a gravelly voice, she asked. "So, tell me lady, did this Freddy character feel you up?"

"What?" Sarah jumped to her feet.

Dee did the same and took off running with Sarah in close pursuit. Out of the cafeteria and down the hall, the two pushed their way past groups of people before bursting out the front door. The chase ended across the street in the park, as both girls fell to the grass. Laughing and coughing, they tried to catch their breath.

Sarah rolled on her back. "He tried," she giggled. "But I stopped him," Both girls held their stomachs as they continued to choke on their laughter.

Dee wiped tears from her cheeks. Looking at Sarah, she smiled. "No matter what happens, let's always be friends."

"Always," Sarah repeated. "C'mon, we have to catch the bus if we want to go riding."

Concluding his remarks, the principal turned. "And now, may I present our co-valedictorian, Sarah Jean Connolly." He stepped forward to offer his help.

Sarah raised her hand. "I'm okay." Bending, she retrieved the crutches from under her chair.

Everyone in the auditorium stood and applauded as Sarah rose and positioned the crutches under her arms. The clapping continued as she made her way to the center of the stage. Keeping one crutch planted, she leaned the other against the side of the podium. Her mom, dad, and sister Nora were seated in the front row. They continued to clap while others began taking their seats.

Sarah nodded to her family. Then, reaching inside her robe she pulled the sheaf of papers tucked in the waist tie of her dress. She laid them on the podium and smoothed out the creases. After a few moments to compose herself, she looked up and declared. "Delores Belle Johnson was my best friend, and I'm going to miss her." Sarah found a new position for her injured foot and steadied herself against the wooden stand. "I thought Deloris would be the one friend I would have my whole life, but now she's gone."

The lump in her throat forced her to swallow. Her tongue searched for moisture in her mouth. "When I…" She stopped. Her hand curled into a fist. *Damn it! If you don't keep going, you'll never get through this.* Her sweaty hands gripped the edges of the speaker's stand. "When I moved to Ely two years ago, Delores Johnson was the first person I met. She introduced herself as Dee. We were both Aries and hit it off right away. I'd missed a lot of classes back in Indiana and had a lot of catching up to do. Dee took me under her wing and guided me through those first scary days. She tutored me for hours, helping me get up to speed in every class. We studied together, ate lunch together, and on weekends we'd hang out at her place or mine. Dee taught me how to ride a horse. Her name was Jubilee. I called her Jubi."

"I recall my first encounter with her. Standing on the bottom rail of the fence and leaning over the top, I held out a handful of alfalfa, hoping to entice the chestnut mare to come. My heart raced as the horse pulled the hay from my hand. With the other hand I stroked her nose as she continued to gently take the last of the greenery. Jubilee had been Dee's horse until her dad brought home Samson, a black stallion, a good two or three hands taller than the mare. Deloris liked Sam's spirit and unpredictability.

Dee and I spent hours riding above the tree line behind her family's ranch. Jubi, as I called her, was perfect for me, a quiet horse that needed coaxing to move beyond walking. It took me a while to let go of the horn and move with the horse. Galloping came as a surprise when Dee cracked Jubilee on the rump. Dee laughed as she and Samson came charging alongside. At first, it scared me to death, but I remembered jabbering like a magpie, telling mom and dad about my first galloping experience.

Looking out at the audience, Sarah realized she was jabbering now. She turned and pointed to the empty chair. "Delores and I were supposed to be co-valedictorians. It was she who dispelled the controversy of how my grades from Indiana were integrated with those from here. I would have been happy to be Salutatorian, but Dee insisted we share the top honor."

"Last weekend we got together and wrote our speeches. Tonight, I'm going to read hers." Sarah smoothed the paper and cleared her throat.

In her opening sentences, Delores thanked Principal Davis, mentioned a few of the faculty by name, and acknowledged members of the school board. She congratulated her fellow graduates and added a special thanks to the people in the audience for coming. Sarah took another deep breath before taking on the heart of Dee's speech.

My fellow graduates, as we finished our last years of school, America began the task of rebuilding a peacetime economy. From 1918 to 1945, two World Wars cost our country many of its finest young men, including men from Ely, and our neighboring towns of Ruth and McGill. We lost fathers, sons, uncles, and friends. We will always remember their sacrifices, but we must also honor them by making sure the country they fought and died for, begins to prosper. It is up to us, the next generation, to make that happen. For many of us, as we go on to college or enter the workforce, we will be expected to bring new ideas and new energy to move the country forward.

Remember when we were studying about the battles of the Civil War? If the flag bearer went down, another soldier would grab the banner and lead the charge. We too must seize the moment. It is our turn to pick up the flag, join with other graduates across the nation and build a strong America.

As we go our separate ways and follow wherever our star of destiny leads, let us not forget where we came from, nor the friends we've made here at this great school. Although none of us is guaranteed a tomorrow, let's look to the future with hope and a desire to make the world a better place for everyone.

Sarah rolled up the paper and bowed her head. The room was silent. Then, one person clapped, and soon everyone joined in. The graduates huddled around Sarah as if believing that holding onto one another would ease the grief each one felt. Dee was everyone's favorite. Many of them had gone the full twelve years of school with her. She'd held every class office, was elected cheerleading captain and voted homecoming queen. Everyone in Ely knew her. People young and old stood, cried, and hugged each other. The town was heartbroken.

Principal Davis was finally able to get people back to their seats. At most graduations, you could count on someone making a foolish remark or gesture when receiving their diploma. No one did. As their names were called, thirty-three graduates solemnly walked across the stage, shook hands with the principal and the president of the school board, before accepting their diplomas. Sarah remained seated. Physically and emotionally drained, she knew by accepting her diploma it would seal her friend's fate in this moment of time. There'd be no miracles. No coming back to life.

Seeing the girl slumped in her chair, Prof. Davis motioned for the board secretary to read Sarah's name again. This time Sarah rose and hobbled on one crutch across the stage. She got a hug from Chester and a pat on the back from the school board president before collecting her diploma. There was one green leather clad folder left on the table. The one Dee would have accepted.

"Can I have that one, too?" Sarah said. "I'd like to be the one to give it to her mom and dad."

Chester handed it to her. "That would be a wonderful thing to do."

CHAPTER TWO

A Night at the Movies?

The band started unevenly. The trombones and drums came in a half beat ahead of the woodwinds. The graduates stood and descended the stage in pairs. No one seemed particularly interested in stepping to the music. Sarah refused Robbie's offer for a lift. Going crutches first and good leg second, she navigated the steps one at a time. Rising, the audience applauded as the young people hurried up the aisle. No one bothered to walk to the music.

Congregating in the courtyard outside the gymnasium, the graduates began shedding their robes. There wasn't the frivolity one would expect on an occasion like this. Girls with tear-streaked cheeks hugged one another. Boys patted each other on the back, as they waited to be joined by friends and family. People filed by, said little, and let a nod and a smile express their feelings. The students nodded to show their appreciation.

Nora reached Sarah first. "You did a wonderful job," she whispered, in the girl's ear. "We're so proud of you."

The Jensen's waited their turn to congratulate their foster child. John was not an overly expressive person. He seldom showed affection, but he too hugged Sarah as any true father would.

Harriet seemed more concerned about Sarah's foot. "Is it hurting? I've got some aspirin in my purse. Would you like a couple?"

The girl waved off the suggestion. "The foot is fine."

"Why don't you sit for a minute?" her mom said, pointing to a nearby bench.

Sarah stood her ground. "Mom, I'm okay." She repositioned the crutches and headed towards a group of students. "I'll be right back. I want to say goodbye to my friends."

"It's hard to believe," Harriet said, looking directly at Nora. "I know there is no blood between you two, but she's just as stubborn as you are."

Nora put her arm around her mom's shoulders. "It's because you raised us. We're both a product of your upbringing."

John snorted a chuckle.

Harriet swatted his arm. "You think that's funny? Am I to blame for everything?"

"Mom, that was a compliment. Look what a fine young lady Sarah's grown to be. That's a tribute to you. When I brought her home, she was a frightened child, unsure of herself. You've made her into a strong young woman."

"And she'll need to be, if she's ever going to get over losing Dee." Harriet pulled a hanky from her purse. "Those two girls were so close. They could have been twins."

Nora watched Sarah hug and speak to the other grads, moving effortlessly between the boys and the girls. "That's the one thing I regret."

"What's that?" Her mom asked, not taking her eyes off Sarah.

"Not being here to witness her beautiful transformation." Nora smiled and hugged her father. "Thank you for being a great dad. You and Mom did a wonderful job raising her."

John drew back uneasy with Nora's embrace. His face reddened. "The Sheriff is sending a couple of us into the canyon tomorrow to bring out Samson. We can't just leave him up there."

"It's too bad they had to shoot him." Harriet wiped her nose and threw her hanky into her purse.

"Everyone is going over to the drug store," Sarah said, as she glided up on her crutches. "Can I go with them?"

"Do you think you should?" Harriet protested. "What about your foot?"

"Her foot is fine, Mom." Nora said. Then addressing the girl, "Go and enjoy your friends. Call when you're ready. Dad or I will come to pick you up."

Sarah turned and crutched off before Nora finished her sentence.

Retreating to the car, John opened the door for his wife. Nora climbed in back.

"Do you think it was wise to let her go?" Harriet asked, settling in the passenger seat.

"It will do her good to be among friends," Nora said. "They're all struggling with Dee's death."

"She still will have to get through the funeral on Tuesday." John said as he got in and started the engine.

It was quiet the rest of the way home.

The recent grads packed the Economy Drug Store's soda fountain. The mood had changed dramatically. Kids were downing bottles of Cokes, spooning the cherries off hot fudge sundaes, and licking ice cream cones. They laughed, congratulated one another, and talked about what they planned to do now that they were "set free."

Sarah slid the crutches under the table and claimed a seat in the corner booth.

A flush of emotion swept over her and tears threatened. She missed her friend. If Dee was here, there'd be a crush of kids hovering around. Her happy-go-lucky spirit made her the backbone of the class. The one everyone counted on to lend a hand or bolster spirits. In the school annual, she was voted "the one destined to do great things."

Sarah crossed her arms on the table and buried her face in the crux. Principle Davis's words about *moving on* swirled in her head. This is going to be hard. She missed Dee so much already.

"Mind if I sit?" The words came out of nowhere. Without waiting for an answer, Robbie slid in next to her.

This isn't right. She slid closer to the wall. He moved too, and in doing so, his leg brushed against hers. The wall blocked her escape. *If Dee were here, she'd have a fit.* Sarah stared straight ahead, not offering any encouragement.

Robbie swirled his hands on the table. "I can't believe she's gone."

"Me neither," Sarah sniffled and wiped her nose with her hand.

"You and Dee were such good friends. Did she ever say anything…about me?"

"All the time. The two of you have been going together since second grade. You were the perfect couple."

"Perfect? That's probably what it looked like to everyone."

What is he trying to say? "My God, the two of you were like the king and queen of the school. I thought you two had plans. She mentioned, once she had her degree, you might get married."

"That's what I thought but she'd never commit to anything. Lately, I got the feeling that was no longer a part of the plan. Is that all she said?"

It would be too cruel to tell him of their lunchroom conversation. Anything about Lucille Barry was better left unsaid. "Just that she loved you." Lying felt ugly, but the truth solved nothing and would surely have left a lasting hurt.

Robbie shifted to face her. "What about you? What are your plans?"

Sarah shrugged. "I'll probably head to Chicago to become a nurse like my sister, Nora. And You?"

"My Dad can get me a decent job at the mine…if I want it. Dee always talked about wanting to get out of Ely. Maybe I need to do the same. I do have a scholarship offer."

"For football?"

"Yeah, a coach from Arizona State said they'd love having me play linebacker for them." He took hold of her hand. "Are you leaving right away, or are you staying the summer?"

She felt a gently squeeze. "I haven't decided. Why?"

I thought we could take in a movie sometime, or maybe go riding?"

"What! I can't do…" Sarah pulled her hand free and reached for her crutches. "My foot is beginning to really hurt. I'm going to call my folks to come and pick me up."

"Hey, I'm sorry…I didn't mean…you don't have to call, I can give you a ride." He slid out, pulled out the crutches, and offered his hand to help her out of the booth.

"Don't you want to stay?" She took the crutches. "I'm sure the guys would love to talk to you."

"Nah, I'm good. It's been a long day."

Sarah was out of excuses. "Are you sure this won't be any trouble?"

"It would be my pleasure."

It was a beautiful June night, unseasonably warm. The night sky provided a theater of twinkling lights. Robbie had borrowed his dad's 1947 Studebaker Champion. It still had the new car smell. As a show of good manners, he held the door while Sarah slid onto the front seat. He waited for her to bring the crutches next to her before closing the door. Sarah rolled down her window and filled her lungs with the sweet smell of freshly mown grass. She stared at the mountains that held Bristlecone Canyon and thought about Dee.

Jumping behind the wheel, Robbie inserted the key, hit the starter button, pulled the gear shifter into low and eased off the clutch. The narrow-nosed sedan pulled away from the curb and headed down the main drag.

When they passed Oak Street, Sarah shot him a puzzled look. "You should've turned there."

Robbie grinned "I thought we'd take a little ride."

Sarah felt the heat of anger but kept her cool. "Maybe some other time. I'd really like to go home. My foot is killing me." Her words froze the air.

"Sorry, I just thought…" Robbie must have felt the chill of her words. He flipped on the blinkers and turned down the next street. Pulling in front of Sarah's place, he shut down the engine and turned off the lights. He swung his arm over the back of her seat. Before he could make another move, Sarah open her door, grabbed the crutches, and jumped to her feet. "Thanks for the ride," she said, slamming the door close and hurriedly moving toward the house.

"I'll call you sometime," Robbie yelled.

Sarah waved one of the crutches. "Don't bother," she mumbled to herself.

The porch light came on and Nora and Mrs. Jensen stepped through the opened doorway. "Who was that?" Nora asked. "Why didn't you invite him in?"

"Nobody." Sarah said curtly as she maneuvered her way onto the porch.

Nora sent a puzzled look to her mom before reaching out to her sister. "Are you hungry? Would you like something to eat?"

"No thanks. I'm going to my room. My arms can't take any more of these stupid crutches." Once in her room, she closed the door, flung the crutches aside and flopped face down on the bed. At first the tears came slowly, but as the memories of Dee flooded her mind, she could no longer contain her emotions. Her chest heaved with each sob. "Why her? Why just her?"

Nora knocked softly. "Sarah Jean, may I come in?" Getting no answer, she cracked open the door and heard the sobbing. Without speaking, she sat on the edge of the bed and stroked the girl's hair.

"It's all my fault." Sarah wailed, before wiping her nose on her sleeve. "I was the one that wanted to go riding. She'd still be alive if it wasn't for me."

Nora pulled the girl into her arms. Sarah willingly gave into the embrace and continued to cry. Her warm tears soaked Nora's blouse. "It was an accident. You shouldn't blame yourself."

Sarah pushed away. "It all happened so fast, there wasn't anything I could do. Why did it have to be her? Why didn't God take us both? Why just her?"

"None of us knows what God has in store for us." Nora took a handkerchief from her pocket and wiped the girl's cheeks. "Maybe he wants you to do something special with your life." Nora felt her own tears coming. She too, had plenty of unanswered questions for God, most of them dating back to the war, but her struggles could wait. Right now, it was Sarah who needed help getting past this tragedy.

"Why am I always the one left behind? He took my father, my mother, and now my best friend. Why is God punishing me?"

"None of this is your fault. God is not blaming you or trying to punish you. I know it's hard, but we have to accept this as his will." Nora lost count of the times she asked God these same questions but hoped Sarah would find solace in her words.

John poked his head into the room and saw the watery eyes and tear streaked cheeks. "Are you girls okay?"

Nora nodded. "We're fine. We needed a good cry."

"I just got off the phone with the office. The sheriff wants to know if you'd feel up to going to the canyon tomorrow and walk us through what happened?"

"You've got to be kidding," Nora shrieked. "How much does he think this girl can take?"

"There's been a death, we have to make a report."

Nora jumped to her feet. "You tell him he can take his report and…"

Sarah grabbed Nora's arm. "It's okay, I'll go." She wiped her eyes with her hands. "It might help me deal with what happened by retracing the path we took."

John smiled. "I'll let the sheriff know."

Nora closed the door. "Are you sure you want to do that?"

"It's fine. I'd have to do it some time. It'll be best to get it over with." She slid off the bed. Balancing on her good foot, she unbuttoned her skirt and let it fall. Nora knelt and helped get it from under the cast. She laid the skirt over the chair. Then, taking the nightgown from the hook on the back of the door, she waited for Sarah to lift off her sweater and remove her bra. She handed Sarah the gown and hung the rest of her clothes over the skirt. Nora pulled back the covers. "A good night sleep will do us all some good."

Sarah sat, swung her casted foot onto the bed, and laid her head on the pillow.

Covering Sarah's slender body, Nora felt inadequate for not being able to take away some of the hurt the girl was feeling. "Are you sure, you're okay?"

"I'm fine, I just need sleep."

"I smell coffee. I'll have a cup," Nora said, walking into the kitchen.

Harriet had just placed a plate of cookies on the table. "I can make you a sandwich if you want. Is Sarah going to be alright?"

"Cookies and coffee will be fine." Nora poured herself a cup and sat at the table. She took a cookie, dunked it in the coffee, and took a bite. "When I made plans to come for Sarah's graduation, I certainly never expected anything like this. The poor girl is heartbroken."

"The whole town is," John said. "Losing Deloris affects us all."

"And just two days before graduation." Harriet set a cup in front of John.

"You've both done a terrific job of raising Sarah," Nora said. "I'm sorry now I wasn't here to experience more of her school years. She grown up so fast."

Harriet poured coffee in John's cup and some in her own. "You've had some growing up yourself. It's taken this long for you to get your own life in order. The war really had you messed up."

Nora cradled her cup in both hands. "I know," she said between sips.

"Have you and Duke talked any more about getting married?" her mother asked. "Just living together must have the people in Pine Lake talking. They certainly would be around here."

"It's none of their business," John said.

Nora put her hand on his. "We're still talking about it." Nora took a sip of coffee. "Has everything been settled with Indiana?"

"Yes, we were back there this summer," Harriet said. "The judge gave us full custody. We brought back Sarah's money from her father's GI insurance and put it in the bank. Of course, she'll soon turn eighteen, and none of that will matter. She'll be able to make her own decisions."

Nora picked up her cup. "I'm going to sit on the porch. It's a beautiful night. You don't get many June nights as nice as this."

"You go ahead, dear, I'm going to shower and say my prayers. Heaven knows we are going to need His help to get through all of this." She looked at John. "Are you going with her?"

"Nah, I'm going to catch the news and come to bed." He walked into the next room and turned on the radio.

Nora stepped onto the porch and plopped into a wicker rocker. The heavens sparkled in a cloudless sky. A full moon crested Murry Peak. She thought about the tortured young girl inside and remembered the bus ride from Chicago to Ely, two years earlier. She smiled as she recalled buying them each a pair of sunglasses to help conceal their identity, thinking the law was after them. She remembered how Sarah, tried to put on a brave front, but had to be wondering what was going to happen to her. God, how much can one person endure? Her father dies in the war. cancer claims her mother, and then the whole episode with her Uncle Bob and Aunt Betty. That should have been more than enough. But now, she loses her best friend. Nora took a drink of coffee, shut her eyes and recalled the night they met, at the bus station in Indianapolis.

Chapter Three

A Pinky Promise

Sarah tried to shift her position in bed. The bandaged ankle made it difficult. Her mind would not rest. The same thought kept recurring. Why did she make such a big deal about going for a ride? Dee didn't seem enthused, and they would have all summer to ride. They could have hung out at school, signed yearbooks, or had a soda and listened to the jukebox at the drug store. What was so damned important about taking a stupid ride? Nothing. No good reason. Sarah wished over and over they had done something else. She dreaded tomorrow.

The memories of that day were hers, and hers alone. They were private, known only to the two of them. Each word spoken, each facial expression, each moment of their time together was indelibly etched in Sarah's mind. She still couldn't fathom how, on a day she and Dee shared so many thoughts and feelings about themselves, and what the future had in store for them, it could have ended, the way it did.

Yes, she'd go with the sheriff. She'd give them every detail of the final few minutes of Dee Johnson's life. They'd get what they needed for their almighty important report. What they wouldn't get, is everything that happened up until those tragic last minutes. Those memories would never be shared.

She closed her eyes as the fateful day came back to her, one snapshot at a time. They had made plans to spend the night at Dee's.

The school bus had dropped them off at the Johnson driveway a little after two. The pair were in no hurry on the mile walk to the ranch house. Normally they'd push and shove, laugh and joke about things that happened at school. Sarah sensed things were different. Dee seemed within herself, troubled. She barely said a word on the bus. Sarah prodded her. "Hey girl, why so glum? We're free. We're through with school. We have our whole lives ahead of us." What a lie that turned out to be.

Dee checked the mailbox. "I guess we beat the mailman."

"We're here way earlier than usual." Sarah said.

Dee pulled on the hem of her sweater and gave an impish smile. "Did you ever go all the way with a boy?"

"What?"

"Only teasing." Dee turned and walked backwards. "Do you think maybe Lucy has the right idea? Do you ever lie in bed and think about doing it with a guy?"

"No, of course not." The lie caused Sarah to look away.

"I do. Don't you ever wonder what it would be like to lie naked next to some handsome cowboy?"

"Deloris!" Sarah feigned shocked. "You shouldn't…"

Dee put both hands on Sarah's chest, cupping her breasts. "Having the guy's hands all over you, feeling your breasts, touching between your legs and putting his business inside you."

Sarah pushed Dee away. "What's gotten into you?" She said, half serious, while trying to hold back a laugh. "I've never heard you talk this way."

"Aw, come on, tell me the truth. Did you and Freddy Stone do it after the Homecoming dance? Did you?" Seeing Sarah come at her, Dee laughed, turned, and ran up the road with Sarah in hot pursuit.

Sarah caught hold of Dee's shirt just as she stumbled and fell into the ditch, pulling Sarah down on top of her. They both laughed so hard tears rolled down their cheeks. Sarah rolled to the side. Breathing heavily from the exertion, she felt the warmth of the afternoon sun on her face, her chest, and her legs. She unbuttoned the top of her shirt allowing the moisture from her body to escape, along with the sweet aroma of lilac perfume.

"Deloris Belle, sometimes you come up with the darnest things to talk about." There was a long pause. "Did *you* ever do it?" She asked.

Dee rolled on her stomach. "Came close."

"Close?" Sarah choked as she blurted the word.

Dee let a long pause smolder. "It was after the spring concert," She hesitated, as if deciding if she should continue. "Harold Gregory gave me a ride home."

"The football player from Ruth?"

"He also has a beautiful baritone singing voice." Dee got to her knees and looked up the road. "He stopped his car right about there." Dee pointed to a large bush. "It's in the gully, so the folks wouldn't have been able to see us from the house."

Sarah sat up. "What did you do?"

Dee came down and lay on her side. "At first we just kissed." She brought her head up, cocked her elbow and rested her chin in her hand. "You know what a French kiss is, don't you?"

"With the tongue, right? Sarah laid on her side and mimicked her friend.

"From there, he started squeezing on my breasts."

"You let him?"

Dee closed her eyes, the corners of her mouth turned upward. "I didn't want him to stop. It made me feel like…a woman. Then, before I knew it, he'd unbuttoned my blouse and was trying to reach around to unhook my brassiere. I had to help him."

"You helped him?"

"I didn't want him to rip the darned thing. How would I explain that to my mother?"

Sarah giggled. "I can't believe you helped him?"

"Have you looked at his hands? They're huge. He cupped my whole breast in it."

"How did that feel?"

"Scratchy." He works part-time at the mine. At first, it hurt when he'd rub those rough calloused hands across my nipples. But at the same time, I felt this all-over warm sensation. It was as if my body was on fire." As if reliving the moment, Dee's chest expanded, and Sarah felt her friend's warm, slow, exhaled breath on her face. Her own breathing came in uneven mini gulps. She wanted to hear more but resisted the urge to ask.

Dee fell over on her back. "God, when he put his hand under my skirt, I froze. My mind was yelling, 'Stop him' while my body yearned for his touch. His hand moved up my thigh. When his fingers started probing, first on the outside, and then inside my underwear, I thought I was going to explode." She covered her eyes with her hands. "It was terrible—no, delightful."

Sarah's heart danced the conga in her chest. "Was that it?"

"Hardly." Dee sat up, turned and sat on her knees. "He loosened his belt and unzipped his pants. I didn't know what was coming next. He took my hand and put it around his business. It was hard and throbbing. With his hand over mine he stroked it up and down. Suddenly, my hand's wet and he's squirming around. For a moment, I thought he was having a heart attack. The next thing I know he's lying back against the seat with this big smile on his face.

"Oh my Gosh, was—'"

Impishly, Dee grinned. "That was pretty much the end of it. That wet stuff is what makes babies." Dee stood up and pulled Sarah to her feet. "You have to promise me you'll never breathe a word of this to anyone."

"I promise," Sarah said, as they both began walking up the road. "Did you ever go out with him after that?"

"He asked a couple of times, but I said no. I don't want no babies. But the truth is, I didn't think I'd have the will power to keep him from going all the way. I don't want to lose my cherry in the back seat of some car.

Sarah kicked the dirt as they continued their trek to the house. "I didn't get that far."

Dee caught up to her friend. "What are you telling me? You and Freddy? Homecoming?"

Sarah blushed. "He *is* a great kisser."

Dee used a hand jester to coax Sarah. "Come on, I want all the juicy details."

"They pale compared to you and Harold. I was wearing slacks and a heavy sweater. He never got inside my clothes. It also didn't help to be parked in front of the house. His kisses were like Robbie's, first it was just lips, and then he sent his tongue deep into my mouth. I almost gagged."

"Isn't that the truth." Dee laughed? "Why do they think that's so romantic? Did he feel you up?"

"He squeezed my breast, and then his hand slipped between my legs. I don't know where things would have gone from there. Mom flicked the porch light on and off. That was end of story."

"That's it, just a few squeezes?"

Sarah pushed Dee. "You have to promise me you won't say a word about it."

"You don't even have to go to confession for that little bit—unless you enjoyed it. Did you enjoy it?" Dee giggled and danced in front of Sarah. "Oh look, you're blushing. You did enjoy it, didn't you?"

Sarah chased after Dee grabbing hold of her belt. "C'mon, say it. Promise me you won't tell anyone."

Dee smiled and put a hand on Sarah's shoulder. "I'll never tell a soul."

The Johnson house sat just below the tree line. It was a rustic looking log house with a porch that stretched the full length of the front. The railings and post were logs taken from young trees, with the bark removed and made smooth with a draw shave. Smoke rose from the large field-stone fireplace that extended from the left side. Wicker chairs and a bench swing hanging from the ceiling, adorned the porch. The whole setting would have made a fine Currier & Ives print.

Dee climbed the three steps and plopped down on the swing. Sarah took a seat on the railing. "I don't want to be stuck here in Ely raising babies," Dee said. "I want more out of life. What about you?"

Sarah nodded. "I'm thinking of becoming a nurse like Nora. A family friend, Gladys Iverson, is the head nurse at Chicago General Hospital."

"I'm going to get my degree from Reno and then it's off to Washington," Dee said. "I hope to get a job with the FBI, or maybe with the State Department. It would be fun to travel to far off places."

Sarah jumped off the railing and grabbed a seat on the swing. "They need nurses in some of the poorer countries. Maybe we could travel together. You could help in the government and I could minister to the sick."

Dee tickled Sarah. "And maybe we could share the Nobel Peace Prize—just like being co-valedictorians."

Sarah jumped off the swing to escape Dee's attack. "C'mon, let's go for a ride."

Dee hung back. "I don't feel like riding."

"Don't be an old poop. C'mon, it will be fun."

Nora turned on the light. "Are you okay,"

Sarah faked waking. She squinted into the light. "Yeah, I'm fine."

"You know, you don't have to go to the canyon, you can give your statement right here at the house and let them figure out the details."

"No, it's best if everyone knows exactly what happened."

"People think they have to know everything." Nora said, as she flicked off the light. "Good night, I'll see you in the morning."

"Good night." *That may be true, but they're never going to know everything.*

CHAPTER FOUR

Returning to the Canyon

"Good morning," Sarah said, as she shuffled into the kitchen. Nora swung around on her stool. John took his face out of the morning paper long enough to give the young girl an inquisitive smile.

Her mom quickly pulled her hands out of the sink and toweled them dry. "Good morning, Sweetie. How's your foot?"

"The foot is fine. It's these stupid crutches, they're nothing but a nuisance."

"Are you hungry? What can I fix you? Cereal? Oatmeal? How about some scrambled eggs?"

"Toast will be fine," Sarah said, leaning the wooden supports against the counter.

"Toast is not enough. You've hardly eaten a thing in two days. You need to put something in your stomach. Your father had eggs."

"I'm not that hungry. Toast will be *fine.*"

Harriet lit the burner and slid the frying pan over the flame.

"Mom-m-m." Sarah rolled her eyes.

Nora dunked a cookie in her coffee and took a bite. "Don't fight it," she whispered. "Eggs and toast will be good for you." Having grown up in this house, Nora learned there are times when it's useless to argue a point—and now seemed to be one of them.

Sarah stuck her tongue in her sister's direction.

Nora, trying to hold back a chuckle, choked, and spit coffee and a piece of the cookie into her hand.

Harriet shot a puzzled look at the girls. "What's going on between you two?"

John, no doubt sensing a war of wills was about to erupt, got up from his chair and gulped down the last swig of coffee. "I've got to run." He gave Harriet a peck on the cheek and patted both girls on the top of their heads. Addressing Sarah, he said, "I'll call to let you know when we'll be heading up to the Johnson's place. I'll swing by to pick you up."

Sarah nodded.

"Want some juice?" Harriet didn't wait for an answer. She poured some in a glass and set it in front of Sarah. "How do you want your eggs?"

Sarah shook her head. "Mom. Please. No eggs. Just toast and peanut butter."

Harriet turned off the stove and clanged the frying pan on the sink. "Toast and peanut butter are not a proper breakfast. Don't blame me if you get sick."

Nora choked again.

"I won't get sick," Sarah argued. "Maybe I'll eat something more, later."

Harriet rinsed the frying pan. "I was just trying to help," she muttered under her breath.

Nora took a bite of her cookie. Leaning forward she searched to make eye contact with Sarah. "Are you feeling better?"

"I couldn't get to sleep," Sarah said. "Too many thoughts about Dee. She had her whole life planned—go to Washington—work for the FBI. She desperately wanted to make something of herself." Sarah bowed her head. "So much for having dreams."

Nora stroked the girl's hair.

"It was terrible." Sarah sniveled. "I keep seeing her crushed body wedged between the rocks.

"Seeing death is never easy, Nora said. "I watched young soldiers die horrible deaths in the war. I still struggled to understand God's plan about who lives and who dies.

Harriet handed Sarah a hanky. "Here Sweetie, wipe your nose."

"Mom please, leave her be," Nora pleaded. "She needs to let it out."

"I know that, but she has snot coming out of her nose."

Sarah raised her head. A long string of mucus hung from her nose. She choked, laughing and crying at the same time. The women all laughed together.

Sarah blew her nose and wiped her eyes. "I'll never have another friend like her. I miss her so much, already."

"You'll make new friends," Nora said. "But no one has to take Dee's place. She'll always be with you in the wonderful memories you have of her. You will cherish the things you did together, for the rest of your life. Let Dee be your inspiration to do something with your life."

"Maybe I will," Sarah said, blowing her nose one more time. "Dee would have liked that."

Sarah was waiting on the porch when John drove up.

"Are you sure you want to do this?" her dad asked, as he helped her into the car.

"It's okay. I'll probably cry, but people need to know what happened."

John put the crutches in the back seat and got behind the wheel. "One good thing, Dee's dad took his tractor, dragged Samson out of there, and buried him in the field. So, you won't have to deal with seeing him."

"I thought about that," Sarah said. "Everyone is thinking about Dee, but the poor horse died, too."

Her dad put the car in gear and drove off.

CHAPTER FIVE

It was Supposed to be a Fun Afternoon Ride

The sheriff and another deputy were already at the ranch. Sheriff Blanchard was short, not even as tall as Sarah. The deputy stood a head and a half taller. The sheriff carried his weight around his mid-section, the other was as skinny as a beanstalk. Both looked to be in their middle forties, and in street clothes they resembled the cartoon characters, Mutt and Jeff. They'd already unloaded the horses, had them saddled, and tied to the fence.

Dee's dad was there, too. Earl Johnson was tall and had the angular body of a hard-working rancher. His deep tan and sandy blond hair added to his rugged good looks. He was clad in typical ranch attire, levi's, western shirt, Stetson hat and boots. He came to the car, helped Sarah out and gave her a big hug. "Are you sure you can do this? I can take the boys up there if it's too much for you?"

She adjusted the crutches. "But you weren't there. They'll want to know how it all happened. I'm the only one who knows."

Sarah made her way to the corral and unlatched the gate. Stepping inside, she leaned the crutches against the fence. She whistled and snapped her fingers. A chestnut mare sauntered over.

"Let me get that for you," Mister Johnson offered.

"I can do it," she said, as the men gathered to watch. Sarah, balancing on her good foot, pulled the bridle off the fence. She pushed the bit into Jubilee's mouth, put the leather headpiece over his ears and swung the reins around the fence board. Johnson grabbed the Indian design saddle blanket and placed it on the horse's back. He reached for the saddle.

Sarah stepped in his way. "I can do that." She pulled the saddle off the fence and threw it onto the horse's back. Losing her balance, she fell against the fence. All three men took a step forward. "Don't," she commanded, holding up her hand. "Please, I have to do this myself." She hung the stirrup on the saddle horn and reached under to bring up the cinch. She looped the strap through the rings and pulled it tight. She gave it an extra yank to make sure the saddle was secure.

"You do that like a pro," Johnson said.

Sarah gave him a big smile. "I had a great teacher." She unloosed the reins from the rail.

Mister Johnson came around the back of the horse. "Need a hand getting up?"

"Nope, Jubi and I can handle this ourselves." Sarah gave the reins a gentle tug. "Down," she commanded. "Jubilee, down." The horse went down on its knees and gently laid on its side. Sarah sat on the saddle and hooked her right leg over the horn. "Up," she said. "Jubilee, up." The horse rose. Sarah swung her leg off the horn and found the stirrup. Reaching forward she brought up the reins and tried to find a comfortable position for the bound foot.

"I take it, Dee showed you that trick," Johnson said. "When she was a youngster, that's how she'd get on and off Jubilee."

"The first time Dee invited me out to go riding, I was scared to death. I'd never been near a horse, much less getting on one. Getting on Jubi that way helped me get over my fears. That was two years ago, I hadn't used it…until the other day."

Johnson untied the scarf from his neck. "Here, let's tie that bum foot to the stirrup. It's not the best situation. Just be careful, okay?"

"I'll be fine. The foot doesn't hurt all that much. It's more of a nuisance." Sarah used the reins to give the horse a light slap on the rump and guided him out into the yard.

The look on her dad's face was somewhere between pride and astonishment. The men untied their horses and mounted up.

"Okay, young lady," the sheriff said. "Lead the way."

Sarah moved the reins to the right and gave Jubi a kick in the ribs with her good heel. Jubilee dug into the loose dirt and trotted out of the corral. Reining him to a walk, the girl started along the fence. The other riders fell in line and followed close behind.

The noon day sun felt warm on Sarah's face. A soft breeze teased the tall weeds along the path making them dance. The light air, the smell of freshly mown hay, everything seemed to be an exact repeat of three days ago. There was one marked difference. Instead of leisurely walking their horses, she and Dee had raced to where the trail turns and goes uphill through the trees. The whole thing played in Sarah's mind like an action-packed cowboy movie. The race was no contest. Dee was a superior rider, on a bigger, faster horse. She and Samson were waiting at the tree line when Sarah and Jubilee came galloping up.

Sarah remember Dee hooking her leg over the saddle horn as they walked the horses through the Juniper pines. Their conversation was nothing the sheriff, or anyone else, needed to hear.

"You going to get married?" Dee's question came out of the blue.

After the whole Robbie thing in the lunchroom, Sarah wasn't sure what Dee was getting at. "I don't know, I suppose—if I meet the right guy."

"My Grandma Belle was married three times—lived to ninety. That's how I got Belle for a middle name. She and her first husband went to Alaska during the rush of 1897 and struck it rich."

"They found gold?"

Dee laughed. "They opened a saloon and dancehall in Skagway. Grandma said her girls did a little more than just swing to the music. She said those mining boys had their 'needs' and were willing to part with a pinch of dust to get it."

"She told you that. She had girls?"

"Grandma Belle told me lots of stuff. Some of it she made me promise not to tell mom and dad. She died two years ago."

Sarah remembered bringing her horse close to Samson. "What else did she tell you?"

"That first guy got gold fever, took off for the mountains, and was bushwhacked while digging his claim. Husband number two was a hot-blooded Spaniard she met on the ship coming back to the States. Grandma said he knew how to please a woman."

Dee's impish smile left Sarah wanting more. "How…"

"She didn't give me any details. His name was Fernando del Prado Villanueva. It took him less than a year to blow through her money—spent it on a cattle ranch, south of Juarez, Mexico. Seems there was a problem with altered brands on some of his cattle. Her Spanish bed partner ended up on the noose end of a rope and Grandma Belle was lucky to escape back across the border.

"Is Belle from your mom's side of the family?"

"Dad's. Grandma landed on her feet in Tucson. Got a job cleaning railroad cars. It's where she met Fred Johnson. She came with him to Ely to help build the railroad in 1906. He worked in the procurement office. Grampa Fred and Grandma built the house we live in.

To Sarah, it felt as if their conversation had happened just moments ago. "Your grandmother had quite a life," she said. "Married three times…"

"She also named a few lovers that never quite made it to the altar," Dee said, as they broke clear of the trees. Bringing her leg off the horn and finding the stirrup, "C'mon," she yelled. "Let's run them to the canyon." She slapped Sam's behind and kicked his stomach. The big black stallion took off like a shot.

Sarah leaned forward and continued slapping the reins across Jubilee's front shoulders. The mare responded with a burst of speed. She would never forget the exhilaration, the mixture of delight and petrifying fear, of hanging on as this muscular animal galloped at full speed for the length of a football field. The look she got from Dee when she caught up, is one Sarah would treasure for a lifetime.

"I do believe that ride qualifies you as a bona fide cowgirl," Dee said, with a full-face smile.

No one could have paid Sarah a higher compliment. "You were a good teacher."

Sarah reined Jubilee to a halt and leaned back in the saddle. The men stopped, too.

"Is this where you entered the canyon?" the sheriff asked.

Sarah looked around. "Yes. We usually took the trail over on the low side, but for some reason, Dee started up the trail on the left."

"Do you know why she went that way?" he asked.

"No, I don't. I figured she knew where she was going. I just followed."

"Should we go that way?" the sheriff asked.

"No. That trail narrows when you get around that outcropping of rock up ahead. We're better off going over on the low side."

The troupe followed Sarah. They weaved along the trail going down into the canyon for what the sheriff estimated to be a quarter mile. Sarah continued to watch to her left. "When we started up that trail," she said pointing to the opposite wall, "it was plenty wide. The farther we went, the narrower it got. It was deceiving. We weren't going up, but the canyon floor was dropping below us. When my left stirrup scraped the canyon wall, I knew we were in trouble."

"Didn't either of you realize you might be heading to a problem?"

"I guess we weren't paying attention. We were just chatting and enjoying the afternoon."

"Chatting? What about?" the sheriff asked.

"Just girl stuff and graduation." *Nice try sheriff. It's none of your business.*

Sarah continued thinking of all the things Dee told of her grandmother's exploits, her laissez faire trips to Las Vegas, Tonopah and Virginia City, and her rendezvous with some of the famous and not so famous men of her time. She smiled to herself when she remembered Dee saying, "I want a life like that, full of adventure, excitement, and fun."

A familiar mound of stone caught Sarah's eye. She pulled Jubilee to a stop. Untying the bandana to free her bandaged foot, she brought her leg up and slid out of the saddle. Leaning against the horse, she waited for the men to dismount.

Her dad came and helped her hop a few steps to the side of the path. Then, pointing thirty feet up the far canyon wall she said, "See that bush. That's where Dee raised her hand. 'It's too narrow,' she said. 'We can't get through here. We have to back up.'"

"I was about ten feet behind her. I pulled on the reins. 'Back!' I yelled. "'Jubilee back!' At first, I couldn't get her to move. I kept jerking on the reins, pleading with her to back up. I looked ahead. Dee was having trouble getting Sam to back up, too. It all happened so fast and yet I saw it all in slow-motion. Samson reared. The edge of the trail gave way under his rear hoof. The horse's leg kept threshing trying to gain footing. When his other leg buckled, his rear turned, and he began falling off the side of the trail taking Dee with him. For a split-second Dee looked my way. I'll never forget the look on her face. It was as if she was asking, 'what do I do now?'"

"Was Deloris still on the horse?" the sheriff asked.

"It probably would have been better if she could have jumped off. There just wasn't time." Sarah closed her eyes, remembering the final look on Dee's face. She took a deep breath and did her best to suppress the urge to cry. "Samson must have come down on top of her when they hit the canyon floor."

Earl Johnson wiped tears from his face.

"I'm sorry," Sarah said. "There wasn't anything I could have done to help her."

"I know," Dee's father said. "I know."

Sarah's dad gave her a hug.

"I'm okay," she assured him.

"What did you do then?" the sheriff asked.

"Once I was able to back Jubilee to a wider part of the trail, I got her turned and I looped around to here." Sarah leaned on her father's arm to climb a small embankment. "By that time Samson was up and standing over there. She pointed to a spot six to ten feet away. He had a long gash on his neck. The red blood was a stark contrast to his black coat. He seemed unsteady and favored his back leg, I knew he had to be hurt, too.

Using a large boulder to steady herself, she pointed to a crevice between two huge angular shaped rocks. "When I got to her Dee was wedged between those rocks. They probably protected her from taking the full force of Sam landing on top of her."

"When you got here, was she awake?" the lawman asked. "Were you able to talk to her?"

"Not at first. Her right arm and leg were bent funny. They had to have been broken. I knelt beside her." Sarah eased herself to her knees. "I lifted her head. My hand felt warm and sticky. When I pulled it out, it was covered in blood. I took off my jacket. She groaned when I put it behind her head."

Dee's father knelt and put a hand on Sarah's shoulder. "That's just the way I found her."

Sarah rocked back. "Then all of a sudden, she slowly opened her eyes and smiled at me. She didn't cry or show any sign of being in pain. She had this…peaceful look on her face."

Sarah paused. Then, facing the men, "It was all surreal. I didn't panic. In fact, I was surprised how calm I felt. There was no way to get her back to the house by myself and I figured it would be best not to move her. I took her hand and told her I was going for help."

"She squeezed my hand. I barely felt it. 'That's okay, she whispered. Grandma Belle is here with me.'"

Earl Johnson's shoulders sagged. He buried his face in his hands and sobbed. It was Sarah's turn to console the grieving father. She laid her head on his back. "I'm so sorry," she said. "It's all my fault. I was the one that wanted to ride."

"It's not your fault," he said. He rose and pulled Sarah up with him. He hugged her. "Dee was doing what she loved to do…ride. It was just a terrible accident."

The sheriff stepped forward. "When did you hurt your leg?"

Sarah looked at her bandaged foot. For a moment, she had forgotten about her stupid ankle "On the way back to the house." She pointed to her horse. "I jumped on Jubilee and took off at a full gallop. When I turned to go down through the trees. I misjudged my speed. Jubilee turned quicker than I expected. She went on one side of a tree and I went flying past the other. A branch spun me around and when I landed, the foot bent backwards. It stung like crazy. I tried to stand, but the ankle gave out."

"I'm assuming you used the same method as in the corral to get back on the horse?" The sheriff said.

Sarah nodded. Once Jubilee got us up, I just held onto the horn and said "Jubi go home. Go home girl."

"Mister Johnson was driving up to the house when we came into the yard. "I told him Dee was hurt bad and so was Samson. I explained the best I could of where to find her. He's the one who called your office. Mrs. Johnson waited with me for the ambulance. Mister Johnson took his rifle, hopped on Jubilee, and rode off."

"Is that pretty much the way you saw it, Earl?" The sheriff asked.

Johnson nodded. "When I got here…she had already passed. Samson's back leg was broken clean through. I had to put him down. I laid Dee over Jubilee's saddle and walked her back to the house.

The sheriff extended his hand. "I want to thank you, young lady. I know this has been hard on you. Will you be all right?"

Hell no. I won't be all right. A part of me died right here in this canyon. How do I separate two hearts that beat as one, or fill the void of never being able to see, touch, or to talk to my friend ever again? No, dammit, I won't be all right. Sarah offered a thin smile.

CHAPTER SIX

One Last
Goodbye.

Sarah rolled to her side and dried her eyes with the sleeve of her pajamas. The morning sun peeked around the drawn shade casting a long shadow on the bed. She'd spent a restless night. Sleep had come in two-hour blocks. It wasn't the foot. The swelling had gone down considerably. No, each time she woke, she thought of Dee and another round of tears followed.

She didn't want to think about the funeral. She dreaded the thought of having to look at Dee lying in the casket or having to touch her cold body. Until she confronted that moment, the door was still open for Dee to miraculously spring to life and declare it was all a mistake. Or God could choose to intervene and restore her friend to life. Impossible? Improbable for sure, but still, it was something Sarah desperately prayed for. She felt alone, longed to hear Dee's infectious laugh, or watch her eye-roll after making some outrageous pronouncement. Sarah knew it would be all the little things she'd miss about her friend. Life, at the moment, lacked purpose. *This funeral thing is going to be hard.*

Sarah came into the kitchen using one crutch.

Nora took her face out of the newspaper. "The foot must be feeling better."

"A lot." Sarah opened the refrigerator and took out the jug of orange juice.

"It's still hard to believe what's happened," Harriet said, walking into the room clipping on an earring. "The Johnson's must be devastated." She stepped aside as Sarah sat and poured juice in a glass. Seeing Sarah's sad face, her Mom brushed the girl's auburn curls off her shoulder. "If this is going to be too much for you, you don't have to go to the funeral."

"Of course, I do," Sarah shot back. "It would haunt me the rest of my life if I didn't."

"I'm only thinking of you, dear," Harriet said.

"Sarah's right," Nora said. "We all have to go. The Johnsons will need all the support we can give them."

Cars lined the street in front of the Wilson-Bates Funeral Home when John pulled up to let the women out.

"It appears the whole town is here," Nora said as she helped Sarah out of the back seat.

Sarah put a single crutch under her arm and glanced at the large gathering of people on the sidewalk leading up to the building.

Harriet was the last to exit. "This has affected all of us." She poked her head back into the car. "We'll wait for you to find a place to park, and we can all go in together."

Nora put her arm around Sarah. "Are you going to be alright?"

"I guess." Sarah said, meeting glances of the people standing there. "Do you think they blame me for what happened?"

"Don't be silly," Harriet said. "Everyone is just sad."

"They're concerned for you," Nora added.

Sarah wasn't so sure. She felt all eyes were on her as she navigated the two steps up. The gathering room was filled with more people. Sarah pressed her way to the chapel doorway. The pews lining both sides of the center aisle were nearly full. An open casket sat under an archway against the far wall. She could see the cream-colored padded lining on the inside of the cover. A bronze Crucifix hung from one of the pleats. Deloris' profile barely showed above the rim of the copper colored casket. A dozen flower displays stood on either side, flooding the room with color, and a fresh floral scent. Sarah wanted to continue, to go to her friend, but her feet felt frozen to the floor. Her good foot finally moved forward a few inches. The bandaged one swung ahead a half dozen more. Each step went a little farther, more fluid, less tentative. Still, it seemed to take forever to make it to the front.

Sarah kept her focus on the crucifix, not wanting to look directly at the still figure lying in the casket. When she reached the kneeler in front, her head began to swirl. She grabbed the velvet armrest. The crutch fell to the side, as her knees drop onto the cushion. *Dear God, I don't want to look…I can't…I won't…I have to…I want to.*

She slowly raised her head. Her eyes focused on the rosary laced between Dee's fingers. Hands that were never still and demonstratively expressive, now rested quietly on what was surely going to be her graduation dress. Sarah slowly took in the full countenance of her friend, as a smile broke across her face. Dee had the same peaceful look she'd witnessed when her friend lay between the rocks. Still, she couldn't hold back the tears that streamed down her cheeks as she clutched Dee's cold hands. She had to grab the kneeler to keep from crumbling into a heap. Nora and her mom arrived in time to steady her.

Nora knelt beside Sarah. She put her arm around her sister's waist. Looking at the girl in the casket, she whispered, "Oh my, she looks so peaceful."

"It's her Grandma Belle," Sarah said. "It's the same look I saw when I told her I'd have to leave to get help. She told me it was okay because Grandma Belle was at her side."

Harriet leaned forward and straightened a perceived wrinkle in the collar on Dee's dress. "How wonderful, her grandma was there to welcome her into heaven." John stood behind the women. He stayed for a moment, then turned and walked to the back.

"Your father is having a hard time dealing with this," Harriet said, combing her fingers through Sarah's long auburn hair. "He said you did a very good job in the canyon. He was so proud of you, but said, but for the grace of God, it could have been you instead of Deloris."

"He's always been like that," Nora said. "The only time I ever saw him cry was when his mother died." She bent, picked up the crutch and handed it to Sarah.

"I think you're right," Harriet said as she led the girls toward an open pew.

Sarah kept her head down, raising it just enough to see where she was going. It surprised her when she made eye contact with Harold Gregory sitting in the second row. His eyes were glassy. She couldn't help noticing his large hands resting on his lap. His eyes locked in on hers. Sarah broke the hold. *He couldn't possibly know that I know—or could he? I just pray to God that he respects Dee's life and memory and never utters a word of that one encounter.*

The service was beautiful. The minister's sermon dwelt on how much life Dee packed into the few years she was with them. Friends and family spoke of how Deloris touched their lives, sharing memories they had of her.

At the cemetery, while others tossed handfuls of dirt or rose buds on the lowered casket, Sarah dropped a goodbye letter she had written. In it, she not only reminisced about all the fun they had but promised to keep Dee's memory alive by returning once a year to put flowers on her grave.

The reception was held at Elks Lodge. The ladies put out a fine spread. Slowly, the mood changed, became more upbeat as subdued laughter filled the room. Once again, people took up the matter of living. They made plans and talked of things to come.

Principal Chester Davis came and sat at the Jensen's table. "Well, young lady," he said to Sarah. "What are your plans? Are you still going to Chicago to become a nurse?"

Sarah shrugged. "I guess so."

"I'm not trying to change your mind," he continued. "It's just, as co-valedictorian, you'd be in line to receive the four-year scholarship to the University in Reno. It's a thought."

Sarah looked at Nora and then at her mom. "I couldn't. That was Dee's."

"I know how you feel," he said. "But it can only go to the valedictorian. You are the only other person we can give it to.

Harriet sensed her daughter's anguish and touched Sarah's arm. "You don't have to decide right now." Then turning to Chester. "We'll talk about it and let you know."

"September is a long way off," he said, getting up from the table. "But, if you're interested, you'll need to allow time to schedule classes."

Nora didn't wait for Sarah to react. "A full scholarship. Wow. That is something you should consider."

"Yes, it is *something*, but nothing has to be decided this minute," Harriet said. "We have the whole summer to decide."

*****

Nora folded her sweater and laid it in her tattered brown suitcase. Looking up, Sarah stood in the doorway.

"Do you have to go?" she asked.

"I stayed a couple days longer for the funeral," Nora said, putting a pair of slacks in the bag and closing the cover. "I really have to get back to Pine Lake. I'm the only trained emergency room nurse at the hospital. Heaven only knows what went on while I've been gone."

"May I come with you?"

The words hit like a crack of thunder. Nora stopped fiddling with the straps on the case. "What? Sure. Have you talked to Mom?"

Sarah rushed into Nora's arms. "I don't think I can stay here. It's terrible," she wailed. "Everything reminds me of Dee."

Harriet heard Sara's lament and came running. "What's going on? Is she okay? Why is she crying?"

"She's okay," Nora said, holding a hand to her mother. "The pain of losing Dee is just too raw. She needs to get away. Maybe come back to Pine Lake with me."

"I think that would be a wonderful idea." Harriet said.

Both girls registered their surprise.

"Would it be alright?" Sarah said, with a burst of excitement.

"A change of scenery will do you good," her mom said. "Besides, I think Nora would love to have you stay with her for a while. You two have been apart for nearly two years."

Nora gave Sarah a super squeeze. "I'd be thrilled to have you come…and Duke would be, too. The summer season is just getting started. There is so much to do. It'll be fun."

"Well, you two better stop dilly-dallying around and start putting something in a suitcase for her," Harriet said. "What time is your bus?"

"Three thirty. We've got two hours," Nora gave Sarah a push. "Mom, do you still have Sarah's suitcase? Let's get this girl packed."

The bags were standing by the door when John came home. Harriet didn't wait before spewing out the whole chain of events, ending with, "Sarah is taking a trip with Nora back to Pine Lake."

John's big smile indicated he wholly agreed with the move.

CHAPTER SEVEN

Heading Back to Pine Lake

The Pony Express bus rolled to a stop in front of the Economy Drug Store. John waited for the driver to open the luggage bay before sliding the girls' suitcases to him. "When are you guys going to get some new buses?"

"They've been telling us any day," the driver said. "But they've been saying that since the war ended—two years ago. Where are you all heading?"

"She and I are going to Chicago," Nora said, releasing from her mother's hug and pointing to Sarah.

"I can get you as far as Salt Lake," he said, picking up the first bag. "Greyhound will take you the rest of the way."

Nora nodded. *We know. This isn't the first time making this trip.*

"Call us when you get to Pine Lake." Harriet said, as she put her arms around Sarah and squeezed tight. "I made some cold chicken sandwiches to take with you." Handing her a brown paper sack, she also slipped an envelope in the girl's pocket. "Extra spending money."

"I have my graduation money, Mom," Sarah protested.

Harriet wiped her eyes with her hanky. "I know, I know. It's money I squirreled away to give you a party. I won't be needing it now." She pushed John. "Better give the girls a hug before they get on the bus."

"Take care of your sister," John said, embracing Nora. "Be good," he said, before giving Sarah a quick kiss on the forehead.

"Get on if you are coming," the driver yelled from his seat. "I gotta make up some time if you want to catch the midnight Greyhound to Chicago."

The girls boarded and grabbed seats by the windows. They waved until they could no longer see their folks.

The bus lumbered down Main Street, made a left turn and headed out of town. Nora got up, settled in the aisle seat next to Sarah and tucked her purse between them. "Well, here we go again, another long bus ride, just like two years ago."

Sarah chuckled. "Remember on our way out here, you thought the police might be after us. You panicked and bought us sunglasses and we acted like we weren't traveling together."

"And we stuffed your long hair under a bandana hoping you wouldn't be recognized."

The girls continued to reminisce as Sarah pointed to things she remembered seeing on the earlier trip. Neither thought about sleeping. The driver made good on picking up time and they were able to make the transfer to Greyhound in Salt Lake. It was a much smoother ride on the newer bus. Soon the constant roll and sway of the bus melted their excitement and lulled them to sleep.

Nora rubbed her neck and blinked her eyes. It took a little time to adjust to the sunlight. "Gosh, what time is it?" she asked, surprised to see Sarah sitting upright and looking out the window.

"A little after seven."

Nora brought her seat forward. "Where are we? Have you been awake long?"

Sarah talked to the window. "My body is still on school time. My eyes flew open at six."

"Any idea where we are?" Nora stretched her neck to look around.

"We just left Rawlings, Wyoming. A sign back there said a hundred and thirty miles to Cheyenne."

"Are you hungry? Nora asked. "We'll probably make a breakfast stop in Cheyenne.

"We still have the sandwiches Mom made for us."

"This is probably the first time I'm ever going to turn down one of Mom's cold chicken sandwiches, but right now, I'm thinking hot coffee, a couple scrambled eggs, and toast. Especially the hot coffee." Nora waited for Sarah to respond. The girl continued to watch the passing scenery.

"Orange juice," Sarah finally said. "I'm not much of a coffee drinker, but orange juice sounds good."

Nora got out of her seat, stood in the aisle, and flexed her legs. "You seem deep in thought." Her nurse's training kicked into gear. "It's best if you can talk about it."

"It's about the scholarship to Reno. If I take it, maybe it will help me keep Dee's memory alive."

"I chose to become a nurse. It's not for everyone, and it would be wrong if you thought you had to do it just to please me. I think a college education is invaluable, but again, you should pursue it for the right reasons. Nothing is going to bring Dee back."

Sarah nodded and looked out the window, not to see anything, but to hide the tears welling in the corners of her eyes. "Working for the FBI is all she ever talked about. We'd play detective and try to remember things about people we saw, like their height, weight, clothing, hair and eye color. We'd pretend to be in a crime scene and see who could come up with the most details of the surroundings. I could never beat her."

Nora plopped back into her seat. "I can tell you everything about your Uncle Robert the night he came to Gladys' place. I can describe the gun and how many shots he fired. I can describe the barn and if I had to, I could probably tell you how many pieces of straw were on the floor. Some things just stick in your mind."

Sarah faced her sister. "Wouldn't it be neat to solve some big murder mystery?"

"Maybe, but not if you're the one being shot at."

Sarah was like a magpie at breakfast. She related one story after another about Dee and the things they had done. None of the personal conversations, but just about every mundane moment they shared over the past two years. Nora had to remind Sarah to keep eating so they wouldn't be late getting back on the bus.

When Sarah continued talking about her friend across all of Nebraska and halfway through Iowa, Nora had to remind herself that it was she who said it was best to talk it out. It was late in the day when the bus rumbled out of Des Moines. Sarah appeared to be deep in thought and was content to watch out the window.

Nora put her seat back. "It'll be close to midnight when we get to Chicago. I'll give Gladys a call. Hopefully, we can hang out at her place until we catch a bus north in the morning."

"She probably won't like that."

"You're right. I'm sure she will piss and moan about it, but it will feel great to shower and catch some sleep…in a bed."

"That sounds better than spending eight or ten hours in the bus station."

As the last sliver of sun dropped behind the rolling hills, Nora could only wonder what was going through her sister's mind.

CHAPTER EIGHT

Spending the Night with Gladys

Instead of being upset, Gladys excitedly drove to the bus station to pick up her friends. Jumping out of the car, she couldn't stop fusing over Sarah. "Look at you…you've grown so. She twisted a curl of the girl's hair. "You're beautiful."

"Gladys, remember me?" Nora said, opening the trunk and putting in the suitcases. "Your best friend, your star pupil."

"Oh, be quiet, I see you all the time in Pine Lake. I haven't seen Sarah Jean in two years."

When they reached Gladys' apartment, Nora called dibs on the shower. Gladys dragged Sarah to the kitchen and peppered her with questions. They were both crying when Nora, dressed in her pajamas, came into the kitchen toweling her hair.

"Why didn't you tell me what happened to her friend?" Gladys didn't wait for an answer. "That is so tragic."

"I was going to tell you when we got here. It's probably best you heard it from her."

"You should have called." Gladys protested.

"Wasn't time." Nora threw the towel at Sarah. "You'll feel great once you've had a shower."

Gladys and Sarah got up from their chairs together. The older lady had lost the gruffness Sarah remembered. "Yes, go jump in the shower. We'll have cookies and milk when you're done.".

Nora pulled out a chair. "Can we get a head start on the cookies and milk?"

"That poor girl," Gladys said, setting a plate of chocolate chip cookies on the table.

"I thought about calling you. It's just not a thing you can explain over the phone. I'm concerned about her. She could be suffering some type of mental trauma from it."

"She seemed fine telling me about it. She cried, but hell, she had me crying, too."

Nora took a bite of cookie. "She talked my ear off on the trip here. I think it's good she's able to talk about it, but maybe it's a sign of something else."

Gladys poured them each a glass of milk. "Like what?"

"Remember when I came to you after the war and had those sessions with the shrink. Doctor whatchamacallit?"

"Stewart."

"Yes, and he said I was suffering the same thing as the soldiers who fought in battle. It's dealing with a life and death situation. It's possible Sarah is experiencing the same problem."

"What can we do for her?"

"I'm hoping a fun filled summer in Pine Lake will help her get over losing her friend.

"Are you two talking about me?" Sarah asked, entering the room. She finished winding the towel around her hair and took a seat.

"Nora was just saying she thinks a summer in Pine Lake will be good for you." Gladys pushed a glass of milk in front of Sarah. "I baked those cookies this morning…er…Oh hell, it's two o'clock in the morning. I baked them yesterday."

"Not good for the waistline." Nora said, dunking her cookie a second time. "Especially if we're going to jump into bed right after."

Sarah followed Nora's lead and dunked her cookie in her milk. "I love chocolate chips."

Nora glanced at the clock. She stuffed the last piece of cookie in her mouth and proceeded to unfold the bus schedule she grabbed while waiting to be picked up at the station.

Gladys stood. "You two okay bunking together? I'll open the hide-a-bed. You're hardly going to be there long enough to warm the sheets? What time is your bus?"

"I'm checking." Nora said, as she reached for another cookie. With her nose deeply involved in the schedule, her finger slid across an empty plate. She looked up and saw Sarah with a cookie in each hand.

"I told you, I love chocolate chip cookies.," Sarah said with a sheepish grin.

"I've got meetings the next few days and a class with nurses that are about to graduate," Gladys said. "If you're not in a big hurry and want to wait until Saturday, we could all drive up to the lake together."

"Can't," Nora said. "There's a northbound bus leaving at ten-oh-five. I should have been back to work three days ago."

"In that case I can drop you off on my way to work." Gladys glanced at the clock. "We might as well get a little shuteye. You can crawl in together or one can take the couch."

"I'll take the couch," Nora said.

Gladys stood by the light switch. "Just leave those dishes, I'll clean up in the morning." She chuckled at the silly reference since it was already early morning.

Sarah was slow to get off her chair. "Could we check on a bus to Indianapolis?"

The light went out and came back on.

Gladys shot a puzzled look at Nora.

"I'd like to go to Danville," Sarah said. "To see my mother's gravestone."

The room fell silent.

"I have my own money," she said. "It would only take a couple of days."

Sarah's request caught Nora by surprise. *A couple of days? I've got to get back to Pine Lake.* "Let's sleep on it," she said. "We can talk about it in the morning."

"If you are back here by Saturday, you can ride to Pine Lake with me," Gladys offered.

Nora shot daggers at her friend before curling up on the couch.

Gladys waited for them to get settled before turning off the light.

CHAPTER NINE

"Are you sure about this?"

Gladys was already in the kitchen when Nora rushed in, wiping the sleep from her eyes. Leaning to see the clock, she shouted, "Dammit, why didn't you wake me?"

"Are you always this pleasant in the morning?" Gladys poured some coffee in a cup and shoved it in Nora's direction. "It's only six-thirty, for criminy sakes. Drink some coffee before you blow a gasket."

Nora took a deep breath. "Sorry, this Danville business is really bothering me. I don't think I slept ten winks."

"What's the big deal? Like Sarah said it'll only take a couple of days."

"The girl is only seventeen years old," Nora protested.

"About the same age you were when you took that big bus ride all the way from Nevada to start your nurses training here in the big city of Chicago."

"That was different, I was…"

"What?" Gladys took a sip of coffee. "I seem to recall you being a timid, shy girl who was basically scared of her own shadow."

"I still don't like it," Nora said, flopping down on a chair.

"What don't you like?" Sarah yawned and stretched her arms in the air as she walked into the kitchen.

"You going to Danville by yourself." Nora rubbed her forehead. "What if…"

"The sky falls?" Gladys smiled, set down a glass of milk, and handed Sarah the last two chocolate chip cookies. Then, turning to Nora, "Be serious, she's not going to China. It's a three-hour bus ride. She'll be back Friday night and the two of us will drive to Pine Lake on Saturday."

"I know the way," Sarah said. "You and I have gone there twice before. I'm sure Mrs. Halstead or Mrs. Canterbury wouldn't mind picking me up at the bus station."

"Friends of the family?" Gladys asked.

Nora pursed her lips. "One took care of her mom when…the other runs the boarding house where her mom worked."

"Sounds to me like she's got things all worked out."

Nora shot her friend a menacing look.

Gladys turned and muttered. "Time for me to keep my big nose out of this."

Nora turned to Sarah. "Are you sure you're comfortable with doing this?"

"I'd really like to see my mom's gravestone—I saved for a year to pay for it. It would mean a lot to me."

Nora scratched her chin. She sensed the two sets of eyes were focused on her, waiting for a response. "Okay then," she said, picking up the bus schedule. "Let's see when the bus leaves for Indianapolis."

Sarah jumped off her chair and hugged Nora from behind. "Thank you. Thank you."

"Here you go," Nora said. "There's a southbound leaving at eleven-fifteen."

Gladys gave Sarah a big hug. "Make sure you have my number. Just call when you get in on Friday and I'll come and pick you up, okay?"

Sarah gave her a big smile and a small nod to affirm the instructions. She put her glass in the sink and darted out of the room.

Nora grabbed Gladys' elbow and spun her around. "If anything happens to that child, I'll never forgive you."

*****

The girls said their goodbyes at Gladys's place, so it was nothing more than a stop at the curb and a quick "See ya," before Sarah and Nora jumped out of the car and grabbed their suitcases.

One would think there wouldn't be a lot of people traveling on a Thursday. Wrong. The Greyhound depot was crawling with people.

Both ticket windows had a half dozen people waiting in line. "Shit," Nora said, before covering her mouth hoping no one had heard her cuss. "After the Army, I vowed to never again stand in line." She grabbed a spot in the one line and shoved Sarah to the other. "Let's see which one moves fastest."

The line Nora picked came to a standstill as a foreign-speaking couple tried to negotiate tickets to who knows where. A call for a supervisor meant Nora's would not move for the foreseeable future. Sarah had continued to move up and was next to step to the window. Nora jumped in line behind her. She brushed off the disgusted look the man behind them gave her. She leaned over Sarah's shoulder. "Do you want me to get the tickets?"

"I'll get my own," Sarah said stepping to the window. "One round trip ticket to Indianapolis, please." She turned back to Nora. "I have to learn to do these things for myself."

The clerk, a man in his fifties, eyed her up. "One round trip to Indianapolis for the pretty young lady." He stamped the ticket and tore it from his book. He eyed her again as he handed her the ticket and again when she turned to walk away from the counter.

Nora stepped up and without flinching, yelled in the man's face. "You keep your lecherous eyes off that girl, or I will pull your scrawny head and neck through this window and blacken both of them." She took in and exhaled a huge breath of air. Then calmly said, "A one-way ticket to Pine Lake, Wisconsin." She paid, grabbed the ticket and turned to leave. She glared at the man in line who gave her the dirty look. "If you say one word, I'll knock your block off." The man leaned back, raised his hands as if to surrender, and shook his head.

"What was that all about?" Sarah asked when Nora caught up to her.

"The ticket guy had an *eye* problem. I gave him some corrective advice." Nora nudged Sarah to some nearby bench seating. "Now just be careful, okay? Have you got Gladys phone number?"

Sarah tapped her purse.

"Have you got mine in Pine Lake?"

The girl again tapped her purse and then held up her bus ticket anticipating the next question. "I'm going to be fine," she said and patted Nora's hand.

Nora looked at the big clock on the far wall. "My bus leaves in twenty minutes—yours, not for another hour or so. Are you sure you want to do this?"

"Would you stop worrying," Sarah said, defensively. "I'm going to be perfectly fine. I'll see you on Saturday in Pine Lake."

Sarah stood on the curb and blew a kiss to Nora as her bus lumbered away from the terminal. She continued to wave as the bus reached the corner and made a left turn. A brief chill caused her to shudder. The feeling was much like that of a child, while lying in bed, waiting for the moment Mom turns out the light. She wasn't scared. At least she wasn't ready to admit she was scared. She reaffirmed her grip on her suitcase, lowered her head and turned to go inside the terminal. She felt surrounded. People moved in both directions. Some entering the terminal while others scrambled to leave. Everyone was in a hurry. Two sailors jostled her as they ran past. One smiled sheepishly and blurted, "Excuse me," as he hurried to keep up with his buddy.

Once inside, Sarah found a seat near the wall. She put her suitcase between her legs and locked her knees tight against it. She closed her eyes. She hadn't fully thought out this part of her journey. It's one thing to be lonely but being alone is entirely different. She tried to recall the last time she felt this alone in the world.

In a flash her mind took her back two years to the moment she gave her mom a final kiss and boarded the bus to go live with her Aunt Betty and Uncle Robert. A smile started in the corners of her mouth and soon pulled to the full width of her face. Sarah opened her eyes and envisioned Nora offering a seat next to her. From that moment on Nora had been her protector. The Jensens took her in and treated her like one of their own. She also had the good fortune to meet her friend for life, Deloris Belle Johnson.

The thought of Dee sent a surge of energy through her body. She straightened in the chair and began taking note of her surroundings. She checked her watch. *Twenty minutes to departure.* The man sitting across from her looked like he had slept in his worn, brown suit. *Five foot -ten, hundred sixty pounds, sandy hair, blue eyes, thin mustache and wire-rimmed glasses.*

She was about to turn her attention to the woman sitting two seats to the man's left when she quickly went back to subject number one. "This one's for you, Dee," she said under her breath. *He's probably a bachelor. No wife would let her husband out of the house with mismatched socks.*

Before she could focus on the woman, she noticed the two sailors had taken seats next to her.

Sailor one's mouth moved in conversation while sailor number two appeared to be looking at her. She turned and checked others in the room, making quick mental notes of each as they came into view. With each glance in the sailors' direction, she found number two's eyes on her. Her quick peeks painted a clearer picture of him. *Cute, dark hair—cut short. Eyes... alluring. Oh, good night. Dee is probably laughing her butt off with that description.*

Sarah recalled when her own father, dressed in his Navy whites, kissed her and her mom goodbye. She was ten years old. All through the war years, every time she saw a sailor, she imagined it was her dad coming home. Her dreams never came true.

The announcement came. The bus to Indianapolis was now boarding. Sarah picked up her bag and got in line.

CHAPTER TEN
On the Bus to Indianapolis

Among the first to board. Sarah put her suitcase on the overhead rack and took a window seat four rows behind the driver. Her ears tingled warmly as she watched the two sailors board. The cute one looked directly at her. She turned away and focused her eyes out the window, watching the driver of the bus next to them load suitcases into its lower bin. She couldn't be sure he looked at her while walking up the aisle but imagined he did.

As the bus left the cars and concrete of the city behind, the Chicago skyline gave way to rolling hills and green fields of early corn and wheat. After two years living in the high desert of Nevada with its mountains and rugged terrain, she'd almost forgotten how beautiful this part of the country looked in the early days of summer. To seeing farmers on tractors, pulling wagons or cultivators, and kids playing in yards gave her a comforting window into where she used to live. Her shoulders relaxed and a feeling of contentment filled her senses. It was hard to feel alone or be lonely when everything looked so familiar.

Watching farm after farm pass by, lost in the moment, Sarah suddenly lean forward and glued her face to the window. She saw a large black horse, munching on grass on the other side of a white rail fence. He brought his head up and looked straight at her. The word, "Samson," burst from her mouth. She spun her body around to get one last glimpse as the bus lumbered past. The animal reared, his front hooves pawed at the air. Sarah fell back against her seat and shook her head. *There's no way…*

The angle of sunlight coming through the window produced a reflection of her in the glass. The image changed briefly to a likeness of Dee, standing next to her big, black stallion. She had the same bright eyes and trademark effervescent smile Sarah had seen a thousand times. Sarah returned a smile of her own and whispered. "I miss you so much."

"Mind if I sit?" The voice was manly but soft.

Sarah looked up at the sailor standing in the aisle. For a split second, it was her father, holding out his hand and saying the words she longed to hear. "I'm Home." Struggling between past and present, any response was stuck deep in her throat.

He used his rolled-up cap to point to the empty seat. "Would you like some company?"

Sarah straightened in her seat. "I…I…guess so." *Oh, jeez, if Nora were here, she'd kill me.* She looked straight ahead.

The young man slid into the aisle seat. "Are you getting off in Indy, or going beyond?"

Sarah took a quick peek at him. *Brown hair, nice nose, blue eyes, dreamy blue, definitely dreamy.* "I'm getting off…going to Danville." *Ugh! Too much information.*

"Do you need a ride? I'm heading that way myself."

Girl, don't be dumb. "No, that's alright, I have someone picking me up." *Liar.*

"Okay, that's good." He extended his hand. "I'm Jeremy, Jeremy Fletcher. The guys call me Fletch."

Sarah couldn't stop the giggle that escaped from her mouth. "What should *I* call you?"

Her question took a moment to register. "Jeremy, I guess. Yeah, Jeremy is fine."

His easy manner was softening her defenses, and after all, he was a sailor just like her dad.

"You look familiar. Like someone I should know. Have we met before?"

Oh right, I'll bet he says that to all the girls. She continued building a description of him. *Six foot, a hundred ninety pounds—of muscle, black hair, and of course, those dreamy blue eyes. I'd guess him to be nineteen, maybe twenty.* Do you live in Danville?"

"My folks have a farm, two hundred and twenty acres, six miles south of Danville."

"That's good farmland." She remembered the oft-repeated description of the land south of town.

"Best in Indiana." The man leaned forward in his seat. "Are you familiar with the area? Are you from Danville?"

"I grew up there. Been gone for a couple of years."

"Going back to see family?"

"In a way, my Mom is buried there." She got a faraway look in her eye and stared out the window. The fleeting image of her mom flashed through her mind and caused a tear to gather in the corner of her eye.

His shoulders sagged. "Geez, I'm sorry. I didn't mean to pry." There was sincerity in his voice. "If you want, I can go back and sit with my buddy." He put his hands on the armrest and made a move to get up.

Sarah touched his sleeve. "That's okay, you don't have to." She thought how she would explain her forward response to Nora. *She'd think I'd completely lost my mind. Dee on the other hand, would probably get a big kick out of it.* She faced him. "Do I really look familiar, or are you just saying that? Is that your pickup line?"

The man blushed. "Nah, you really do. Did you go to school in Danville?"

"Through my sophomore year, but I missed a lot because my mom was sick. I moved to Nevada two years ago—after she died."

"I'm sorry. That must have been tough."

The memory of those final moments with her Mom at the depot raced through her mind. "It was cancer. She fought hard, but in the end, I had to watch her slip away a day at a time.

"What about your dad? It must have been hard on him, too?"

"My dad died in the attack on Pearl Harbor. I was eleven years old." She watched the color drain from his face.

He shook his head "God, I am sorry. How did you…"

Sarah put her hand on his arm. "I know it all sounds bad, but really, I'm doing fine. I've got a wonderful foster family, including a big sister I never had. Believe it or not, I have a lot of wonderful memories of my time in Danville." Neither spoke as the minutes ticked away.

The sailor finally straightened in his seat. "I'll have to get out my yearbooks and see if I can find you."

Sarah bounced in her seat and rolled her eyes. "Oh God, I was tall and skinny, and my hair was a lot shorter. I don't look anything like I did back then."

"Yeah, you probably wouldn't recognize me from my yearbook picture either. I was on the chunky side, one of the goofball farm kids that everyone made fun of."

I doubt anyone would make fun of you now.

The bus growled as the driver downshifted. Sarah looked out the window. "Are we there already?"

Jeremy looked past her. "Nah, this is Lafayette. It's another hour and half to Indy. It's probably just a rest stop. Do you want to get off and stretch your legs?"

Sarah scrunched up her shoulders, surprised how much tension she felt in her shoulders and neck. "Yes, I think that would feel really good."

Jeremy chuckled as he followed her off the bus. "You've got a little bit of a western twang in your voice. It's cute. I like it."

Sarah didn't need a warning from Dee. Farmer boy was showing himself to be one smooth talker.

Walking took the kinks and stiffness out of her legs. Jeremy excused himself to find the nearest men's room. Sarah watched him trot off. The thought came to mind. Should she continue talking to the guy or nip this in the bud. In her head, she posed the question to Dee. *What do you think? He seems nice enough, but I'm only going to be here a day and a half, and God only knows where he's going.* She searched the inner confines of her mind for an answer. *It would be great to know your answer, but you have to admit he looks darn good in that uniform.* She didn't hear him come up behind her.

"Would you like a coke?" he said handing her a bottle.

Startled, she reached and then withdrew her hand. "I'd love one, but first I have to make a run to the ladies' room. I'll never make it another hour and a half on the bus.

*****

Standing in front of the restroom mirror, she brushed a few strands of hair to their rightful place and added a fresh layer of lipstick. Her reflection morphed into a mental picture of Dee. Sarah pointed the bright red tube at the mirror. "Okay, now that you're here, are you going to help me? Should I continue, or should I give him the cold shoulder and move on?"

A woman came out of one of the stalls, looked around and then at Sarah. "Who are you…" She never finished. With raised eyebrows, she straightened her dress and hurried out of the room. Sarah could hear Dee's infectious laugh as she picked up her purse and walked out the door.

The bus was loaded when Sarah got there. The driver looked exasperated. Jeremy stood by the door, still holding the two bottles. "I was beginning to worry about you."

Sarah's face flushed as red as her lips. "I'm sorry, I didn't mean to keep everyone waiting." She accepted the coke and climbed the steps into the bus.

The sailor followed and waited until she settled in the window seat. He looked at the open seat and then at Sarah. "Would it be alright if…I…" The bus lurched forward, and Jeremy grabbed the seatback to steady himself.

Sarah smiled and nodded. Looking out the window she mouthed, "You're no help," barely making a sound.

The sailor sat, held out his bottle, and waited for Sarah to clink hers to his. "Did you say something?" he asked.

"No, not really, just talking to the little voice in my head." *Sarah Jean, will you pul-eeze stop acting like a nutcase.*

"Does it have anything to do with me? Is my head on the block here?"

Sarah suppressed the urge to laugh and kept a straight face as she studied her small green bottle. She had a feeling both Nora and Dee would shake their heads. *I really should end this—now.*

The sailor slumped in the seat. No doubt deflated by the lack of a response. "Geez, Maybe I should dig the pea coat out of my duffle. It's getting pretty chilly in here."

Sarah swung to face him. A giggle escaped. She knew exactly what he was hinting at. "That's not true. I've been friendly."

"Oh yeah? Then how come, I still don't know your name?"

Sarah raised an eyebrow. "Did you ask?"

"I think I did," Jeremy scratched his head, "but, maybe I didn't."

The pause gave Sarah one last chance to decide. *This is it. Once I give him my name there's no turning back.* "It's Sarah Jean," she blurted. "Sarah Jean Connolly."

The man in the white uniform laid his head back. "Sarah Jean." He said it slowly. Then paused.

"What? Did it ring a bell? Do you remember something about me?"

"No," he said drawing a broad smile. "I just think it's a pretty name." He mouthed it again.

Sarah rolled her eyes at the sailor's theatrics. *Girl, you better be careful.* It was as if the thought came straight out of Deloris Belle Johnson's mouth.

"Where are you staying in Danville?"

"At Center House."

"With Florence Canterbury?" He practically coughed up the words.

Sarah spun in her seat. "You *know* her?"

"She's my Aunt."

Excited, she grabbed his arm. "You're kidding me." Two sets of eyes focused on her hand gripping the stark white sleeve. She slowly let go but pressed on. "I don't believe that. My mother worked for Mrs. Cant…your…Aunt Florence—for years."

"That's it." He pointed a finger in her direction.

She jerked backwards, hitting her head against the window. "What?"

"That's where I saw you. I knew you looked familiar. It had to be three or four years ago. Mom and I stopped for a visit. We stayed mostly in the parlor, but I came into the kitchen to get a drink of water and you were sitting there—off to the side—by the cupboard with all the little drawers."

Oh my God. The little drawers. My little drawers. "I'd sit there while my mom fixed meals for the roomers." Her lip curled with emotion. "That corner was my pretend office. I kept my stuff in those drawers. I think at one time, they were used to hold herbs and spices."

"Do you remember me coming in there?"

"Kind of." She wasn't lying. She did remember a kid getting a glass of water. Unfortunately, the only thing she really remembered, is that he stunk like the barn.

He relaxed. His smile no doubt reflected his satisfaction of finally remembering where he had seen her before.

Sarah's drift to the past were memories of her mom. How she stood. How she walked. The images were vivid. Her mom's favorite thread-worn green dress with the small flowers was also a favorite of Sarah's. She swallowed hard, remembering her mother's soft brown eyes and how they became dull and sunken as the cancer ravaged her body. *I'm coming mom, see you soon.*

Sarah rummaged in her purse and brought out the hanky with the small rose embroidered in the corner. She dabbed her eyes and remembered what Florence Canterbury told her after her mom died. "Every time you see a rose, it's a sign that your mom is watching over you."

Approaching Indianapolis, Jeremy excused himself. "I'm gonna say goodbye to my buddy. We just finished boot camp. He's shipping out, got to be in Norfolk in ten days. I probably won't see him for quite a while."

Sarah ran through her game plan for when they reached Indianapolis. Nora had called from Chicago to let Mrs. Canterbury know Sarah was making the trip, but she still had to locate the shuttle to Danville. Sarah gazed out the window. She felt good about making the trip and being on her own. Was this a first step in becoming an adult. Grownup or not, both Nora and Dee would question the wisdom of being so friendly with Seaman Fletcher. She chuckled. *Don't worry, He's a nice guy, but I'll end it when we get off the bus.*

CHAPTER ELEVEN

A Ride
to
Center
House

Things got hectic as soon as the driver shut down the engine. Everyone jumped up and clambered for space in the aisle. Elbows flew as people wrestled to get their bags down from the rack or from under the seats. Sarah thought better of joining the fray. She waited for the mob to finish their hand-to-hand combat. Once the aisle cleared, she gathered her things and stood.

In the back, Jeremy and his friend were locked in a bear hug, each patting the other's back. "I'll see you, man," Jeremy said, as he started to leave.

"You too," his buddy shouted, "Good luck with the lady." Jeremy waved without turning. He pulled his duffle off the rack and made his way down the aisle.

Sarah put her sweater over her arm, grabbed her suitcase, and walked out ahead of him. She cornered him in front of the bus. "Good luck with the lady?" she teased. "Was he talking about me?"

The sailor's cheeks turned red. "What? Nah, that was just…swabbie talk."

Sarah arched her eyebrows.

"Well maybe…you know how guys talk."

Wrong. I don't know how guys talk, but I'll take it as a quick lesson. She held out her hand. "I guess this is where we say goodbye."

"Goodbye? No—wait. Don't go." He pointed to a couple standing on the curb ten feet away. "Come, I want you to meet my mom and dad." She barely had time to grab the handle on her suitcase before he took her arm and began pulling her in that direction. "Mom. Dad. I want you to meet someone. This is Sarah Jean Connolly." They say a look is priceless, but one would be hard-pressed to find the words to describe the facial inquiry they dropped on Sarah.

Sarah first glanced at Jeremy and then at his folks. *Oh no! They must think I'm a new girlfriend, or a wife even.* "This isn't what it seems," she stammered. "We met on the bus and both happened to be going to Danville—separately." The couple's tense shoulders relaxed and collectively they breathed a sigh of relief.

"Her mom worked for Aunt Florence," Jeremy blurted. "We met three or four years ago. I thought I knew her but couldn't remember how or where."

"Hold on, son," Mr. Fletcher said in a calm voice, "let's slow down and get back to the introductions." He extended his hand. "It's nice to meet you, Sarah. I'm Harold Fletcher and this is my wife, Pearl." Sarah shook their hands. "Your mom worked for Florence?"

"Yes, helped with meals—before she passed away."

"Of course," Pearl said, putting her arm around Sarah's shoulders. "You're Audrey's daughter. Flo said you were coming." The woman held Sarah's hand. "My, look how you've grown." The woman drew her fingers through one of Sarah's long tresses. "You look just like your mother, except for your dad's beautiful Irish auburn hair."

Sarah smiled. *When Mrs. Fletcher talks, she sounds just like Mrs. Canterbury. They have to be sisters.*

Jeremy looked around. "Has your ride showed up?"

Sarah felt the heat of embarrassment warm her face. "I fibbed. I'm taking the shuttle."

"The shuttle. Don't be silly." He passed his duffle off to his father and picked up her suitcase. "We'll give you a ride right to Aunt Florence's doorstep."

Do I refuse? They seem like nice people. "I don't want to be a bother"

All three Fletchers insisted it was not.

The thirty-minute ride to Center House was filled with questions. Mom and Dad Fletcher did most of the asking. How long are you staying? Where did you come from? What's it like in Nevada? Where are you going from here? Jeremy sat in the back seat with Sarah. He mostly just listened. At one point he took hold of her hand…and she let him. Her long held desire to hold her father's hand may have affected the decision.

The sky was a brilliant orange. The sun had fallen behind the buildings on Danville's four- block main street giving them a haloed glow. The Fletchers stayed in the car and kept the motor running. "Tell Florence we've got cows to milk," Harold said. "She'll understand."

Jeremy retrieved Sarah's suitcase from the trunk. "Can I call you…later…or tomorrow."

The question caught her by surprise. This was all supposed to end back at the bus station. "I need to spend some time with Mrs.—I mean Florence."

"How are you going to get around? You don't have a car. I could drive you wherever you want to go."

"I do want to go to the cemetery—to see my Mom."

"Tomorrow? I'd be happy to take you."

Sarah nodded her agreement.

"Great. I'll pick you up at nine." He hopped in the back seat, rolled down the window and waved as the car drove off.

Sarah stood on the sidewalk and looked skyward. *Don't blame me. I'd tried to end it, but how was I supposed to get to the cemetery?* She picked up her suitcase and climbed the stairs.

CHAPTER TWELVE

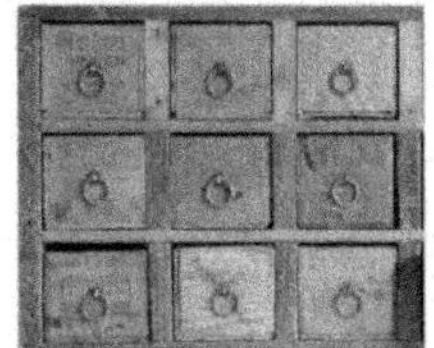

Filled with Memories

Center House was a large, two-story Victorian with a domed spire, shutters, and lots of ornamental wood trim along the upper eaves and the overhang of the long-covered porch. Two old gentlemen sat off to the side, rocking in wicker chairs. "Nice evening." one said, nodding his head

Sarah smiled. "It is." *It's like coming home. Everything looks the same. It's as if time stood still for the past two years.*

The house was home to a half dozen senior gentlemen. Mrs. Canterbury began taking in boarders as a way to sustain herself after her husband passed away some fifteen years ago. For a monthly sum, the men got a room, clean sheets once a week, and three nourishing meals a day. They were all like one big happy family. No one ever left. Openings came on the heels of a one-way trip to the undertaker. Mrs. C. would always serve a candlelight dinner in honor of the "dearly departed."

Sarah turned the doorbell lever and heard the familiar ring. When the lady of the house opened the door, her face lit up. "Sarah Jean." She wiped her hands in her apron. "My, my, look how beautiful you are." She looked up and down the street. "How did you get here?"

"The Fletchers gave me a ride."

The woman looked puzzled. "Harold and Pearl?"

"I met Jeremy on the bus. They said they had cows to milk."

"That they do, and a lot of them. I thought Jeremy was in the Navy." Mrs. Canterbury took the girl's suitcase. "Come inside, it's so good to see you."

"He just finished boot camp." Sarah followed the woman.

Mrs. Canterbury smiled as if she knew what that meant. "Your sister Nora called to let me know you were coming, but I wasn't sure when you'd get here."

Sarah thought about correcting her relationship to Nora but decided to let it slide.

The woman set the suitcase to the side. "Turn around, let me have a good look at you." When Sarah completed the turn, the woman hugged her. "Your mother would be so proud." She took Sarah's hand. "Are you hungry? We're about to serve dinner." Florence didn't wait for an answer. She pulled the young girl into the dining room where four elderly gentlemen sat at the table with their hands neatly folded in front of them. They all smiled and nodded to her.

"Sit here," Florence said, pointing to a chair on the end. "Give me your sweater, I'll hang it over the stair railing." Sarah couldn't help but chuckle. Mrs. Canterbury had always reminded her of a hummingbird, always on the move, flitting here and there.

Florence scurried back into the room, took a quick look at the table and ducked into the kitchen. A minute or so later she came out carrying a large platter of steaming hot fried chicken. Sarah drew in the wonderful aroma and could almost taste Mrs. C's signature chicken dinner. The two men from the porch hurried to their seats.

"Listen everyone," she said, putting the chicken in the center of the table. "I know some of you remember Audrey Connolly, my helper for many years. Well, this is her daughter, Sarah Jean."

The eruption of applause embarrassed Sarah. She smiled, gave a quick wave and sat.

"You sure are a pretty one," one old gent said, with a broad smile on his face.

Mrs. Canterbury slapped his bald head with the hot pad. "I bet you wish you were sixty years younger, don't you?" It was a toss-up whose face was redder, Sarah's or the man's

Another octogenarian winked at her. "Just because there's snow on the roof doesn't mean there ain't fire in the furnace."

Sarah looked puzzled.

Florence, on the other hand, knew exactly what he meant. "Will you old coots behave yourselves and stop embarrassing this poor girl." She pushed the kitchen door open with her backside. "One more peep like that and you'll all go to bed without supper." She left amid a chorus of chuckles and groans.

Once the food was in front of everyone, Florence led a brief prayer of thanksgiving. Following the loud "Amen," the chatter spoke to the beautiful weather and bemoaned the shape of local politics. On the national scene, Tom Dewey seemed favored to beat "the buck stops here" Harry Truman for President. The fried chicken with mashed potatoes and corn was the best meal Sarah had since leaving Ely. She cleaned her plate.

Pushing their empty dishes forward, the men rose as a group and congregated on the front porch for their customary after-dinner smoke. Sarah stood and gathered the silverware. Florence brought the coffee pot and filled her cup. "Want some?"

Sarah shook her head. "No thank you." She pointed to her glass. "Water is fine."

"Leave that stuff be, we can get to it later. Sit with me for a minute." The woman took a sip of coffee and waited for the girl to sit. "How long are you staying?"

"I have to be back in Chicago by tomorrow night." Sarah saw the disappointment on Florence's face. "I know, I hate to just pop in and run, but I'm spending the summer in Pine Lake, Wisconsin. I have to catch a ride there with Nora's friend Gladys. Coming here was a spur of the moment decision. I came to see the headstone I bought for mom."

"I've seen it," Florence said. "It's very nice, sort of a mauve color. When I'm out traveling about, I often stop for a quick chat with your mom. When the roses bloom, I put some there in your memory."

"That's sweet. I remember what you told me about roses. I believe it's true." Sarah touched the woman's hand. "What can you tell about them? I was so young when daddy left for the navy, and then soon after that, mom got sick. I really don't have a lot of memories of them being together."

Mrs. Canterbury started with how her folks met at the county fair, leading to stories of a rocky courtship. "Your Mom really loved your dad," the woman said, "but they could get into some real knock-down, dragged-out fights. Your father was a good man, would help anybody, give the shirt off his back, but he was Irish and would sometimes drink too much. Your mother was sweet, loving and caring, but she had a backbone of her own. I remember her stomping into the tavern and dragging him out by the ear."

Sarah knew he drank, but for her it was not a problem. He'd always bring home candy when he did.

"Drinking is how he ended up in the navy. Some guys got him drunk and they all went down and signed up. It about broke your mother's heart." Mrs. C stopped and looked at the clock, "It's way past eight, you've been traveling all day, and I'm prattling about things I probably shouldn't. All I know is your mother loved your dad and she loved you, with all her heart."

Florence picked up her cup, "Come. We can talk while I clean the kitchen. I normally have a high school girl helper, but she's on a graduation trip to Washington, D.C."

Sarah finished her water and picked up a handful of silverware. "Someday I hope to go there."

"They say there is a lot to see." Florence took a handful of plates and marched off to the kitchen.

Sarah paused for a moment. *Do I want to see it, or do I want to work there?* She finger-locked three empty glasses together and butt-pushed open the door into the kitchen.

For her, this room was hallowed. Her fingers tingled, and her breathing came in rapid gulps of air. A glance in every direction produced images of her Mom. Sarah's legs were unsteady. Her arms trembled. She put the glasses and silverware in the sink before grabbing the counter with both hands to steady herself.

Mrs. C came to her side. "Are you alright."

Sarah took a couple of deep breaths before speaking. "Just…a lot of memories…to deal with. Give me a minute—I'll be okay.

The kitchen hadn't changed a bit from the memories that were tucked in the far reaches of her mind. She'd spent countless hours here, waiting and watching her mom cook. She drew in a huge breath of air and savored every familiar smell. Sarah paused before walking to the corner cupboard. The one holding the small spice drawers. She opened the top one. It was empty save for a paper clip and stubble of a pencil. She closed it and opened the next. This one held a small folded piece of paper. Sarah recognized it. It was a hand drawn valentine she'd made for her mother. The crayon masterpiece had a big red heart and the words, "Be My Valentine" in uneven letters. It was signed, "Love Sarah." Tears fell as she ran here finger across the backward *h*.

Florence put dishes away in the adjourning cabinet. "You spent a lot of time playing with those little drawers."

Sarah handed her the paper. "Look at this. I probably drew it in second grade. Would you mind if I take it?"

"Oh heavens no. Please, it's yours. You can show it to your kids when you tell them about your mom."

Sarah opened the other drawers hoping to find anything that might connect her to the past. In one, she found her mother's ruby ring. The one her father gave to her mom on their wedding day. Sarah loved looking at it on her mom's finger. She loved the bright red stone. She recalled her mom would take it off to knead dough or mix meatloaf. *Did you forget to put it back on or did you leave it there for me to find.* She put the ring on her finger. It was a perfect fit. She showed it to Florence "Mom and I have the same size fingers." She twirled the ring knowing it was another golden link to her past.

The last drawer contained the real treasure, a letter her mom had written to her, dated three days before she died.

A dried rose petal fell to the counter, as she unfolded the note. She put the fragile blossom to her nose, there was still a hint of fragrance. The pink stationary bore a water-color print of a single red rose in the upper right corner. The penmanship was scratchy, no longer her mother's beautiful, free flowing script that Sarah remembered. She paused and ran her finger across the two water spots on the bottom of the page. She fought to keep her lips from quaking, knowing these blemishes could be her mom's tears. Sarah took a moment to stabilize her breathing, before reading aloud.

> My Dearest Sarah,
> I'm sorry to have to leave you. I so wanted
> to be there when you graduated from high
> school and to watch you grow into the
> wonderful person I know you will be.
> Although I won't be there to see all the
> fantastic things you do with your life, please
> know that I will be watching every step you
> take along the way.
> With all my love,
> Mom.

Sarah held the letter to her chest. "I love you too, Mom," she whispered.

Florence handed Sarah her handkerchief. "That is so beautiful. What a treasure." She wiped her eyes with her apron. "There are some photo albums in the parlor. We've kept pictures of our guests over the years. There are probably some of your mother. You're welcome to take whatever is there."

"I'll be sure to do that," Sarah said, running a finger across her mother's signature.

Florence left the room, only to return moments later with Sarah's purse, sweater, and suitcase. "Come, let's find you a place to sleep."

Sarah hadn't moved, she still had the letter pressed to her chest.

Mrs. C turned out the overhead light. The small glow over the sink silhouetted the girl's still figure. The woman waited.

"Come, I know you must be agonizing over a thousand things but getting a good night's sleep will help."

Sarah finally stepped forward. *It's not agony. Sorrow yes, but a lot of wonderful memories, too.* She followed the woman into the back apartment.

"I'm sorry. The couch is all I have to offer. Every bed in the place is taken." Florence pulled a clean sheet from the cabinet and tucked it around the cushions.

"This'll be just fine," Sarah said, loosening the top button on her blouse. I appreciate you letting me stay here and I'm grateful for all the stories of my mom and dad. These are memories I'll treasure for the rest of my life."

The woman pushed the air. "I'm delighted you came. Your parents were good people. You remind me so much of your mother. I know she's looking down from the stars above and saying, 'that's my baby.'" She laid a blanket over the couch back. "Get some sleep. We can talk more in the morning. I'll leave the light on in the bathroom so you can see your way around."

"Good night," Sarah offered. She closed her eyes and hung on every word the woman had spoken about her parents.

CHAPTER · THIRTEEN

Hello Mom,
It's me.

Sarah finished breakfast and sat in the parlor going through photo albums. Florence was correct. There weren't many photographs of her mother, but she carefully removed the half dozen she found and put them in her purse.

When the front doorbell made its chattery ring. She could see it was Jeremy through the clear part of the etched glass window.

Mrs. Canterbury came out of the kitchen wiping her hands in her apron.

Sarah jumped to her feet. "That's okay, it's Jeremy. He's taking me to see Mom's grave."

"You'll come back before you leave, won't you?"

"Of course, my bus doesn't leave until six." Sarah opened the door.

Without his Navy whites, Jeremy didn't look quite as impressive, although he looked comfortable in his blue jeans and checkered shirt. His demeanor hadn't changed from the day before. "Sorry, I'm a bit early." He puffed, no doubt from running up the steps. "Are you ready to go?"

"Sure, let me grab a sweater. I'll be right back."

She and Florence met at the kitchen door. "Here," Florence said. "It's only a bud. The roses are just starting to bloom, but I'm sure your mom will like it just the same."

Sarah put the flower to her nose. "I'm sure she will."

"This isn't the same car we rode in yesterday." Sarah said as she descended the front steps.

"Nah, this is mine." He opened the passenger side door. "The one yesterday belongs to my folks."

Sarah waited for him to get in and start the car before rubbing her hand across the cloth on the front seat. "Is it new? It smells new."

I've had it a few months. It's a '47 Chevy Fleetline."

"Did your parents buy it for you?"

"Bought it myself," he said leaning forward to tune the radio. "I raised three head of beef. One of them was last year's grand champion at the Hendrick's county fair." Sarah's mind hung on the words, county fair. *That's where my dad and mother met.* She missed some of what Jeremy said, but tuned in as he continued. "It drew a pretty penny at auction. From selling all three, I was able to buy the car."

"I like the color," Sarah said running her fingers across the dash.

"It's new, it's called Seafoam Green. The accent color is Volunteer Green. It's got these little silver specks in it." He continued to work the dial on the radio. "Do you like country and western music?"

Hillbilly music! Oh my gosh. "Back home mom has the radio tuned to things like Bing Crosby, Perry Como and Nat 'King' Cole, I like Hank William's ballads, but not the twangy stuff.

Jeremey turned off the radio. "After we're done at the cemetery, I'd like to show you our farm and maybe have lunch at the Blue Bonnet diner. They have a terrific hamburger."

Sarah twirled the rose under her nose. "Sure, but can we do the cemetery first?"

Jeremy shifted up into second gear, stuck his arm out the window, and made a left turn.

The car pulled through the cemetery gate. "Do you know where your mom lies?"

Sarah looked around. She had only been there once. "I don't know. Darn, I should have asked Mrs. Canterbury for directions."

"I'll ask the guy over there pushing the lawnmower." Jeremy said. "He might know." He got out and trotted to the man.

Sarah stood by the car and looked to get her bearings. A warm breeze blew her chestnut hair away from her face as she walked up the driveway. She held onto a few strands as she scanned the different shapes and sizes of grave markers. Up ahead and a little to her right, a deep maroon stone caught her eye. It was smaller than those around it, but something drew her to it. As she approached, she saw the word *Connolly* etched in large letters. Her heart fluttered. There it was. Her mom's resting place. She dropped to her knees and let the smell of fresh mown grass fill her senses. Touching a finger to the stone, she traced each letter in the name

Jeremy came running. "I see you found it. The guy said it was over here."

"I think Mom led me to it." She placed the rose bud on the bottom ledge. Her hands gripped the outer edges of the stone, as if it could take the place of an embrace "Hello Mom," she whispered.

Jeremy backed away. "I'll leave you alone…I'll be in the car."

Sarah turned and smiled. "Thanks. Mom and I have a lot to talk about."

It was more than an hour before Sarah returned and got into the car. Her eyes were bloodshot, and her cheeks streaked from crying. She touched Jeremy's hand. "Thank you so much for bringing me here. I'm sorry it took so long. I had so much to tell her."

"It's okay. It's got to be tough to lose your Mom.

"If you want, I'm ready to see your farm."

"We'll take a quick look and then go have something to eat."

CHAPTER FOURTEEN

A Visit to
the Fletcher
Farm

The farm was impressive. The barn and out-building were bright red trimmed in white. They looked freshly painted. "We had a really good year." Jeremy said. "Milk prices are up, so is corn and wheat. Dad had a new roof put on the house and whole inside painted."

They found the elder Fletcher in the milk house washing cans. He pulled off one of his long rubber gloves to shake Sarah's hand. "Did you come to help us milk?"

Sarah smiled and shook her head. *I'm not going anywhere near a cow.*

He laughed out loud. "There's only sixty-five of them." He stripped on his glove. "Pearl says she remembered you winning a blue ribbon at the fair for a pair of rabbits."

Sarah's hand covered her mouth. "I did." She doubled over with excitement. "Oh my gosh, I had forgotten all about that. I was ten years old. Mom would bring the leafy table scraps home from work. Betsy and Barney ate really well." The smile faded from Sarah's face. "Daddy sold them to the butcher. I guess we needed the money. I don't remember what happened to the ribbon." That was a lie and she knew it. Her father spent the money in the tavern and to show her displeasure, she had cut the ribbon in tiny pieces. *I guess I've put that out of my mind.*

Jeremy pulled on Sarah's arm. "Come, I want to show you the new tractor." They left the milk house and walked across the yard to the machine shed. He rolled back the door. "There it is," he said, pointing to a green and yellow behemoth. The rear wheels were as tall as she. It's a Model A John Deere, or as some of us call it, a Poppin' Johnny."

Sarah wasn't sure of what that all meant but had little interest of learning more

Sarah looked at the other pieces of equipment in the building. The one thing she was sure of, the Fletchers were successful farmers.

Pearl Fletcher walked up as Jeremy pulled the door shut. "I was just on my way to grocery shop, but if you want, I can fix you two something to eat."

"That's okay, Mom. We made plans to go to the Blue Bonnet. I've been bragging about their hamburgers."

She turned to Sarah. "If I don't get a chance to see you later, it's been very nice to meet you."

Jeremy was already dragging Sarah to the car. "You, too," Sarah yelled over her shoulder.

CHAPTER FIFTEEN

Lunch at the Blue Bonnet

The crowd had thinned after the noon rush at the Blue Bonnet Diner. Jeremy found an empty booth by the window. He cleared the last of the plates and silverware and set them on a nearby tray stand. They no sooner sat, when a wisp of a woman in her fifties threw a rag on the table and swept the remaining crumbs on the floor. "Can I get you some drinks?"

"A couple of cokes?" Jeremy looked to Sarah for approval. Getting a nod, the waitress dropped a couple of menus on the table and left.

"Your family farm is very impressive," Sarah said. "I can't believe your Mom would remember me getting a ribbon for raising those rabbits."

"She's been a fair judge for years. That's her big thing every summer."

"Milking sixty-five cows is a lot of work."

"Yeah, Dad was pretty pissed…" He stopped to correct himself. "I mean upset when I joined the Navy. He just assumed I'd be there to help out. Now he's had to hire extra help."

Sarah nodded. She understood the pressure of other people's expectations.

"I wasn't ready to settle down. I wanted to see the world. Maybe do something different with my life." He paused. "Now having gone through boot camp, I'm not so sure I made the right decision."

The waitress put down their drinks and tossed a couple of paper straws on the table. "Are you ready to order?

"Sorry," Jeremy said. "We haven't had a chance to look at the menu."

The woman snorted, put her order pad in her apron pocket and stormed off.

Sarah giggled as she put a straw in her soda. "What do you mean—the right decision?"

"After living with a bunch of guys in the barracks for three months and listening to their stories, I'm thinking life on the farm isn't all that bad. In fact, it's way better than most."

I understand totally. Do I become a Nurse or go work for the FBI? "So, what are you going to do?"

He took a swallow of coke. 'Not much to do. I signed up for four years. Right now, I'm due back for schooling at Great Lakes in ten days. Who knows, after that." He cleared his throat. "Could I ask you something?"

Sarah looked up from the menu. "What's that?'

"What are your plans?"

Plans? "Well…I want to spend some time with Mrs. Canterbury." She chuckled. "I just can't get used to calling her Florence. And then…I have a bus to catch at six o'clock."

"That's not what I meant. With your life. Are you getting a job—going to college?"

My life? "I have a scholarship to the University of Nevada in Reno, but my original plan was to go into nursing. I'm basically taking the summer to decide." She took a sip of her drink.

The waitress stepped to the table. "If you want your food sometime today," she said sarcastically. "I suggest you order."

Jeremy folded his menu. "Two burgers, French fries, and two cokes." He looked for Sarah's approval and got it. Once the woman put the pad in her pocket, gathered the menus and hurried off, he leaned forward and took Sarah's hand. "Would you wait for me?"

"What!" Sarah choked on the soda. She yanked her hand free. "What did you say?"

The guy threw back his shoulders. "I'm sorry, I didn't mean to spring it on you that way, but I think I'm in love with you."

Love? "LOVE!" Sarah looked around. People nearby turned her way.

Jeremy was oblivious to the attention. "I think I have been from the moment I saw you in the bus station. I thought, maybe, if you felt the same, we could…sort of…wait for each other?"

Sarah didn't know whether to laugh or cry. Given time, she could come up with a thousand reasons why that wouldn't work, the least being she didn't love him, at least not at the moment. Her silence had to be killing him. She used the straw to swirl the ice in her glass. "Jeremy…" *Geez, what do I say? I don't want to hurt his feelings.* "Listen—I'm flattered—you're a really nice guy—I've enjoyed meeting you and I appreciate all you've done for me, but…you don't even know me."

"I know you're sweet, and caring—"

"I'm seventeen," Sarah blurted, causing the heads to turn, again. "I just graduated from high school." *Dee Johnson, you better not be laughing her butt off.*

She covered his hand with hers. "Listen, I'm emotionally drained from visiting my mom, and shortly before coming here, I lost my best friend. I can barely keep two rational thoughts straight in my head. I'm sorry, I can't make a commitment like that."

"Can I call you sometime? Maybe come for a visit—wherever you are?"

The waitress set down their food. Sarah welcomed the interruption. She tried to further defuse the situation by asking for ketchup.

It appeared Jeremy was not about to let silence be his answer. "Can I write to you—just to stay in touch."

Sarah nodded and spoke through a mouthful of burger. "I…guess that would be alright."

No doubt seeing the futility of pursuing the matter any further, the young man ventured forward with meaningless small talk about the weather, the price of beef on the hoof, and functionality of the new John Deere tractor. Sarah listened, adding an *uh huh* or a *really* whenever appropriate. There wasn't much said on the ride back to Center House.

"I can give you a ride to the bus station, if you need one." Jeremy said as he opened her car door.

Sarah stepped out of the car. "Are you sure you want to?"

"I don't think there's an afternoon shuttle. Is there anything else you'd like to see…or do?"

"I really should spend some time with Mrs. Canterbury. Would it be okay if you came back around four?"

"Sure, I can do that." His half-hearted response trailed off. His spirit deflated.

Sarah stood on the sidewalk and waved as he drove off. She hated to hurt his feelings. *But he had no right to spring such a silly notion on me.*

Mrs. C. was in the kitchen cleaning up after the noon day meal and bringing things out for supper. "Oh, there you are," she squealed, as Sarah entered the room. "Are you hungry, can I fix you something?"

"I'm fine, we ate at the Blue Bonnet Grill."

"Was it good? A cousin of mine owns it."

"Yes, very good. We had hamburgers." Sarah chuckled. "You must be related to half the people of Danville."

"The gal at the diner is a distant cousin, but I guess if you go back far enough, a lot of us in town are related. I'm not sure about your mom, I think her family came from around Terra Haute. Speaking of…how did it go at the cemetery?"

"Mom and I talked for an hour. For two years I've had this void in my heart, but now I feel peace. Her stone is beautiful and now I know she lies with dignity, like all the rest.

"And her soul is up there watching over you." Florence pointed her finger to the ceiling.

"I actually have two, or three, counting my father. My best friend died in a riding accident right before graduation."

"Oh my." The woman touched the hem of her apron to her mouth. "That's so tragic. How did it happen?"

Sarah set her purse on the counter and pulled up a stool. Florence did the same.

When Sarah finished sharing the details of Dee's death, the woman stood and hugged her. "That's so true, between your mom and dad, and your friend, you've got three wonderful people looking out for you. Do you want to help set the table?" She handed Sarah a handful of silverware. "What time do you have to leave?"

Sarah put a knife and a fork next to the first plate. "Jeremy is coming at four o'clock."

1947 Chevrolet Fleetline

CHAPTER SIXTEEN
Heading Back to Chicago

Jeremy pulled his Chevy to the curb as Sarah walked down the Center House steps. Mrs. Canterbury stood on the porch with her arm around one of the posts. "Travel safe," she said waving her hanky. "Come back and see us, won't you?"

Sarah turned and waved back. "I will. I promise." She blew a kiss to the woman.

Jeremy jumped out, ran around, and opened the passenger side door. "Is that a promise for me too? Will you come back…sometime?"

Sarah handed him her suitcase and settled in the front seat. She waited for him to put the case in the trunk and get behind the steering wheel before answering. "I'm sure I'll be back. I just can't tell you when. I've got a lot going on in my life and I need time to sort things out."

Jeremy said he understood but Sarah knew he took her reply as a 'no.' Nothing she could say now would change his deflated ego. The conversation on the ride to Indianapolis was intermittent and centered around mundane things like the weather and what fields were beginning to sprout. She didn't intend to hurt his feelings but felt emotionally drained. Her only thought, get on the bus, and head back to Chicago.

Their goodbye at the bus station was quick. He handed her the suitcase and said it was wonderful to have met her. She did the same. As she turned to leave, he grabbed her wrist and placed a piece of paper in her hand. "It's my address. If you get a chance, write me sometime. "

Sarah set suitcase on the walk and put the note in her purse. "Sure." They both knew that would probably never happen. She smiled and picked up her case. "Thank you for everything. You've been more than kind. Good luck in the Navy." She stepped back and headed for the terminal door, turning one last time to wave before entering the station. His half-hearted wave came from waist level. The young man turned slowly and got back into his car. Sarah stood for a moment. *I probably shouldn't have burst his bubble that way but leading him on seemed crueler.*

Sarah fumbled in her purse looking for her return ticket. Panic gripped her until she located it in the side pocket. She made a quick stop at the ticket counter to make sure the bus would leave on time and then found a seat against the outer wall. Another of Dee's rules: *In a crowded place, be aware of who or what is behind you.*

Taking out her mother's letter, she sniffed the dried petal. Danville was already drifting from her mind as if locked in the far distant past. She spent time reading and re-reading each word, taking special note of each curve and curly-Q in her mother's handwriting. A finger brushed away the tear that gathered in the corner of her eye.

She wasn't sure when she noticed the man staring at her. He was sitting off to the side and had to turn his head to see her. She made a few inconspicuous glances in his direction. Spying a row of phone booths, along the far wall, she decided to call Gladys to let her know she would be arriving around six in the morning. Bus schedules listed arrival and departure times but taking into consideration traffic and breakdowns, they could be off by as much as an hour. It would also provide an opportunity to find a different seat, away from prying eyes. She picked up her suitcase and hurried to the first open booth. She locked the case between her legs and shut the door.

She felt her panic level raise a notch seeing him walk by and had to caution herself to remain calm, even as he stopped and looked her way. As if Dee's voice prodded her, she ran through a quick description of the guy. Creepy, white male, late twenties, one hundred seventy pounds, closely trimmed blond hair, some kind of tattoo on his right forearm, wearing red and green plaid shirt and dark trousers. *Whoops, sorry Dee. I know, do a facial description.* Dark eyes, set deep, could be brown. Narrow roman nose, wide lips, rounded chin, and two to three days of facial hair.

The loudspeaker crackled. The bus to Chicago was loading at Gate Five. Sarah reached down, grabbed the handle of her suitcase, and opened the door. She'd have to wait and call Gladys when she got to Chicago.

She glanced to see if Mister Creep was anywhere in site. His chair was empty. A quick scan of the room failed to locate him. *Hopefully he's going somewhere else.*

Sarah handed her suitcase to the driver, who turned and slid it into the lower compartment. Being among the first to board, she grabbed a window seat four rows behind the driver. She crossed her fingers and watched as people took seats in front of her or moved to the back. *So far, so good. No sign of Creepy.*

The driver climbed aboard and flopped in his seat. He turned to face the back. "This bus is going to Chicago and points north. If that's not where you're wanting to go, I suggest you get off now."

Sarah chuckled along with everyone else. She kept her eye on the driver. *C'mon, close the door. Let's get out of here.* She barely finished the thought, when the driver reached to his right and pulled the door handle. Sarah exhaled a big breath of air at the sound of the door closing. The driver's hand dropped onto the shifting lever and as he searched for reverse gear, a loud knock rattled through the bus. Someone was pounding on the door. The driver abandoned the shifter and pulled on the door lever. A young man jumped onto the first step.

Sarah's heart sank. It was Creepy in the flesh. *Dammit.* She turned and looked out the window as he came up the aisle. There was no way she was going to make eye contact. From the slight bounce of the bus, she figured he plopped his butt in a seat two rows behind her.

The driver turned to the passengers. "If y'all are settled down back there, we'll get this show on the road." Again, there was a sprinkling of laughter. Sarah was not in the mood. She pulled her sweater tight around her waist and wedged her purse between her body and the armrest. *Stay calm, he's not going to try anything on the bus.*

After jockeying his way out of the terminal and through heavy downtown Indianapolis traffic, the driver soon had the bus headed north on highway 65.

The farms and fields of early corn and wheat reminded her of the Fletcher place. Jeremy was a nice guy. He deserved a girl who would enjoy being a farmer's wife. Sarah smiled. *It's just not a life for me.*

As the miles rolled by Sarah felt more at ease. She chided herself for being so silly. Outside of a few glances her way in the terminal, he really hadn't shown any interest in her. She was the one floating all the bad guy stuff. He's probably a decent person. Maybe he's not even going to Chicago. He could get off anywhere along the way. Lafayette is coming up.

A dozen or so got off during the brief stop in Lafayette, but the man in question was not one of them. Not only was her nemesis still on board, but he had moved to the seat right behind her. Sarah grabbed her purse and inched forward. *Move! Go! Grab a seat up front. Go!* The bus jerked forward as the driver began going through the gears. Sarah slowly settled back into her seat, angry at herself for not making the move. It didn't take but a few miles up the road before the guy put his hand on her seat back.

"Where you headed?" His voice had a raspy tone.

Sarah moved forward in her seat and continued to look out the window. She had no plan other than to completely ignore him and hope he would get the message and back off.

"You from Indianapolis?"

He didn't get the message. Sarah fumbled with her purse and closed another button on her sweater as further evidence she was ignoring him.

"Are you going to Chicago?"

Without turning, she spit out a curt reply. "It's none of your business." She grabbed her purse, got up and moved to the front seat across from the driver.

The man behind the wheel turned and smiled. "Did you come up here to keep me company."

Sarah gave him a blank look. She wasn't sure if he was just making small talk or if it was some shady remark from another pervert. She chose to ignore him. She leaned her head against the window and closed her eyes. She was spooked. Nora had expressed her misgivings about making the trip, saying there were a lot of crazy people in this world. *I guess this is what concerned her.*

CHAPTER SEVENTEEN

Welcome to the Windy City

As the bus made its way into the heart of downtown Chicago, Sarah checked her watch. It was just past four-thirty. Daybreak was still hours away. *Geez, we're getting in early. Gladys won't even be up.* There were barely a dozen people left on the bus. Many who boarded in Indianapolis had gotten off along the way. Unfortunately, Creepy was still curled up in his seat.

The majority of the city's residents hadn't yet crawled out of bed. The sparse street traffic moved at a steady pace. Soon, the driver pulled the bus into the parking area behind the terminal and shut off the engine. He pulled the lever to open the door as he came up out of his seat and lumbered down the steps. Sarah jumped from her front row seat and followed him out. It was dark. The lot was dimly lit. Sarah fidgeted as she waited for the driver to open the luggage compartment. She certainly didn't need another encounter with the creepy jerk in the plaid shirt. The moment the driver had the door secured upright, Sarah grabbed her bag and hustled into the building.

The terminal was quiet, not many people milled around, but then again it was early. Sarah zig-zagged her way past rows of empty benches and took a seat at the far end, close to the front door. Another of Dee's warnings: always have an escape plan. The door would offer a quick getaway if one was needed. It also provided a clear view for when Gladys arrived. The minute hand on the large wall clock clicked to ten after five. Sarah debated if it was too early to give her friend a call.

A row of phone booths lined the wall on the right. Picking up her bag, she scurried over and ducked into the first one. Sitting, she shut the door and peered out the window. No sign of a plaid shirt. She opened her purse, pulled a slip of paper from the side pocket and deposited a nickel in the slot. Before rattling off the number to the operator, she took another glance around the room. Her heart leaped in her chest when she heard Gladys' voice. "I'm so glad you're up," she blurted. "This is Sarah. We got in early. Can you come and pick me up?"

She heard Gladys's concerned reply. "I'll leave right now. Is everything alright? You sound anxious."

"I'm fine." It was a bald-faced lie, but she tried to sound calm. "Just get here as soon as you can, okay? I'm right by the front door."

Gladys' last words before hanging up, "I'll be there in fifteen minutes."

Holding the receiver to her ear, Sarah pretended to be still conversing as she looked for any sign of her creepy admirer. Seconds ticked off before she ended the charade and hung up. She swung the door open, found the handle on her bag and stepped out. A man came out of the next booth at the same time. It startled her. *Geez!* Her heart stopped until seeing it was a balding, sixtyish-year-old, a whole head shorter than she.

Reclaiming her seat by the door, she locked her suitcase between her legs. It was too early for the business day to begin, none of the ticket windows were open and neither was the coffee counter. Soon she could only count a handful of people. Thank goodness no one wearing plaid shirt and dark trousers was among them. At least he was nowhere to be seen.

An elderly woman she recognized as being on the bus from Indianapolis was greeted by a gray-haired man who had just come through the front door. They hugged, kissed, and hurried out the door.

A bus, leaving the yard, drove past the front of the building and disappeared up the street. *God, I hope the creep is on it.*

Sarah felt the urge and wished she had gone to the ladies' room as soon as she got off the bus. It would have been the perfect time. *Dang it.* She couldn't wait until she got back to Gladys's place. She spied the restroom sign at the other end of the terminal. Hesitating would only make things more pressing. *Dammit!* She cursed her poor planning. Taking a final look around the room, she slung her purse over her shoulder and picked up her bag. Doing her best to avoid the few remaining people, she bristly marched to the far end of the terminal and bolted through the restroom door. Resting her hands on the sink counter, she took a deep breath in an effort to slow her breathing. *Why am I letting this guy freak me out?*

Relief brought a sigh. It wasn't until she stood at the sink and splashed water on her face, that she felt her breathing return to normal. She pulled a couple of sheets of paper towel from the dispenser and wiped her face.

Suddenly, plaid covered arms wrapped around her, locking hers to her side. *What the...* She felt his hot breath on her neck and down the front of her shirt. His whiskers scratched her ear and cheek. She tried to pull free but couldn't match his strength. *How did he—where was he hiding? Why didn't I hear him?*

"Well, little Miss Stuck up, what are you going to do now?" he growled in her ear. She heard a click and saw the silvery blade spring from a pearl-handled switchblade. He brandished it menacingly close to her face. "You make one peep and it'll be the last sound you'll ever make."

He spun her around, pushed her against the wall, and jammed his forearm under her chin. Holding the point of the knife beside her nose, he pressed the blade against her skin. Bringing his face within an inch of hers, he whispered, "Just relax and you won't get hurt." His moist breath shot up her nose and down her throat. The foul smell choked her.

Her mind raced. *Don't scream. Wait your chance.* Her eyes darted around the room.

He chuckled, low and sarcastic. "Ain't nobody here. It's just you and me." His hand ripped down through the buttons on her blouse. Some popped open, while the cloth around others tore loose leaving her shirt gaping open. He yanked her bra strap off her shoulder and tore at the lacy cloth until her left breast was fully exposed. His hand slid up her stomach.

Sarah instinctively grabbed it before it reached it's target. *You bastard.*

The creep pressed the knife to her nose, nicking the nostril. She took it as a warning not to resist. She let go of his hand and wiped the trickle of blood from her nose. *You're going to pay for this.* His coarse fingers rubbed across her nipple before cupping the breast. He squeezed it once, twice.

She pushed his hand away and sneered, "Stop it, you're hurting me."

Using his body, he again, drove her against the wall. "You want hurt? I'll show you hurt." He reached down and brought his hand up under her skirt. She could feel his fingers grabbing for the elastic in her underpants. Anger burned to her core. She grabbed his hand and held it from going further. *You'll have to kill me...get your filthy hands—*

The sound of the door opening froze the man in place. An elderly woman walked in.

The man took one look and yelled, "Get the hell out of here. G'wan, git."

Seeing the knife and Sarah's chest laid bare, the woman shrieked and backed out of the room.

It was all the distraction Sarah needed. She brought her knee up into the man's groin with all the strength and fury she could muster. He groaned, doubled over, and grabbed his crotch. She brought her fists above her head and came down hard on his back. "Here's some hurt for you."

He grabbed for her.

She swatted his hand away and kicked him again in his privates, sending him stumbling backwards over her suitcase. The knife flew and made a clicking sound as it slid across the tile. He ended up sprawled on the floor, moaning and writhing in pain.

Sarah had one thought. *Get to the door.* She held onto the counter as she moved to get past him. *Just a few steps more.* As she bolted to make her escape, the man made a desperate lunge, caught her ankle, and sent her crashing to the floor. "I'm not done with you, bitch."

She kicked his hand and yanked her foot, but he held tight.

"I think it's time we have a little fun," he said, as his free hand moved up her leg. She felt his rough fingers on her calf, and then above her knee. It reached mid-thigh before she brought the other knee up.

"Fun is over," she said, and sent the foot squarely down onto the bridge of his nose. Blood spurted everywhere.

"Sonofabitch," he yelled, letting go and grabbing his nose.

Sarah scrambled to her feet and stumbled to the door. She had it half open before he came crashing into her back. He pushed her to the side. His face was covered in blood. He wiped the crimson off his chin and studied his bloody hand. "You bitch!" He glared and lunged for the shoulder strap of her purse. "Whada you got in there? Money? Let me have it."

"Go to hell." she yelled, yanking the strap out of his reach.

In a split-second response his fist caught her square under her left eye sending her reeling backwards. Flailing, she fell awkwardly on her backside and slid against the sink counter. The creep stood over her. He tore the purse from her grip and snarled, "So long Miss Stuck Up. It's been nice knowing ya." He pulled the door open and ran out.

Sarah sat up and covered her eye with her hand. Even the slightest touch made it hurt worse. Her lip started to quiver. *Dammit. How did this happen? Where was he hiding?* She couldn't stop the tears that flooded her eyes and rolled down her cheeks. "This was so stupid." She moved her bra strap up over her shoulder. "I'm stupid. I let my guard down." *Dee said it a hundred times, be aware of your surroundings.* She pulled her blouse together and buttoned the ones that still had a matching hole intact.

She recoiled at the loud crash and seeing his plaid shirt come flying through the door. This time he came in backside first. The Creep struggled to gain his footing but fell to his butt and slid against the wall. Blood continued to drip from his nose. More covered his chin from a wide gash in his lip. A large woman, dressed in a white uniform, stormed in with two hefty men on her heels. "Sit on him until the cops get here," she instructed. "If he moves, punch his lights out." She bent and pulled the purse strap from the bloodied man's grip. "Let go of that or I'll kick your teeth out." He quickly let go.

Kneeling next to Sarah, she brushed the tear-soaked strands of hair out of the girl's face. "Are you alright?'

Sarah nodded before throwing her arms around the woman. "Oh Gladys, I'm so happy to see you. I was so scared. He had a knife. He tried to…I thought he was going to kill me." Her shoulders jerked uncontrollably as she sobbed.

"Everything is going to be okay. He can't hurt you anymore." The nurse got up and wet some paper towels. Sarah flinched as Gladys applied the cold compress to her eye. "It looks like you're going to have quite a shiner. He caught you a good one."

Two police officers came charging into the room. Before either could speak, Gladys pointed to the creep, "Get that asshole out of here."

Seeing the man's bloody face, the one officer turned to his partner. "Jesus, What the hell happened to him?" One of the men holding the guy down, chuckled. "He tried to pull something, and those women cleaned his clock."

One officer cuffed him while the other put his hands on his knees and bent towards the women. "Can someone tell me what happened here?"

"Are you blind?" Gladys shrieked. "That dirtbag assaulted this girl. Take your choice. You can write it up as attempted rape or attempted murder." Gladys pointed to the switchblade. "All with a deadly weapon. And, if that's not enough you can add battery and purse snatching."

The officer stifled a laugh. "By the looks of him, he got the worst of it."

Gladys pointed to Sarah, "I'm guessing she busted his nose. Then waving her fist, "I'll take credit for the split lip." She helped Sarah to her feet. "Come on, let's get you back to my place."

"Wait," the officer said. "We need to fill out a report."

"Screw your report." Gladys' tone left no room for argument. "Can't you see, this girl is in shock. You run the guy downtown and we'll come by later to do your *report*. This girl needs time to decompress. Check the books, medical needs supersede those of law enforcement." Then turning to the two men. "Thanks for your help fellas. Will one of you grab her bag and bring it along." Gladys held Sarah close as they walked out of the room.

The policeman scratched his head and muttered. "Is that really a law?"

Looking Beyond the Moment.

Gladys navigated her trusty '40 Ford through the busy Chicago streets. Sarah sat holding her torn blouse tight to her chest with one hand, while the other kept the wet towel pressed against her eye

"Are you doing okay?" Gladys knew the symptoms of a person in shock. "You'll feel a lot better once you've had a chance to shower and get into a change of clothes." It was hard to determine if Sarah nodded or if her head movement was just part of her whole body shaking. "I still have a few of those chocolate chip cookies left. Milk and cookies always make things better." Gladys was not happy when Sarah failed to respond. She reached and lifted the towel from Sarah's cheek. "Yep. That's going to be one doozy of a shiner."

"What am I going to tell Nora?" Sarah's voice was just above a whisper.

Gladys winced. "You're right, she's going to be madder than a wet hornet. Maybe it would be best if we changed our names and moved to Mexico."

It took Sarah a moment to catch the humor. At first, it was just a small giggle that rattled in her throat. Soon they were both laughing out loud.

"Maybe she won't notice." Gladys said

Sarah sat up and pulled the rearview mirror around so she could see her face. "Are you kidding? Look what I look like. The whole world is going to wonder what happened."

"Let them wonder," Gladys said in a serious tone. "The main thing is, I think you're strong enough to put this behind you." Gladys laughed again. "Imagine that guy trying to explain it to the other jailbirds."

"I hope he gets what he deserves," Sarah said quietly.

Gladys was right, the warm shower felt wonderful. She soaped up three times, making sure she washed every inch of her body. She spent extra time scrubbing where his grubby hand touched her breast. She probably would have stayed in the shower for the rest of her life if Gladys hadn't knocked on the door. She was standing holding her purse when Sarah came out of the bathroom wrapped in a towel with another wrapped around her hair.

"I've got to go into work and make sure everything is running smooth. We've got some dynamite makeup we give to people to hide bruising. It should help cover up that shiner. I should be back around lunch time. If you're up to it, we can go down to the station, fill out the report and then head up to Pine Lake. Are you okay here until I get back?"

Sarah nodded. "I'll be fine."

"Scrounge around. Eat whatever you want. I left the cookies and milk on the table."

Sarah towel dried her hair. She hadn't paid that much attention to the apartment when she and Nora had arrived. It was nicely furnished, not ritzy, more on the comfy side. She walked to the wall of pictures near the front door. Gladys was the only one she recognized in most of them. Right in the middle was a picture taken two years ago when they all were in Danville for the custody hearing. She put her finger to the glass. *Look how young I look...and innocent.*

"I'm not feeling sorry for myself." Her outburst was a retort from an imagined question from Dee. "And where were you when that guy was all over me?" She tossed the towel across the room. "I don't believe it. You were enjoying every minute, weren't you? Dee Johnson, if I could get my hands on you, I'd…I'd…" Sarah flopped on the couch. A smile spread across her face. "I'd hug you to death." She got up and picked the towel off the floor. "And you're right, I'm not going to let this incident rule my life. If I do, I'm the one who loses."

The makeup did a fairly decent job of camouflaging Sarah's black eye. The average person might not notice, but neither woman believed it would fool Nora. "She'll see it for sure," Sarah said.

"You're probably right," Gladys added, "but it does make it less noticeable."

*****

One of the arresting officers led Gladys and Sarah to a private office off the main lobby of the police station. A tall, slender man got up from the desk and introduced himself as Lieutenant Morrison. He offered them chairs. "I've already got a statement from the attending officers. Do you feel up to filling out your part?"

Sarah nodded. "I'm over being sad or frightened. I'm at the mad stage. All I want is to make sure this creep isn't free to attack anyone else." She was also encouraged that he hadn't stared at her face or commented on her black eye. *Maybe Nora won't notice either.*

"I don't blame you," Morrison said. "He appears to be a pretty bad apple." He pointed to where he wanted Sarah to begin. "Just give us a brief account of what happened. Your name, and how we can get in touch with you are most important. We've already got a lot of info on this character. He's a prime subject in a string of similar assaults. There's also an open murder case with a possible fingerprint match. This investigation will take time. You probably won't hear from us until the end of summer."

No bail, right?" Gladys asked coming forward in her seat.

"Oh, hell no," the officer said. "He'll sit in jail until the trial. I'll give you a heads up when we get to that point."

He waited for Sarah to sign the form before handing her a business card. "If you want to call to see how things are going, or have any questions, you can reach me at this number." He walked them to the front door. "The officer's report says the perp gave your eye quite a wallop. Your makeup does a nice job of concealing the bruise."

Sarah just smiled and thanked him for his help.

Gladys got behind the wheel and started the car. "You did a good job. I have a feeling that piece of crap is going to spend the rest of his life behind bars."

"The makeup didn't fool him. Nora is sure to zero in on it."

"Let's not worry about that until we get to Pine Lake." Gladys pulled away from the curb and merged into traffic.

Sarah studied the lieutenant's card. "I'll have to testify, won't I?"

"Probably," Gladys said, "but that's a long time down the road.

"What if I'm already back in Nevada?"

"You've already given them your statement. Besides, it sounds like they have a mountain of evidence against him. I wouldn't worry about it. Let's go back to my place, gather up a few things, and head north to the lake."

"Do you think we should call Nora and let her know what happened?" Sarah asked.

"No-o-o-o." Gladys tapped her fingers on the steering wheel as if pondering the question. "You know she's going to blow her stack. She'll be mad at you for wanting to go to Danville and me for saying it would be all right. I think it'll be best if we plead our case face to face."

Sarah conjured a laugh. "I think you're right."

CHAPTER NINETEEN

"Let's plead
our case
face to
face."

Gladys normally made the boring, five-hour trip to Pine lake by herself. Today, she was happy to have Sarah along to keep her company, and the girl didn't disappoint. She was like a magpie, talking about every part of her trip. The visit to her mom's grave had the older woman digging in her purse for her hanky. Gladys's ears perked up as Sarah talked about meeting Jeremy on the bus. She coaxed the young girl, wanting to hear every detail. "When he asked if you'd wait for him, was that like a proposal?"

Sarah laughed. "It caught me by surprise. I'm not sure what he wanted."

"For men, it all leads to one thing, a romp in the sack."

Sarah choked on a giggle. Her cheeks warmed.

Gladys appeared oblivious to the girl's reaction. "So, where is this encounter going? Do you plan on seeing him again?"

"I'm not sure what my plans are," Sarah said, checking her cuticles. "For the past two years, I planned to follow Nora and become a nurse. Then when Dee…died and I got the scholarship…I thought about…" Sarah stopped mid-sentence. A mental image of Dee's bleeding, contorted body, wedged between the rocks, brought her to the edge of tears.

Gladys let the pause simmer.

As if awaking from a trance, Sarah continued. "I'm hoping to sort things out over summer, but right now, I don't picture myself being a farmer's wife…milking cows…in Indiana."

They both laughed.

It was close to four in the afternoon when Gladys pulled her car in front of Duke and Nora's place. She shut off the engine. "Are you ready to go in and face the music?"

Sarah looked up at the house. "I know she's going to kill me."

Gladys opened her door and slid off the seat. "C'mon, she'll have to kill the both of us."

Sarah took one last look at her eye in the overhead mirror, got out and retrieved her suitcase from the back seat. "She'll see it right off the bat, but I guess the sooner she knows what happened the faster she'll get over it."

"Right, but maybe it'll be best if you let me handle this. I'm bigger than she."

By the time the women reached the top step of the porch, Nora was there to greet them. She didn't wait for Sarah to set down her case before wrapping her in her arms.

She let go and took the suitcase from Sarah. "I see you made it okay. How was your trip?" Sarah kept her head turned so the bruised eye was out of Nora's line of vision. "Come inside, Duke and I have been waiting." She turned to Gladys. "Duke is cutting up some cheese and salami. We thought you might want a little something to hold you 'til supper."

"I'll take a beer and pass on the snacks," Gladys said, as she followed the other two to the kitchen.

Duke set down his knife and opened the refrigerator door. He held out a bottle to Gladys. "Got time for a beer?"

"Thanks," she said, as he passed by. "I think I'm going to need this." She opened the drawer and took out an opener.

Duke rushed to Sarah. He gave her a quick look before wrapping his arms around her. Then, taking a step back, he said, "Wow, where did you get the shiner?"

Nora yanked Sarah around. "Shiner? Where?" She used a finger to wipe away some of the makeup. Her eyes grew as big as saucers. "What happened…how did you?"

Gladys took the moment as her cue to step between the girls. She raised a finger to Nora. "Before you fly off the handle, I want you to take a deep breath."

Nora pushed the finger away. "What about…"

Gladys put her finger to her lips as you would to quiet a child. "Sarah had a wonderful trip except for one small incident."

"Small? What do you mean, small?" Nora grabbed a washcloth from the sink and wiped away more of the makeup. "Look at that," she shrieked. "How did that happen?"

Gladys took a quick sip of beer. "Sarah and Mrs. Canterbury had a nice visit. She saw her mom's grave and she met a nice Indiana farm boy."

Nora latched onto the word boy. "You met a boy?"

She actually met two." Gladys took another drink.

"Two?" Nora searched Sarah's face for answers.

"Yeah," Gladys continued. One wanted to marry her and the other tried to rape her."

Nora pulled Sarah into her arms. "What! Rape!" The words shot from her mouth. She studied the girl's face. "Are you alright? Did he hurt you?" Her voice trailed off as if she neither wanted to finish the question nor hear the answer.

Sarah shook her head. "I'm okay."

Nora hugged her sister. "I knew it. I should never have let you go to Danville by yourself." She spun and marched up to Gladys. Jamming her finger into the woman's chest, she shouted. "Let her go you said…she'll be fine. Well, this doesn't sound fine to me."

Gladys backed away and took another swallow of beer. "If you're done ranting and ready to listen, it's not as bad as it sounds. Look at her. She's fine. She was mugged but nothing happened. In fact, the guy got the worst of it. She broke his nose and I busted his lip. It appears the jerk is facing a lifetime in jail.

"But I…I…" It was evident Nora had conflicting emotions. She came up behind Sarah, wrapped her arms around the girl and rested her head on the back of her shoulder. "You've been through so much. I can't bear the thought of you being hurt anymore."

Sarah squeezed Nora's arms and laid her head against Nora's. "It's okay, I'm fine and I had a really good time. Mrs. Canterbury told me so many things about my mom and dad." She turned to face Nora. "They were down-to-earth people, not perfect, but now I feel a strong connection to who I really am." Sarah showed her the valentine she made in second grade and let her read the letter her mom wrote. "I also found my mother's wedding ring." She extended her hand. Pulling it back, she admired the pretty red stone. "I would have missed all of it, if I hadn't made the trip."

Gladys clunked her empty bottle on the counter. "That's it for me. I'm going. Mom's probably wondering what happened to me. I'm sure Sarah is dying to tell you the rest of the *nice* things that happened on her trip."

Duke put his arms around both women. "All is well that ends well."

"Don't bother breaking up your little pow-wow," Gladys said. "I know my way out."

Sarah spent the next hour giving Nora and Duke a minute by minute recap of the entire trip. She even gave them a blow by blow of her encounter with the creep in the ladies' room and her trip to the police station.

"And if you have to testify against the jerk," Nora said. "We'll go with you."

CHAPTER TWENTY

Pie & Coffee at the Bay Side

Nora took Sarah's hand. "Come, I'll show you your room. Duke finally finished the upstairs, at least the guest bedroom and bath. There's enough room up here to make a whole apartment, but that will have to wait." At the top of the landing, Nora opened a double door. The room was spacious and bright. A white four poster bed accented with a pink chiffon canopy and matching bedspread graced the far wall. A matching white provincial dresser hugged the wall to the left. On the right, next to the window hung with pink curtains, stood an ornately carved armoire, with its white doors trimmed in gold pinstriping.

"Wow," Sarah said, as she put down her suitcase. "This looks like something out of the movies."

"Duke picked up these mis-matched pieces at estate sales, stripped the old dark varnish and refinished them in white just for you."

Sarah ran her hand up and down one of the bedposts. "For me? But I've—"

Nora touched the girl's shoulder. "We've always hoped you'd come and stay with us." She went to the window and opened it. The curtains billowed into the room. She quickly pushed it down, leaving a three-inch opening. She drew in a deep breath. "There's a nice cool breeze coming off the lake."

Sarah opened the door on the armoire and looked at her suitcase. "I don't have much to put in here."

Nora chuckled. "We can call Mom and have her send a bunch of your stuff. It would only take about a week. In a pinch, you can raid my closet for anything you need."

"Seriously?" Sarah asked, wondering if it was an actual offer.

"Of course. We're pretty close to the same size." Nora looked at Sarah, then said, "but we're not getting on the scale to prove the point."

Sarah giggled as she opened her suitcase and began putting stuff in the armoire.

"If you still have some of that graduation money left we can go over to Penney's in Middletown and do a little shopping."

"I could use some blouses—and a new bathing suit."

Nora sniffed the air. "Come, it smells like Duke is cooking the pork chops."

"You gals are just in time." Duke said, as he put a bowl of mashed potatoes in the center of the table. "The chops are ready."

Sarah put her hands on a chair back. "The table looks beautiful and everything smells so good."

"Sit." Nora pulled out her chair. "With my crazy schedule, Duke does a lot of the cooking." She glanced in his direction. "It's one of the reasons I keep him around."

"Is that all?" Duke smiled and fluttered his lashes.

Nora flushed and nodded in Sarah's direction. "Shall we eat?"

Sarah sat and unfolded her napkin. "I know all about the birds and the bees, if that's what you two are talking about."

"That's wonderful," Nora said. "But we don't have to discuss it at the dinner table. Would someone please pass me the potatoes?"

Sarah caught Duke looking at her. They both squelched a laugh.

Duke passed the bowl to Nora and the platter of meat to Sarah. "So, what are your plans? How long are you staying?"

"The summer, if it's alright with you guys."

Nora took the platter and handed Sarah the bowl of potatoes. "Have you made a decision on school?

"Not really."

"Green beans, anyone?" Duke passed the bowl. "Nora said you were class valedictorian and got a college scholarship. That's quite an accomplishment."

Sarah's fork stopped in mid-air. "It was supposed to go to my friend."

Nora moved quickly to change the subject. "Maybe tomorrow, you can come to the hospital, I'd love to show you around and introduce you to some of the people."

Sarah smiled. Her head nodded approval.

"If you want to know anything about boat refinishing," Duke said, "you can tag along with me."

Nora cut in. "I doubt if she wants—"

"No," Sarah said quickly, "I'd love to see how you do that. You did a beautiful job on the furniture in my room. I love it."

"See," Duke said with a big smile on his face. "This girl has a taste for the finer things in life. Hell, anyone can save a life, but not everyone can make a Chris-Craft look like new."

Nora buried her face in her hands. "Okay, hot shot, but do you have to swear to make your point."

I'm sorry," Sarah said. "I didn't mean to cause a ruckus between you two.

Nora laughed. "You didn't, Duke just gets a little full of himself at times. You do what you want. We just want you to enjoy your time with us."

"Nora's right," Duke said. "We love having you here, but refinishing *is* an artform."

Nora rolled her eyes. "See what I mean. For dessert, what do you say about walking down to the Bay Side Coffee Shop for a slice of apple pie—ala mode?"

Sarah's eyes widened. "I love apple pie."

Duke jumped to his feet. "I'm for that. Give me two minutes to corral the leftovers. The dishes can wait until we get back."

It was a beautiful evening. A cool breeze came off the lake. The three large lilac bushes bordering the sidewalk, gave off an intoxicating fragrance. The splash of purple blossoms would make a wonderful painting. Duke pointed and named the trees and plants they passed, while Nora identified the homes and businesses. People milled on Main street, some just out for a stroll, while others window shopped in the shuttered stores.

A large group of people laughed and chatted as they streamed out of the coffee shop. Duke stepped back and let them pass. "I hope they still have some pie left," he said, holding the door for the girls.

The waitress greeted Nora by name, cleared a table, and tossed down some menus. "Coffee?"

"And three slices of apple pie," Nora said. "Warm them up and add a scoop of vanilla ice cream."

"I'll have milk," Sarah interjected.

"Make that two coffees and a milk," Duke said.

Nora waited until the waitress had set down the pie and drinks. "Blanche, this is my…baby sister. She's here for the summer."

"If she's looking for work, we can use some help. What's your name, dearie?"

It's Sarah," Nora quipped, "and she's not looking for a job."

"Too bad," Blanche said. "We normally get a few college girls from Middletown, but so far no one has come to apply." She leaned forward. "That's quite a shiner, you've got."

"She ran into an opened door," Nora said quickly, not wanting the town gossip bittys to get hold of the story.

Blanche smiled as if to say, good story, but I don't believe it.

Nora turned to Sarah. "You weren't thinking about getting a job, were you?"

"I did work the ice cream counter at the drug store. It would be a chance to make money for school clothes."

"If you're interested," Blanche said. "Stop in and fill out an application."

Sarah nodded and picked up her fork. She sniffed the air. "The pie smells delicious."

"You know, you don't have to work if you don't want to," Nora said. "With everything you've gone through, it might be nice to kick back and enjoy the summer."

"There's no hurry, you have plenty of time to think about it." Duke said. "Take a few days to have a look around."

"I think that's a splendid idea." Sarah put a forkful of pie in her mouth.

CHAPTER TWENTY-ONE

Starlight Stage in Lakeside Park

Sarah followed Nora out of the coffee shop. She walked to the curb and gazed at the large red brick building across the street.

"That's the Marshall County Courthouse," Nora said, and she continued to name buildings and businesses as she pointed to each of them.

"I love your downtown," Sarah said. "It's smaller than Ely, but the shops look pretty much the same. Can we look in some of the store windows?"

"I have the early shift at the hospital," Nora said. "Maybe some other time."

"Let her go walk around," Duke said. "She's a big girl." Then turning to Sarah, "Can you find your way back to the house?"

Sarah looked in the direction they had come. "I'm sure. I won't be long. I'd just like to see what Pine Lake has to offer."

Nora begrudgingly nodded her approval. "We'll leave a light on—and Duke will probably still be up."

"There's a lot to see," Sarah said. "I'd also like to walk down and have a look at the lake."

Duke took Nora by the arm. "Enjoy yourself, we'll see you back at the house."

Nora forced a smile as Duke escorted her up the street.

Sarah understood Nora's apprehension, but this was small town USA, not a bus depot in Chicago. Looking up, she felt comforted at seeing the night sky filled with stars and having the same constellations visible in Ely. People she passed on the street voiced pleasant greetings or just nodded and smiled. One of the first shops she came to, had a display of bathing suits. A white one, with small navy polka dots caught her eye. She bent over and crooked her head in an effort to read the tag. *They always hang them, to hide the price.* "Seventeen fifty!" The words came out louder than she intended. Embarrassed, she casually glanced around to see if she had raised anyone's notice. Shocked at what had to be tourist pricing, she hurried down the street. *My God, I paid six dollars for the suit I bought last year.*

She passed a hardware store and a barbershop before pausing to look in the window of Warner's Gift Shop. It was filled with a variety of Pine Lake trinketry. *If that charm bracelet with the fish and boats is Sterling, it might be a nice souvenir to have.* Sarah continued until she came to the end of the street. From there, she could look beyond the park and see the lake.

Dodging a car, she ran across the street to the park entrance. A large white welcoming sign supported by a post on either side and fronted with a box of red geraniums, stood to the left. She took a moment to read it. *Lakeside Park and Starlight Stage. Band Concert - 7 PM on Wednesdays. Free Movie - 8 PM on Fridays.*

She walked toward the lake. The light from the three-quarter moon sparkled like a thousand diamonds as it reflected and danced off the rippling water.

A large structure stood in the shadows off to her right. She turned and walked slowly to it. Standing in front of the waist-high stage platform, she was taken by its size and beauty. The roof slanted upwards from back to front and the side walls angled out creating an acoustical clamshell. Wing walls on either side concealed the stairs leading to the stage floor. Sarah went to her right and climbed the four steps. Walking out onto the stage she looked through the dark at the grass clearing.

At first it was a simple twirl, then a full pirouette followed by two more. With arms outstretched, she spun her way to the other end of the stage and finished with a deep bow. She held her pose to the imagined applause of her adoring fans. She giggled as made her exit. In a moment she bounded back on stage for a final bow and to blow kisses into the night stillness.

Clap, Clap.

Sarah stiffened and searched the darkness.

"Great performance." A tall figure jogged up to the platform. "Are you going to be performing here all summer?"

Sarah walked to the edge of the stage. "I was just being silly. I didn't think there was anyone around."

"I thought it was pretty good, but you might want to work on the pirouettes."

"You mean, like take dance lessons for the next ten years before I come back."

The man jumped up and sat on the edge of the stage. He strained to get a better look at her. "Haven't seen you before, are you a tourist or local?"

"Somewhere in between." Sarah took a few steps upstage putting a little distance between them. "What about you? Are you some kind of kook? Do you always spook around in the dark?"

"I was going to ask you the same thing." The man laughed and slid off the stage. "I'm sorry if I've interrupted your dance. The pirouettes need work." He jogged off.

Sarah watched him disappear into the shadows. *A kook and a dance critic. What does he expect, my last dance lesson was ten years ago?* She giggled at her silliness and jumped down from the stage. walking to the lake, she climbed onto a nearby picnic table, she sat on the top and rested her feet on the seat. The aquatic lake smell was intoxicating and a far cry from the arid earthy smell of the high desert of Nevada or even the agricultural tilt of Indiana. The breeze moved her auburn hair off her forehead and away from her cheeks, a feeling she thought similar to riding Jubilee at a full gallop. She closed her eyes and relived the day Dee died. *It would have been neat if you could have come here with me.*

Still lost in thought, she never heard the three boys until they were thirty feet away. She saw the cherry of their cigarettes bobbing in the dark before hearing their muffled laughter. She saw them before they saw her. They appeared to be no more than fourteen or fifteen years old.

"Whoa, what have we here?" the bigger one said as he flicked his smoke into the lake. He walked unsteadily to the table. His breath reeked of alcohol. The other two held back. "What are you doing here all by yourself?" He asked, pushing a half pint bottle of whiskey to her face. "Want a drink?"

Sarah pushed the bottle away and slid off the table. She attempted to step to her left, but the boy stepped in her path. "Would you mind? she said, moving to the right.

"Yes, I mind." He pressed the bottle into her chest.

Sarah parried, looping her arm and violently knocking his arm aside. The bottle went flying in the air. It spun around twice, hit the rocky waterfront and shattered, spilling the fiery liquid into the water.

"You stupid bitch," the boy shouted, pushing her down. She landed on her backside and slid on the damp grass. He jumped on top of her and drew back his fist.

Sarah covered her face, expecting the blow.

It never came. His buddies pulled him to his feet. "C'mon," one said. "That's enough, let's get out of here." They tried to run, but their whiskey-fed rubber-legs sent them crashing down on top of one another. Scrambling to get up, they stumbled off into the night.

Sarah rolled to her side, raised her skirt, and got to her knees. She brushed the wet grass from her hands and off her backside. She got up and looked around. *Wouldn't that have been great, a black eye on top of a black eye. Welcome to Pine Lake.*

Sarah had no trouble finding her way back to the house. She was less sure of what she would tell Duke and Nora about her little adventure. Hopefully, she could get the grass stain out of her skirt before having to confess or make up a plausible explanation for how it got there. Things were working in her favor. When she approached the house, it was dark, save for a light in the foyer.

Sarah slowly turned the knob on the front door and stepped in. Slipping out of her loafers, she tiptoed up the stairs. She tossed her sweater on the bed, undid the side button of her skirt and let it fall to the floor. Picking it up, she checked the stain. "It's going to take a lot of scrubbing to get that out." She draped it over the back of the chair and changed into her pajamas. After a long drive from Chicago, dinner, dessert, and two encounters in the park, the bed felt wonderful. Sleep came swiftly.

CHAPTER TWENTY-TWO
Sarah Meets Griff

Duke finished wiping up around the stove as Sarah walked into the kitchen. "Well, good morning, sleepyhead." He tossed the washcloth in the sink. "Can I fix you some breakfast?"

Sarah plopped in a chair and laid her head on the table. Lifting slightly, she shot a glance around the room. "What time is it?"

"Half past nine." Duke opened the refrigerator and brought out a pitcher of orange juice. He poured some in a glass and set it in front of her. "Would you like some eggs, pancakes, or I can make you some of my super delicious French toast?" He grabbed the coffee pot and held it up. "Want some?"

Sarah put her hand around the glass. "Juice will be fine. I've never acquired a taste for coffee. Has Nora left for work?"

"She's got a half day in already. Her normal is six to two. What'll it be? Eggs?"

Sarah slouched in the chair. "Maybe just a couple pieces of toast?"

"I've got fresh raisin bread. Makes great toast, especially if you add some butter and honey." Duke opened the bread box and brought out the loaf. "Did you have a good look around town last night? We never heard you come home."

"I wasn't that late. I tried to be quiet."

Duke pushed the butter dish to her. He took a large jar from the cupboard. "A buddy of mine has bees, this is the best honey you'll ever taste." He turned as the bread popped up from the toaster. Handing her the plate, he continued. "So, what do you think of Pine Lake?"

Outside of a few kooks... "It's nice. I'm anxious to see it in daylight." *No need to bring up the friendly encounters.* "I saw a silver bracelet, with boat and fish charms, in the gift shop window. I thought it would be a nice souvenir to take back to Ely."

"At Warner's? They have a lot of nice things."

She nodded as she buttered the bread and drizzled a generous amount of honey on each.

"I thought I'd take you over to the boat dock and show you where I work. We've got a couple of Chris-Crafts that are about ready to go in the water. I've worked all winter on them. How about it?"

Sarah nodded, not wanting to talk with a mouthful of raisin bread. "Yes," she said after swallowing. "The toast is really good and yes, I'd love to see your work." Sarah stood, picked up the second slice, and gulped down the juice. "Give me ten minutes and I'll be ready to go." She hurried up the stairs, putting the last bite of toast in her mouth before any of the honey could drip. She rummaged through her suitcase before coming up with her toothbrush and paste. Pawing through the rest of the stuff she brought out her last pair of clean underwear. "It's either go shopping or do laundry" She chuckled as she grabbed her comb and hairbrush and hurried off to the bathroom.

She didn't quite make the ten minutes, but it didn't matter. Duke was just hanging up the phone. "That was Nora. She's cutting out early and wants us to meet at one for lunch at Greystone. She also invited Gladys and her mom."

Sarah looked down at her denim skirt and western plaid shirt. "Am I alright to go like this? It's about the only thing I have left to wear…that's clean."

"You look fine. We don't put on airs." He grabbed his keys off the hook and led the way out back. He swung one of the garage doors off to the side before kicking a brick in front of the other to make sure it stayed open. "Hop in," he said going to his side of the pickup.

Sarah pointed to the motorcycle parked off to the side. "You promised to give me a ride when you were in Ely."

Duke opened the truck door only to slam it shut. "That I did. I think it's a beautiful day for a ride."

"You mean now?" Sarah's voice cracked with excitement.

"Yes, now." He righted the bike and kicked up the stand. Throwing a leg over the seat, he straddled it and walked his way backwards out of the garage. He leaned to the side and opened the fuel line. He turned the key, shifted the lever into neutral, and gave the hand throttle a slight turn. In one flowing motion, he jumped and came down with all his weight on the starter pedal. The engine responded with a loud snort, sputtered and nearly died. Duke worked the throttle while feathering the choke. In a few moments the engine settled into a low heart-throbbing rumble. "I haven't ridden lately," he yelled over the noise. "It gets a little grumpy until it has a chance to warm up."

"Is this the same one you brought to Ely?" Sarah asked. "It looks different."

"Do you like it? I gave it a whole new paint job—dressed it up, added some chrome trim."

"It looks brand new."

Duke laughed and pointed to a bar just ahead of the saddle bag. "Put your foot on that and swing your leg over."

Just like getting on Jubilee—foot in the stirrup—and up you go. Sarah felt tentative about putting her hands around Duke's waist but grabbed tight as soon as he took off down the driveway. She quickly found the rhythm and leaned with him as they went around corners. She loved feeling the wind in her face and hair. It was horseback riding with noise. "Hang on, we've got to burn out some carbon." He accelerated up the street. Getting her bearings, she recognized they were going out the road she and Gladys had come into town on. Once they were beyond the city limit sign, his hand slowly turned the throttle grip. Sarah felt the raw power as the cycle sped past fields and farms. She poked her thumbs behind his belt and tightened her fingers around the leather. *What's he doing? We must be going a hundred miles an hour.* No sooner had the thought crossed her mind when the engine quieted. Her body pressed into his back as he lightly applied the brakes. Coming to a full stop, he turned and looked over his shoulder. "Sorry, did I scare you?"

"Maybe a little." *Maybe a lot. Were you trying to kill us?*

"I'm really sorry. You ride so well, I forgot you were back there. I've got to open her up once in a while or the sludge clogs her up. Nora hates when I do that." He checked behind, shifted into gear and made a U-turn in the road. "We'll head back to town."

Duke took a slow cruise down Mill Street and either nodded or waved to just about everyone they passed. "Oh boy," he said turning back to Sarah. "The tongues will be wagging now." He laughed. "Everyone will want to know who I had on the back of the cycle." He turned the corner and went down the street by the park. The bandshell had a more inviting look than it did last night. He pulled to a stop in front of a string of old gray boat houses. He turned the key and the engine shuttered to a stop. "This is it," he said, and waited for Sarah to swing herself off the seat. He put down the kickstand and leaned the bike against it. "C'mon, the boat shop is around back."

Duke led the way, "We had three full restorations over the winter. One twenty-six-foot cabin cruiser and the two Chris-Craft Roundabouts," He talked while he walked. "We put the cruiser in the water yesterday. The other two go in today. They'll need a few days to soak up and be ready for the fourth." They walked past a long stretch of old gray lapstrake clad buildings. Although sturdy looking, they all leaned slightly one way or the other. The faded paint showed areas where it had chipped and peeled. Seeing the inquisitive look on Sarah's face, Duke laughed. "These are all boat houses. They've been here for fifty years."

At the end of the boat houses stood a large cinderblock building with double doors that extended floor to ceiling. Going to the side, Duke opened the walk-in door. A thin red cloud rolled out. "JEEZUS! He shouted, dashing inside. Running first to the compressor, he slammed the switch and popped the air hose.

From there he opened the electrical panel on the wall and fumbled to twist in a fuse. Immediately the whir of a fan motor broke the silence and the rosy cloud began moving toward the ceiling.

"Griff," he yelled at the top of his lungs as he ran to open one of the tall outside doors.

Sarah stepped in and fanned her hand in front of her face. She choked on the strong smell of paint.

In the far corner, a figure came out of a half-open sliding door with a spray gun in his hand. Dressed in brown coveralls, tinged in red, he shook the gun as if to question why it stopped working. With his cap turned backwards, sporting goggles and handkerchief tied across his nose and mouth he looked like creature from some cheap Hollywood horror movie.

"Look what you've done." Duke shouted.

The man raised the goggles and pulled down the handkerchief. He looked up at the cloud of red as it slowly made its way to the ceiling exhaust fan.

Duke swiped his finger across the deck of one of the runabouts. "You've got paint dust on everything."

The man set down the spray gun "I tried to turn on the exhaust in the spray booth, but it didn't work."

"Dang it." Duke said shaking his head. "The switch broke last week. I've been so busy trying to get these boats in the water I didn't take the time to fix it." He put his hands on his hips and stared at the ground.

The young man pulled off his gloves. "I suppose I should have waited for you to get here."

"Yeah, but I know the yacht club has been harping about getting those buoys done, so I can't put all the blame on you."

"I'm really sorry for messing up." The young man stripped off the goggles and began unzipping the coveralls."

Sarah stepped up to one of the boats. "Are the boats ruined?"

"It's nothing we can't fix. We'll just have to bust our tails and wipe down every square inch of those boats. If they don't get in the water today, they won't be ready and we'll have some very unhappy people, including the boss man."

The man stepped out of the coveralls and looked at Sarah. "You're the dancing girl from last night."

Duke looked puzzled. "You know her?" Neither spoke, each apparently waited for the other to explain. Duke broke the impasse. "This is Nora's sister, Sarah Connolly, he said. "She's visiting for the summer." Then pointing at his young helper. "Meet the notorious, Griff MacDonald."

The man wiped his hand on his pants before he extended it. "Please to meet you. Sarah is a pretty name."

Don't give me any of your sweet talk. Sarah turned to Duke "I can help with the boats."

Duke tossed her a rag. "We won't turn down the help." He put a ladder next to the first boat. "Why don't you climb inside and work on the seat cushions and dashboard. Griff and I will do the front deck, sides, and transom."

The rest of the morning, the three worked non-stop to wipe, polish, and shine each boat stem to stern. Griff made a few attempts to engage Sarah in conversation but was met with silence and cold indifference.

Wiping his brow, Duke threw his rag on the work bench, and checked his watch. "Come out of there, girl, we've got a luncheon date." He held the ladder as Sarah climbed out of the boat.

She handed him her rag and brushed off her clothes. "I guess that wasn't so bad." She turned to inspect their work. "No one will ever know there was a problem."

Griff came around from the back of the boat. "Thanks for your help." He tipped his cap to her. "Maybe we can meet up sometime?"

I doubt it. She made no attempt to respond but did give him a smile.

Duke threw Sarah's rag in Griff's face. "If you're around after lunch, you can help me get these two beauties in the water."

The young man snatched the cloth out of the air. "It's the least I can do. Again, I apologize for being such an airhead."

Duke put a hand on Griff's shoulder. "No harm, no foul. I'll see you later." He headed for the door. "Come girl, let's get going. We don't want to keep the women waiting."

"Nice meeting you, Sarah." Griff called as he watched them leave.

She turned and gave him a second smile before following Duke out the door.

CHAPTER TWENTY-THREE

Lunch at Greystone Cottage.

Nora was standing by her car when Duke and Sarah rode up on the motorcycle. Her look morphed between anger and disbelief. "I'm not sure it was a good idea to bring her here on that," she said, as Sarah threw her leg around and stepped off the bike.

"You're right," Duke said, kicking down the stand. "We drove through town, and by now, the telephone wires are on fire. All the busybodies are wondering who Duke Brady had on the back of his cycle."

"That's not what I meant," Nora said straightening Sarah's hair.

"It was my idea," Sarah said. "I reminded him, when he came to Ely, he promised to give me a ride."

"And I'm sure that was all it took for him to drag out the ol' blue bomber. Please tell me he didn't run it up to clean out the engine."

Sarah's look at Duke gave it away.

"I knew it." She gave Duke the evil eye. "He always says, he has to go like a bat out of hell to burn out the sludge. I'd be willing to bet there isn't a pinhead's worth of sludge in the whole damned engine."

Duke smiled. "She rides better than you do. I forgot she was even on the bike."

Nora was about to give him what for when Gladys and her mom approached and defused the situation.

Gladys went right to Sarah and hugged her. "Everything going okay?"

That was a loaded question, but Sarah thought better of launching into a whole dissertation of the last twenty-four hours.

Gladys didn't wait for an answer. She grabbed Sarah's hands and pulled her to her mother. "This is my Mom. She'll want you to call her Mary. Since dad passed, she hates being called Mrs. Iverson."

"With him gone, I'm not a Mrs. anything," the woman said, waiting for Duke to open the restaurant door.

Everyone, including Sarah, chuckled as they followed *Mrs. Iverson* inside.

The Greystone Restaurant sat on the water's edge and occupied the main floor of the last remaining cottage that was part of the Greystone Resort, built five years before the Civil War.

Duke gave a little background as he and the ladies paused to view the many pictures on the wall. "They say the resort could accommodate over three hundred guests at one time. Livery wagons were kept busy shuttling people into town and to and from the train station. Back then, the Chicago Northwestern Railway made two stops a day."

Stopping by a photo of the main lodge, he added. "The first floor held the kitchen, dining room, and a huge ballroom. Guests enjoyed music and dancing, and the occasional traveling minstrel show in the gymnasium sized room. Above, were three floors of sleeping rooms."

The Dining room was crowded. The hostess checked off the name and said the table was being readied. It would be just a few minutes.

Duke continued to regale the ladies with his knowledge. "After the Civil War, people fled the south to escape the scourge of Yellow Fever. Additional cottages were built to handle the surge. This one is said to have been the private residence of the owner, Geoffrey Greenfield."

Nora poked her elbow in Duke's stomach. "Where did you learn about all of this?"

"From Henry Eaton at the historical Society. I've been thinking about writing a book on some of Pine Lake's early History."

"It's too bad," Gladys said. "Dad could have told you a lot. He and Mom farmed here for forty years."

"You've never said anything about writing a book," Nora said over her shoulder, as she followed the hostess toward the porch.

Duke grinned. "See, I'm a man of hidden talents."

Nora and Gladys choked back a laugh at the same time.

Sarah grabbed Duke's arm. "That is so interesting. I love knowing the history of things. What happened to the resort?"

"Unfortunately, one cold December night in 1918, a fire of unknown origin, leveled all but this one cottage. The story goes, Greenfield grabbed the insurance money and lit out for California. The land and everything went on the auction block for unpaid taxes. It's been in the Langdon family for a quarter century. Five years ago, one of their sons turned the place into a restaurant."

Sarah looked around. "It would have been wonderful to have been a guest back then."

"The charm of Greystone, Gladys said, "is eating on the porch. Normally, you have a southwesterly breeze, and it's hard to beat the panoramic view of the lake."

"I thought it would be fun to come and play tourist," Nora said pulling out a chair.

"Mom and I eat here every now and then," Gladys said. "Their southern fried chicken is to die for." She sat, put the napkin on her lap, and gazed out at the Lake. "George Langdon does a nice job, but it's his wife Millie that rules the roost. Food is a little pricy for locals, but the tourist and lakeshore crowd love it. They relax the dress code a bit at lunchtime, but for evening dining it's dresses for the ladies and coat and tie for the men." She held the menu in front of her mouth to mute her voice. "It's a bit of forced snobbery."

"Duke and I came here for our anniversary," Nora said, opening up the cloth napkin. She adjusted her silverware before noticing all eyes were on her, then quickly added, "…of the day we first met…back in forty-one."

"For a minute, I thought you two might have finally tied the knot," Gladys said. "Although I would've been totally pissed, if you'd gone off and done it without me."

"Gladys!" Mary slapped the table. "Is that anyway to talk?" She pursed her lips. "We have a child with us."

Sarah held back a smile. It wasn't a real bad word, but not one she'd use.

Nora swatted Gladys' menu with the back of her hand, a signal for her friend to change the subject.

Duke anticipated the look he got from Gladys. "I plead the fifth," he said holding palms up defensively.

Nora seized control. "I suggest we survey the menu and decide what we'd like to eat." She looked at Sarah, "Does anything look interesting to you?"

Sarah tipped her menu forward. "Is southern fried the same as regular fried chicken?"

Gladys chuckled. "Yes, but this'll be the best you've ever tasted.

"Then that's what I'll have," Sarah said. *Best? I don't know. Mrs. Canterbury's chicken is darn good.*

Gladys was right. The chicken was delicious. Everyone raved about what they ordered. There wasn't enough left on anyone's plate to bother to take home. Even Mary, who Gladys accused of eating like a bird, mowed through her clubhouse sandwich. In between bites everyone watched the activities on the water. A lone fishman sat anchored in a small boat out from shore. Every now and then, he'd pull in another fish. Two sailboats, with their sails billowed, seemed to be racing each other. They tacked around the angler and headed in a new direction. Speedboats, some pulling skiers, kept the waters choppy.

"They're going to swamp that poor guy" Duke said. "But, by the way he's dragging in fish, I'm sure he ain't going to give up that spot."

Duke could have left it at that but decided to move the conversation to Sarah and Griff's meeting in the park the night before. "Seems, Sarah was doing some kind of dance down at the bandshell last night and Griff happened by."

All heads turned her way, her face flushed. "I thought I was alone. It was just a few steps I remembered from dance class when I was ten. And then, he appeared out of nowhere."

"I think at some point," Gladys said. "Every girl, dreams of being Ginger Rogers."

"Not me," chimed Nora.

Duke got off his chair. "I'd love to chat away the afternoon with you charming ladies, but I've got to get back to the boat shop. The aforementioned lad forgot to turn on the exhaust fan and got over-spray dust on two of the boats I spent all winter refinishing."

Nora stood. "Did it damage them?"

"Nah, we got them cleaned up." He pointed to Sarah. "She gave us a hand, but now I've got to get them in the water. He looked at Sarah, "Are you coming with me or going with Nora?"

Before she could speak, Nora cut in. "I thought we'd drive over to Penney's in Middletown. She needs some summer blouses."

"And a bathing suit." Sarah added, coming up from her chair.

Duke gave Gladys a hug. He took Mary's hand. "Maybe we can sit down sometime and talk about what you remember about Pine Lake at the turn of the century."

"Listen to him," Nora said, "my budding author."

Duke winked, "It's called research." He planted a peck on Nora's cheek. "Have fun shopping. I'll see you both back at the house."

"Bye," Sarah yelled. "Thanks for the motorcycle ride."

In the parking lot, the women hugged goodbye. "I'm heading back to Chicago in the morning," Gladys said, "but I'm coming back for the long weekend over the fourth. Maybe we should plan a picnic or something?"

"Sounds good," Nora said. "Call me when you get back into town."

CHAPTER TWENTY-FOUR
Shopping for a New Bathing Suit

Sarah followed Nora to her car. "Is this new?" she asked, before opening the door.

Nora grinned broadly. "Looks new, doesn't it. I bought it used from one of the doctors at the hospital."

Is this a Ford?" Sarah sat and ran her fingers over the mohair fabric on the seat. "It even smells new. Oh my gosh," she squealed. "It even has a radio"

"It's a forty, two door sedan," Nora said, tapping her fingers on the steering wheel. "The doctor was able to get one of the first Buicks that came to the dealership in Middletown after the war. It took automakers time to switch from making tanks and trucks for the Army to get back to making cars. Professional people were given the first chance to buy. I would have liked a different color, but black is okay." She started the car and backed out of the parking stall. "Look at the odometer, it's hard to believe the car is over seven years old and only has fifty-eight thousand miles." She reached and turned on the radio, "Why don't you dial around and see if you can find some music you like."

Sarah leaned forward and turned the knob. "The boy I met in Danville had a Chevrolet. His had a radio, too. The trouble was, he liked twangy, hillbilly music. Back home, mom has the radio in the house tuned to play big-band music. I love Glenn Miller. On Saturday nights, we listened to Jack Benny. He's so funny."

"I see nothing's changed since I left." Nora smiled. "I like Frankie Sinatra. He sang with Tommy Dorsey and Harry James.

Sarah continued to move the needle on the dial. "I'm not sure if I heard any of his songs." Just then, Frank's *Time after Time* coursed from the speaker.

"Wait, that's him." Nora immediately began singing along. She bobbed her head from side to side. Then rolling her eyes to Sarah, "Don't you just love him."

Sarah sat back in the seat and nodded to the beat. When the song ended, Sarah swung her leg onto the seat. "How come you and Duke never got married?"

The question caught Nora by surprise. A slight jerk on the steering wheel sent the front tire off the pavement and onto the gravel shoulder. Stones flew as she over corrected, sending the rear end sliding sideways. The car bounced back up on the road. It swayed first to the right and then left before Nora finally regained control. She braked and pulled to the side of the road. Releasing her death-grip on the steering wheel she took in a deep breath and looked at Sarah. The girl's eyes were as big as saucers. One hand gripped the seatback while the other held tight to the door armrest.

Nora gripped Sarah's forearm. "I'm so sorry. Are you alright?"

Sarah nodded. Her lips moved but no sound emitted.

Nora was first to start laughing. It began with a small giggle before erupting in stomach-hurting hilarity. Sarah, too, doubled over. As the laughter faded, Nora's face turned serious. "With marriage comes commitment and certain things are expected of each person. After the molar pregnancy, I was told I could never have children," Nora paused to give the lump in her throat a chance to go down. "I no longer felt like a real woman and didn't feel I could be a wife to Duke in the true sense of the word." Nora searched her purse for a handkerchief. "Then, it could have had something to do with the war. The shrink Gladys set me up with told me I probably suffer the same battle fatigue as the soldiers do. I saw so many young men die. I thought about the mothers and sweethearts that were left brokenhearted. It seems like I'm always angry. Angry at the world. Angry at God. I think I'm afraid to love. Afraid if Duke and I got married, that somehow I'd lose him." She turned and looked at Sarah. "Does any of that make sense?" Nora wiped the corners of her eyes before reaching for the shifting lever. "Maybe we'll get married someday," she said. "For right now, we're both good with the way things are. Neither of us needs a piece of paper to declare how we feel about each other." Nora poked Sarah in the ribs. "But if we do, you'll be my maid of honor."

Sarah giggled and pushed Nora's hand away. "Maybe I'll work on Duke. Plant a little bug in his ear."

Nora looked straight ahead, not wanting Sarah to see her glazed eyes. "You know, I still have the wedding dress that he bought me–way back then."

Sarah slid over and put her arm around Nora. "I only want you both to be happy."

Nora pulled the shifting lever into low, checked her rearview mirror, and accelerated up the road. "And happy we are."

Penney's store window had a complete display of swimsuits. The bright red two-piece on the center manikin caught Sarah's eye. Her face colored a similar shade. "That's like going swimming in your underwear."

Nora shook her head. "The two-piece suits are becoming popular. Maybe not for the locals, but I have seen a few tourist and lakeshore girls strutting their stuff in one.

Sarah pointed to the blue and white striped one-piece hanging from the knotted rope on a white canvas covered lifesaver. The material had a sheen to it and the two buttons in the center added interest. "What do you think of that one?"

"Cute," Nora said. "Let's see if they have your size." The next hour was spent trying on swimwear and picking through shirts and blouses on the bargain table.

Sarah bolted out of Penney's front door with a broad smile on her face. "Thank you. Thank you. Thank you," she squealed. Spinning in place, she clutched the shopping bag filled with three blouses, two pairs of shorts, and the blue and white striped bathing suit.

Sarah sat on her bed clipping the price tags off her new wardrobe. "I feel like it should be my birthday or Christmas. I've never had so many nice things all at once."

"You paid for a lot of it with your own money," Nora said, hanging a pale-yellow blouse on a hanger. "This will go good with the tan shorts."

"But you spent money, too. I promise, I'll pay you back." Sarah stood and held the blue suit to her chest. "I can't wait to go swimming. I've never had such a pretty bathing suit."

"You're going to be a knockout in that," Nora said. "We'll have to peel the boys off you with a can opener. And don't worry about the money. Seeing that beautiful smile on your face makes up for everything."

"No, I'm serious," Sarah said, giving Nora a big hug. "I can't expect you and Duke to continue shelling out for me, besides, I like having my own money." She folded the suit and put it in the drawer. "I think I will go to the coffee shop and apply. Serving breakfast and burgers can't be any harder than serving ice cream."

"Blanche said she needed help." Nora went back for another hug. "But please don't think you have to work. It'll be just fine with Duke and me if you want to loaf around and enjoy the summer. You have your whole life to work. You're only a kid once."

Sarah pondered the thought. "I'm sure I would still have plenty of time to have fun."

Nora headed for the door. "C'mon, let's go downstairs and have some iced tea while I figure out what I can scare up for supper."

Sarah held her stomach and followed Nora. "It doesn't have to be much. I'm still stuffed from lunch."

Duke waltzed through the back door a little after five and immediately planted a kiss on Nora's cheek. "Did you hear the latest? Someone broke into Foster's Liquor Store last night."

Nora had just pulled a pan out from the cupboard. She banged it on the counter. "Here in Pine Lake? What is this world coming to? Did they take much?"

"The sheriff thinks it was kids. All they took was a fifth of Jack Daniels whiskey and some cigarettes. The bathroom window got left open."

Sarah choked on her drink. *Whiskey? Cigarettes? It could have been those kids I ran into in the park.* Her first thought was to tell of the incident, but she didn't want to accuse anyone without having more information. *Maybe I should try to find the pieces of the broken bottle. Dee's lesson number one collect the evidence.*

"That poor John Foster," Nora said. "Since his wife up and left him, they say he's drunk every night. I feel sorry for their boy, Douglas. That's a lot to deal with for a seven-year-old."

"I see him quite often," Duke said. "The kid will come and hang out in the boat shop. I let him make toy boats with some of the scrap wood." He peeked over Nora's shoulder. "What's for supper?" Then looking a Sarah, "Did someone get a new bathing suit?"

Sarah raised her hand with a big smile and wide opened eyes. "It's blue and white, and I love it," she said. "I also got three blouses and two pairs of shorts."

Nora was at the sink putting water in the pan when Duke came up behind her and wrapped his arms around her waist. He kissed her on the neck. "Did you buy me something?"

"Duke." Nora wiggled from his grip and rolled her eyes in Sarah's direction.

"Sarah," Duke commanded. "Close your eyes. I'm about ready to tickle the living daylights out of your sister."

Sarah giggled and swung her back to them.

Nora moved to the stove with Duke at her heels. She turned and pushed her hand into his chest. "Don't you tickle me. If you do, you'll be wearing this pan of water."

Duke laughed and backed off. "Is that supper? What are we having?"

"Hobo Dinner." Nora said. "Wieners and beans. I didn't think we needed much. Sarah and I are still stuffed from lunch."

"I'm a bit full myself." Duke swung a leg over the chair and sat at the table. "Griff was asking all sorts of questions about you. You might be an itch he'd like to scratch."

Sarah's face reddened. "Were you able to get the boats in the water?"

"Yep, everyone's happy. He's a good kid. He just didn't think about the overspray. No harm, no foul."

Duke was off his chair as soon as he heard the knock on the back door. "Surprise. Look who just showed up," he said, leading the way into the kitchen. Nora turned to see who it was.

Griff stepped forward and immediately smiled at Sarah. "I guess I didn't make a very good impression this morning…or last night. I hope you're not too upset with me."

Sarah stood. *Why would I be upset. I hardly know you.* Her thoughts didn't translate into words.

Duke pulled out a chair and motioned to Griff. "Do you want to stay for supper?"

Nora banged the spoon on the counter. "Duke!" She used the spoon to point at the pan.

Duke was quick on the uptake. "Maybe you'll want to take a pass. We're having Hobo Dinner."

Griff raised his eyebrows. "What's that?"

"Hot dogs and beans," Sarah said, trying to suppress a giggle.

Griff took a step back. "That's okay, my folks are probably waiting to go to supper." He turned to Sarah. "I was thinking about getting the boat out after dinner. Maybe doing a little water skiing. Would you like to come along?"

Sarah looked to Nora, who in turn looked at Duke. He held out a hand to Sarah. "There you go. Your first chance to try out your new bathing suit."

"Water skiing?" Sarah's voice cracked. "I've never done that. Is it hard to do?"

"Not at all," Griff said. "Besides, you're looking at the best ski instructor on the lake." He leaned on the back of her chair. "There's no wind. The lake is smooth as glass, perfect for skiing."

Oh my God. Water skiing? What am I getting into? "What time?" She asked, looking down at her lap.

"About six? It's light until close to nine. Maybe we can stop for ice cream afterwards."

Sarah waited for the nod from Nora. "Okay, I'll be ready." Her response was barely above a whisper.

With that, the young man turned. "Great. I'll see you guys," he yelled as he dashed out the back door.

"How about that, your first date in Pine Lake," Duke said, grabbing silverware and napkins to set the table.

Nora handed him plates. "Check with me before you invite people to dinner. I don't mind, but I'd rather be serving something other than beans and wieners when you do."

He set the plates and adjusted the silverware. "Why do you fret, milady, I have it on good authority that you make the best wieners and beans in the whole county."

Nora ladled a spoonful of beans onto his plate. "And you are the best B.S.er anywhere."

Sarah cut her wiener in chunks and dipped a piece in the ketchup. She raised her eyes to the ceiling. *Well Dee, what do you think of Mr. Griff MacDonald?*

CHAPTER
TWENTY-FIVE
A Driving Lesson

Nora knocked. "It's me," she said, walking into Sarah's room.

Sarah flinched before finishing to button up the white cotton blouse they had purchased earlier.

"Aren't you going to wear your bathing suit under your clothes?"

Sarah gave her a puzzled look.

"If you're going water skiing, there might not be a place to change." Nora stepped to the armoire. "And why don't you wear the pale-yellow top with the tan shorts. They both looked great on you."

Sarah opened the drawer and brought out the suit. "I didn't think about that." Tossing it on the bed, she unbuttoned the white blouse. "I was saving the yellow and tan outfit for something dressy." Then picking up the suit, she dashed across the hall to the bathroom. "I'll be right back," she said, closing the door. She shed her underpants and bra. Holding the top, she stepped into the suit. A brief smile crossed her lips as she drew the soft blue fabric over her hips. Bringing the gathered top over her breasts, she wiggled from one foot to the other until everything felt comfortable. She reached behind, brought the straps over her shoulders, and slid the hooks into the fabric loops. She studied her image in the mirror. The suit clung to her like an extra skin. Her hands rested on her waist before sliding over the roundness of her hips. She smiled. *Oh my gosh, I have hips. When did that happen?*

Ely was always cold. There weren't many opportunities to swim or even put on a suit. In two summers, she could only remember swimming once, and that was at a public pool in Las Vegas when her dad had to go there on police business. It had been four or five years since she'd learned to swim in the pool in Danville. She was a good swimmer, her stroke fluid, but was not a threat to steal any of Esther Williams' thunder.

Sarah moved her hands across her stomach and then under her breasts. She turned, first to one side and then the other. In her mind, Dee had the perfect shape. The kind boys drooled over, and girls envied, but she liked what she saw in the mirror. Sarah spent another moment or two looking at herself before grabbing her underwear and going back to the bedroom.

"Wow." Nora blinked. "I always think of you as the frightened fifteen-year-old I met on the bus two years ago but look at you now. You're a full-grown woman."

Sarah tossed her bra and panties on the bed and twirled in front of the large free-standing oval mirror. "It's the bathing suit. I just love it."

"Maybe we should have a little talk about the birds and the bees."

Sarah giggled. "I know all about that. Mom and I had *the* talk. I've dated some, and I did take biology." Grabbing her navy shorts, she yanked them on, stuck her arm through the sleeve of the white blouse and fumbled to fasten the top button. "Look at the time, Griff will be here any minute."

"He'll wait. Sometimes a little wait is good for them. Just remember, you're dealing with a red-blooded American male. Don't let your emotions get the best of you."

"I won't." Sarah dug in her purse, brought out a pair of sunglasses, and stuck them on top of her head.

Nora giggled. Are those…?"

"Yep. The ones we bought in Cheyenne when you thought the cops were after us." Sarah
bolted upright at the sound of the doorbell. "That must be him." She went down the stairs two at a time.

"Have fun but be careful." Nora yelled.

Griff looked different dressed in a natty pair of shorts and knit shirt. His hair was combed, and his aftershave had a manly smell. His eyes lit up when Sarah opened the door. "Gosh, you look great."

Sarah blushed. *Mr. MacDonald, you say all the right things.*

He grabbed her hand. "You don't mind walking, do you? It's just down to the Boat Dock."

"By the bandshell?"

"Right. I gassed up the boat before I came."

Sarah pulled him to a stopped. "Wait, do I need a towel?"

"That's okay. There are plenty on the boat."

The two walked briskly down the sidewalk. The sun hung high in the sky, no wind, and the air was unseasonably warm for late June. "What kind of boat do you have?" she asked.

"It's just a puddle-jumper. We've had it for a couple of years."

The town was bristling, the sidewalks were crowded. People stood looking in the windows, while others went in or came out of the stores. "Is the town always this crowded?" Sarah asked.

"Not usually," he said looking around. "But with the big fourth of July celebration coming up, the town will be crawling with people."

Griff led the way as they weaved their way down the street, across the road by the park, past the bandshell and over to the collection of buildings and docks. "Watch your step," he said as he led her into the darkened building. There were boats of all shapes and sizes. The walkway was narrow. Sarah heard the water splash against the rocks under the wooden floor. The boats bounced up and down, one after the other, as the waves from a passing boat came ashore. "Ours is in the next building."

Puddle-jumper? These were all large boats, some even had cabins. A few were painted white, one light blue, but most were rich looking varnished mahogany with gleaming decks and sides. Each slip had three or four boat tied in a line.

Griff stopped and took her hand. "We're out on the end, but be careful, the beam is narrow."

Sarah looked down at an eight-inch wide slab of wood. "Wait." *This is like walking a tightrope.*

"Don't look down. Look straight ahead. There's a post every six feet. Just walk one to another." He walked ahead to the first one and stepped around it. "Okay, your turn."

Dee, I know you are up there laughing your ass off, but this is not funny. "I don't think I can do this."

"Sure, you can. Eyes on the post and walk to it."

Sarah put her right foot about six inches in front of her, swallowed hard and in three quick steps made it to the post. Griff had released and was on to the next post before she bearhugged the wood stanchion. She peeked around and counted how many more she'd have to navigate. *Eight! It'll be a miracle if I don't end up in the drink.* Sarah took her time and with a little encouragement from him, made it to the end.

Griff jumped into the boat and extended his hand. "Step here," he said, pointing to a rubber pad on the side deck.

Sarah grabbed his hand and stepped in. She looked from stem to stern. "This is your boat?" She hadn't come up with a mental picture of what his boat might look like, but this was way beyond anything she would have imagine. It had to be twenty feet long. The floor was carpeted and the seat cushions both front and back were upholstered in light tan fabric, trimmed in red and brown. The deep mahogany front deck glistened under multiple coats of varnish. The windshield, trimmed and held in place by chrome brackets, sat above a wood dashboard that housed a cluster of gauges. On the right a large steering wheel with its shiny horn ring, was equal to any fancy car of the time.

The boat rocked as Griff went side to side untying the lines fore and aft. Sarah momentarily lost her balance and parked her butt on the large padded box sitting in the middle of the boat.

Hopping into the bench seat behind the wheel, he reached under the seat and brought up a key tied to a fishing bobber. He inserted it into the switch and moved the chrome lever protruding from the floorboard to a straight up position. He turned the key and pressed the starter button. Sarah jumped as the engine roared and came to life beneath her.

Griff laughed. "You're sitting on the motor cover. There's a Chevy engine under there. C'mon, sit up front with me."

She stepped over and slid into the passenger seat. "You should have warned me."

"I should have." He laughed. "Sorry about that." He pulled the shift lever back and the boat eased its way out of the slip. Once clear, he moved the lever forward, spun the steering wheel to the right and opened the throttle enough to change direction. "We have to go slow until we get out past the channel buoy."

Sarah pulled the sunglasses off her head and fixed them to her face. She wanted to ask him more about the boat, but there was just too much to see. Homes and cottages, some big, some small, lined the shore. The bay harbored dozens of sailboats each moored to brightly painted cubes of wood. The air was fresh, and she felt the hot sun on her skin. She unbuttoned the top button on her blouse. Griff did her one better. He'd already pulled his shirt out and was stripping it over his head. He tossed the shirt under the deck. Leaning over the side, he grabbed a handful of water and splashed it on his arms and chest.

Sarah kicked off her shoes and reached to take off her socks.

"Man, it's going to be a great fourth if the weather stays like this." He sat up on the seat back. "Here, slide over and steer and I'll get out the ski stuff."

"Steer," *Is he nuts.* "I don't know how to steer," she protested.

Griff was already standing behind the seat holding the wheel with one hand. "It's just like steering a car. You turn the wheel to the right, and it goes right, left, and it goes left."

"I don't know how to do that, either." Sarah reluctantly slid behind the wheel.

"Do what?" He waited for her to take the wheel before letting go.

"Drive a car."

"Seriously?" He slipped down on the seat beside her. "Well then, I guess I'll have to give you my crash course in boat navigation. He put his right arm behind her. "First," he covered her left hand with his and moved the wheel slowly to the right.

The boat went right. "See." He brought the wheel back to the left and the boat turned to the left. "Now you do it." He let go and she turned the boat in both directions. "Now, the more you turn the wheel, the sharper the turn."

She continued making turns and giggled as she made a complete circle before heading back towards the buoy. "That was fun."

"Once we get past the buoy and around Grey Stone Point, we can rev it up."

"Is that where the restaurant is? We had lunch there, today."

"One of my favorites," he said. "I love their fried chicken."

"You mean their Southern Fried Chicken?" She gave it her best southern drawl. "That's what I had. It was delicious."

Griff laughed out loud. "y'all take a-likin' to collard greens?"

Sarah looked puzzled. "I don't know what those are."

"Aha, then you are not a true southern belle, just another northern scallywag pretending to be."

"A what—"

"I'm just teasing. Look over there." He pointed to a huge boulder that sat half in the water and half on land. "Hence the name, Grey Stone Point. The restaurant is right around the corner."

Once they cleared the buoy, he reached over and moved the lever in the middle of the steering wheel a quarter turn. The engine immediately responded, lifting the bow up out of the water. "We'll cruise by so you can see what it looks like from the water."

As soon as the large grey building came into view, Griff idled the engine, and helped her steer the boat in closer. Keeping a hand on the wheel he guided the boat along the shoreline.

Sarah let go of the steering wheel and stood. Holding onto the windshield for balance she eyed every part of the structure. "It looks even more beautiful from here. Duke was telling us some of the history of the resort."

Griff pointed up the shoreline. "The eight houses, all the way to that big red boathouse, were all part of the original property.

The main lodge that housed the ballroom sat about where house number six sits."

"It's hard to believe Pine Lake could have had a resort that big, that long ago," she said.

"It was big. When you consider it had its own dairy farm and vegetable gardens, it was quite self-sustainable." He pulled Sarah back to her seat. "Enough about history, let's get back to your driving lesson."

He advanced the throttle. The bow raised and then planed to a smooth glide across the water.

"O-o-o-o-ooh!" Sarah's voice rose an octave. She blinked. Her hands gripped and re-gripped the wheel. She felt a burst of adrenalin. Her cheeks warmed and fingers tingled. "Am I doing okay?"

"Doing fine, just hold it steady." He covered her hand again and moved the wheel a little to the left. "See, when you go faster it doesn't take much to make it turn." He let go. "Now you do it."

I can't," she shrieked. "We'll tip over."

Griff laughed. "Just turn it slowly. We won't tip over."

She gulped for air. Every muscle felt as tight as a bowstring. She let the air escape slowly as the boat responded to every slight turn of the wheel. At first, she made small turns, then as her confidence grew the turns became more dramatic.

Soon she was smiling ear to ear as she brought the boat to a straight-line course. "How fast are we going?"

Griff tapped the large gauge on the dash. "Eighteen miles per hour."

"Is that all? It feels like we're going fifty."

"You're only at half-throttle. Top speed is somewhere around thirty-eight to forty, but eighteen to twenty is a good speed for skiing." He turned and pointed to the left. "Head for that big open space. We'll go down to the inlet and see if we can get you up on skis. The water is shallow. It's easier for first timers."

Sarah brought the bow around and headed for the far shore. *Oh boy, this should be an adventure.*

CHAPTER TWENTY-SIX

A First Time for Everything

As they approached shore, Griff eased back on the throttle. The high-pitched whine of the engine died to a low moan. The boat lost momentum and settled down on the water. He put his hand over hers and steered the bow out from shore. Grabbing the chrome floor lever, he pulled it all the way back, reversing the engine. The boat came to a standstill. "Good job of driving," he said, moving the lever to the neutral straight-up position and turning off the key.

He stepped over the seat, picked up a short ladder and hung it over the side. Sliding his butt over the motor cover, he slipped a pair of skis out from the loop holders attached to the inside wall.

Sarah hadn't moved. She was still trying to decide if she wanted to give this skiing a try or if it was time to chicken out and beg off.

Griff took one ski and began fumbling with the adjustment knob. Looking up, he paused. "Well, C'mon. Sit here on the motor cover so I can adjust the foot bindings to fit you."

Sarah climbed over the seat. "I'm…I'm not…"

He stood the ski upright on the floor and leaned his arm on the rounded tip. "Are you going to be the first?" he asked.

"First what?" She eased her bottom onto the padded box.

"The first one to flunk out of my long standing, tried and true, waterskiing prep course."

"It's just that I never—"

"That's perfect, because my special training is guaranteed and has a 99.9% success rate with girls that have never skied before."

She laughed at his bluster.

He picked up her leg, pushed her foot into the rubber binding, and tightened the knob. "Does that feel okay? It's not too tight is it?"

Yes, it's tight, but how should I know how tight it's supposed to be? She smiled. "I guess it's okay."

"I want to make sure they stay on." He eased it off her foot and adjusted the other to match. Laying them side by side next to the ladder, he took her hand and pulled her upright. "Now, when you get into the water, I want you to sit back and bend your knees." He squatted to show her what he meant. "The important thing is to keep the ski tips up and out of the water."

Not so fast. What was that about ski tips?" She kept mouthing the instructions as best she could remember.

Raising the back-seat cushion, he brought out a long length of rope and began untangling it. He looked up and smiled. "This is the part where you take off your shirt and pants and get ready to go into the water."

"Oh right." She started unbuttoning her blouse.

He continued to untangle the rope but kept checking on her progress.

She pulled the blouse out from the waistband of her shorts and let it drape open. She moved slowly to undo the side button on her shorts. *"What. Is he going to stand there and watch me undress?* "Would you mind?" She twirled her finger in a circular motion.

"Oh, sorry." He turned and continued to fiddle with the rope. "You've got a bathing suit on under there, don't you?"

Her face reddened. "Yes, but—"

"Geez, you had me scared for a moment—"

"Scared?" *What, that I wasn't wearing one?* Sarah folded her shorts and blouse, leaned over the front seat, and laid the clothes under the front deck. When she came up and faced him, his mouth was agape. *Was he watching me?*

Her look seemed to embarrass him. His cheeks turned rosy.

She couldn't decide whether she should be angry or flattered. Adjusting the top of her suit, she lifted her heel, and struck a modeling pose. "Do you like it? It's brand new."

Griff's eyes appeared glued to one particular part. The one just below the ruffled top. He cleared his throat. "Yes. It's…It's a pretty color." Reaching, he brought out a wide white canvas belt from the seat compartment and wrapped it around her waist.

"What's this?" She asked, as he looped the cotton strap through the rings and cinched it tight.

"A safety belt, each of these squares has a block of cork inside. It'll keep you afloat. Well, that's it," he said, taking a step backwards. "Time to get wet."

Sarah hesitated. "I'm really not sure about this."

"You'll do fine." He held the ladder steady as she stepped over the side and found the first step.

Standing on the bottom rung, the water was to her knees. She shivered. "It's a little cold." She waved her hand around in the clear blue water. "Oh, look, I can see the bottom."

"The best way is to just fall backwards and get wet all at once"

Easy for you to say. How did I get myself into this? Go, just do it, he's waiting. Sarah took a gulp of air and let go of the ladder. The initial shock brought her head shooting out of the water. "Oh, my goodness." She wiped the water from her eyes as her toes bounced off the sandy bottom. The water came within two or three inches of her chin. Letting the belt do its job, she laid on her back and continued to move her arms and feet as her body adjusted to the water temperature.

"That wasn't bad, was it?"

She smiled. *If looks could kill, you'd be dead.*

He slid one of the skis across the water to her. "Bring your knees in, pushed the back of the ski down and slip your foot into the binding."

Sarah caught the ski, turned it around and tried to shove it under the water. The ski had a mind of its own and fought her every effort to get her foot into the binding. "I can't get my foot..."

"Do you want me to get in the water and help you?"

His condescending tone irked her. *If I need your help, I'll ask for it.* She continued to struggle with the ski. Between the buoyancy of the belt and the stupid wooden plank trying to float to the surface, she soon found herself turned over and face down. It took no end of leg kicking and arm splashing for her to get to her back. By this time, the devil-possessed ski, had drifted away. All her splashing aided it's escape.

Suddenly Griff's head broke the lake surface next to her. "Here, let me help." Before she could protest, or ask to get back into the boat, his hands were on her waist. "Just relax." He rolled her on her back. Grabbing the ski, he pushed it under the water, and slipped it on her foot. At some point during her struggles he must have tossed the other ski and the rope into the water because it was right at his fingertips. It only took another minute before she was bobbing in the water wearing both skis. "Here's the handle from the tow rope, keep it between the skis. Hold onto it with both hands. Remember what I said, bend your knees and keep the ski tips up. Got it?"

No, I don't "got it." Her brow curled and she shot him a dirty look.

His fingers pushed up the corners of her mouth. "Smile, this is going to be fun."

Despite wanting to bite his finger, she did manage an eye roll and a sarcastic grin. *It hasn't been all that much fun so far.*

"Okay, I'm going to get back in the boat. I'll go slow until the rope becomes taut. Keep your elbows close to your side. At that point, I'll give it the gas and it should bring you up out of the water." He grabbed her ankle. "I want you to push with your heels. Hold the handle tight, and don't lean too far forward. Once you are up, keep your knees flexed until you find your balance, and then slowly lean back and enjoy the ride. You got it?"

Her brief nod should have no way been construed as a solid yes. *How am I supposed to remember all that?* She watched him swim to the boat, climb on board, and take in the ladder. The engine snorted an angry growl as it came alive. Griff sat half on the seat back and half on the side of the boat. He raised his hand. "Get ready." He pushed the shift lever forward with his foot and watched as the rope swirled around on the water.

Sarah too, watched as the rope snaked in front of her. Her mind raced with what she could remember of the instructions—tips up—heels down—rope between… Everything happened at once. She heard the engine, felt the pull, but instead of bringing her up out of the water, it was pulling her sideways. This wasn't right. She let go of the rope. The boat went a short distance before coming around in a sharp turn. Griff stood and idled the engine. "Are you alright?"

She waved. "I guess I wasn't quite ready. I got going sideways."

"Keep your elbows in, it will help to keep you going straight," he said. "I'm going to go around you. The rope will come around. Lift it over your head and get it between the skis."

Sarah could see the rope handle splashing in the water as it came to her. *It's going awfully fast.* The engine whined as Griff put it in reverse and then into neutral. Standing in the back of the boat, he cupped his hands around his mouth. "Have you got it?"

Sarah felt the rope run across her back. She reached to the side and let it slide through her fingers as she put it over her head. The handle came a little quicker than she had anticipated but she was able to put a firm grip on it. She quickly got into her lay back position, brought the ski tips up and could feel the rope pulling her forward.

Griff's yell, Sarah's wave, and the engine roar all came within a split second. Sarah dug her heels. It felt like she exploded out of the water. Her arms were way forward. It felt awkward. The skis were out of control sliding this way and that. Suddenly, the left one decided to go off on its own. About to do the splits, Sarah quickly let go of the tow rope and fell butt first into the water. She surfaced with one ski still on her foot. The other bobbed a few feet away. "Dammit," she said under her breath, as she used the breaststroke to retrieve the ski. *This is crazy. I overcame my fear of horses, learned to saddle, and ride at a full gallop, this waterskiing business is not going to get the best of me.*

She already had the second ski on by the time Griff returned. He idled at a safe distance. "You almost had it."

"I would have made it, but the skis kept going every which way." There was no way she could hide her excitement. "Can I try again?"

"Of Course, I'll bring the rope to you just like before. Just remember, once you're up, lean back, ride the back of the skis."

This time everything felt different. She came out of the water in one fluid motion. With her weight back, the skis tracked in a straight line. She soon found the balance between the rope pull, ski position, and the lean. *Son of a gun, this is fun.* She kept her focus on the back of the boat.

Griff made a big circle before driving along the inlet shore. Sarah figured it was his way of giving her a chance to drop off in shallow water. Taking the cue, she raised her hand and let go of the rope. She held her balance and slowly sank into the water. She watched as Griff brought the boat around. Kicking off the skis, she brought them up and used them like a paddle board to swim to the boat. He'd turned off the engine and was reeling in the rope when she came along side. "You were right. That was really a lot of fun."

He laughed as he hung the ladder over the side. "And not only that but you kept my 99.9% record intact." He reached down and lifted the skis into the boat. "I might have to give you an A with an extra gold star. You really did well for your first time."

"I owe it all to your fine tutelage."

"I was hoping you would go outside of the wake, get out on clear water."

Sarah had her hands on the ladder but made no attempt to come out of the water. "I don't understand."

He reached down and helped her into the boat. "It's no big deal. I could show you if you think you can run the boat and give me a chance to ski." Bending, he brought a couple of towels out from the backseat storage compartment and draped one over her shoulders.

Sarah unbuckled the safety belt and let it fall on the deck. "You want me to drive the boat by myself?" She wiped her face and wrapped the towel around herself. "I don't know if I can do that." She reached for her blouse under the deck and slipped it on.

"You've steered the boat and know how the throttle works." He slid over the front seat and grabbed the silver rod protruding from the floor. "This is the shifting lever. If you want to go forward, you push it ahead. Pulling it all the way back will make you go in reverse. When it's straight up like this, it's in neutral, and you don't go anywhere." He motioned to her. "Come, we'll take it for a test run."

Sarah climbed behind the wheel. "Are you sure you want me to do this? What if I run into something?"

Griff laughed. "We're in the middle of the lake. There's nothing to run into." He slid over next to her. "First, set the throttle as low as it will go. Good. Now, turn the key and press the starter button." Sarah followed the instructions and the engine sprang to life.

She waited for the next command. When none came, she looked at him.

He just raised his hands and shrugged his shoulders. In her mind, it was his way of saying, you're in charge. What are you going to do next?

"I want to go forward, so I push the lever to the front," she said, following her own words. The boat moved ahead slowly. "Oh my God." She quickly turned the wheel when she realized the boat was headed for the shore. Once she had the boat heading to the middle of the lake, she gripped the throttle lever on the steering wheel and began moving it around to the left. The engine's roar increased in measure to how she advanced the throttle. Remembering what Griff said earlier, about eighteen miles per hour being a good skiing speed, she kept drawing the lever down until the needle on the speedometer reached that number. She quickly looked for his approval. "Did I do okay?"

Griff had a big smile on his face. "Like a pro." He got out of the seat. "Bring it down to an idle and put it in neutral." He gathered up the rope and threw it behind the boat. "There's just one thing, When I give the signal, bring that throttle down quickly. I'm going to slalom, so I need a burst of power to get up." He strapped on the safety belt, picked up one of the skis, and made a quick adjustment to the binding. "You can run it about twenty-five for me." He winked. "I like a little excitement."

Sarah was on her knees looking over the back of the seat. "Are you only using one ski? That's crazy. Wait. Where do you want me to go?"

He waved his arm in a circle. "Just make a big swoop and head back towards the inlet." With that, he jumped overboard. Almost as soon as he surfaced, he had the ski on his foot. Then reaching out he grabbed the rope and let it slide through his fingers. "Put it in gear and wait for my signal."

Sarah pushed the shifter forward. With one hand on the steering wheel and the other on the throttle, she looked over her shoulder. She could see the rope handle coming up behind him. *It's almost there.* His left hand went up as the right grabbed the handle. "Hit it," he yelled.

Sarah pulled the throttle to the halfway point. The engine roared and the speedometer needle jumped. A quick look over her shoulder sent a shot of adrenalin through her body. Griff came shooting out of the water and immediately leaned to his right. Crossing the boat's wake, he was propelled high off the water. Coming down, he continued to move out to his right. A rooster tail stream of water rose high behind his ski as he quickly turned and came flying back across the wake. Each time, he'd jump two to three feet off the water.

Sarah's head swiveled between looking ahead and behind, making sure he was still skimming across the water on the one ski. A quick glance at the speedometer shocked her. The needle was pointing straight up at the number thirty. She thought about easing off, but he seemed to be handling the speed nicely. She turned the wheel and began a wide turn back towards the inlet. She marveled at his athleticism. It was like watching a dancer make spectacular jumps and graceful body moves. She noted how much speed he'd generated when racing from side to side. A couple of times, he came around and was almost even with the back of the boat. *That's got to be way more fun than just following behind the boat.*

When she approached the inlet, she turned and ran parallel to the shoreline. Griff did a couple more passes behind the boat before tossing the rope handle in the air and sinking in the water.

Sarah moved the throttle back and made a sharp turn. Griff held the ski in the air to mark his location. As she closed in, she continued to move back the throttle. Keeping her distance, she drove around behind him and aimed the boat away from shore. She pulled the shifting lever into neutral and then momentarily into reverse to stop any forward momentum. Coming back to neutral, she turned off the key and jumped out of the seat. "That was beautiful." She hung the ladder as he swam up to the boat.

He handed up the ski. "And you did a great job of driving the boat."

"I see what you mean about going out beyond the wake. Do we have time, I'd like to try it one more time?"

Griff looked at the sky. "We're running out of daylight, but you if you want, you can ski our way back towards the Boat Dock."

Sarah wasted little time taking off her blouse and strapping on the safety belt. She handed him the ski. "You have to re-adjust this one to fit me." She threw the other ski in the water and jumped in after it. There was no hesitation, she had the ski on and the rope in her hand before grabbing the ski he skidded to her. Griff put on his shirt, jumped behind the wheel, and watched for her hand signal.

She waited for the rope to become taut. The engine snorted and she came out of the water like a seasoned skier. At first, they were just small moves. By leaning and using her ankles, she quickly learned to move in either direction. She had no intention of jumping the boat's wake as Griff did. It was perfectly fine to just let the skis slide over the rolling water. Even so, she momentarily lost her balance on the first attempt, and had to make some wild gyrations to right herself. Once outside, and gliding along on smooth water, she raised her hand and shouted. "Yahoo!, I did it."

Soon crossing behind the boat was second nature. Not to be confused with his spectacular jumps, she was able to put a little air between skis and water on a couple of crossings. Gaining confidence, Sarah soon realized by digging her heels and pushing against the pull of the rope, she could generate more speed. The big smile on her face said it all. She was having fun.

Everything was going smoothly until another boat passed them going in the opposite direction. The opposing wakes and Sarah met at the same time. This time she went airborne. The skis went up over the top of her head. Doing a half-gainer, she hit the water headfirst. Her neck and shoulders took the blunt of the impact. A rush of cold water washed across her chest. She opened her eyes and flailed her arms, searching for sky. Her lungs screamed for air. The thought came with a vision of Dee. It seemed like a lifetime before her head broke through the lake's surface. She gasped and spit out a mouthful of water. She could see the boat, hiked on its side, in a sharp turn. Something felt funny. Her hand was tangled in some kind of string. She brought it out in front of her. It was a blue strap. She looked down. Her breasts were totally visible, floating freely in the water. Her bathing suit was at her waist. She treaded water with one hand while using the other to pull her suit back up into place. She bought one of the straps out of the water and was happy to see the hook was still attached. Putting the strap over her shoulder she matched the slide hook to the loop on the suit. By now the boat was coming up fast. She found the other strap. *Dang. The hook's gone.* Not only was the hook gone but the loop on the suit was torn through.

Sarah heard the engine die and before the boat settled in the water, Griff was in the water next to her. "Are you alright?" He spun her around.

"I'm fine." She held up the strap. "I just tore my suit."

"Man, that was some fall you took. I thought for sure you hurt yourself."

Griff gathered the skis, swam back to the boat, and tossed them in. He lifted himself up on the back deck, hung the ladder and reached to offer her a hand.

She grabbed both sides of the ladder. In coming out of the water the unattached side of her suit slid down exposing her breast. She saw his eyes widen.

"Oops. Sorry," he said, as he quickly turned his head.

Once in the boat, she covered her exposed body part and went to the front seat to find her blouse.

He turned around as she started buttoning it. "I still can't believe you didn't hurt yourself. That's about the wildest fall I've ever seen anyone take."

Oh joy, leave it to me to garner that distinction. "My brand-new bathing suit wasn't so lucky. Thank goodness for the safety belt or I might have lost it completely."

"Wow, wouldn't that have been something." He began gathering in the tow rope.

Oh yes, that would have been something. She smiled at the thought and knew Dee was laughing somewhere. "You wouldn't happen to have a safety pin, would you?"

"No, but I know where I can get you one." He slid into the front seat and started the engine.

CHAPTER TWENTY-SEVEN

A NIGHT TO REMEMBER

Griff started the engine, pushed the lever forward, and advanced the throttle. Sarah grabbed the seat back as the bow came up out of the water. As soon as the boat planed and picked up speed she climbed over the seat and sat beside him. The speedometer needle held steady on thirty. The rush of air, still a little warm from a setting sun, blew the wet hair off her shoulders. It also pressed the wet blouse against her skin. It felt cold on her chest. She shivered and grabbed the towel off the seat. "Brrr. It's getting chilly," she said, as she wrapped it around herself.

Griff reduced their speed to twenty miles per hour. "You're right." He reached under the deck and brought out his shirt. "Hold the wheel for a second." With her hand on the wheel, he pulled the shirt over his head and stuck his arms through the sleeves. Taking control again, he pointed ahead. "It's just a little bit farther."

Sarah slid into her shorts and put on her socks and saddles. She had just finished tying the laces when he backed off the throttle. She looked up. The boat was heading towards a pier. The first thing she noticed was the big red boathouse two doors up on the right. *Is this where the main building of the Greystone Resort stood?* A large two-story house sat on a hill directly in front of them. The clapboard siding was painted pale yellow, accented with white eaves, trim and window shutters. A screened porch extended the full width of the building. It wasn't the largest she'd seen on the lake, but it was bigger and grander than the ones that stood on either side of it. "Is this—"

"My folk's. My grandfather built it in the thirties." He brought the boat to an idle and made a swooping turn to bring the bow around to face the lake. With precision, he reversed the engine allowing the craft to nestle up to the pier, barely bumping the wooden structure. He jumped out, and before the boat could move away, had it tied fore and aft. "Come on, let's find you a safety pin."

Sarah held his hand as she stepped first on the side of the boat and then onto the pier. "You live on the lake?" She wished she hadn't put so much emphasis on the word lake.

Her tone must have confused him. "Why, is that a bad thing?"

"No…no, not at all. It's just that you work with Duke in the boat shop. I just thought…"

Griff laughed. "That I was a local? First of all, I don't work in the shop, at least not as a paid employee. Duke lets me come in and putter around. I love working with wood. I've been doing that since I was twelve years old." He walked uphill through the yard. "Come on, I'll give you the tour."

"Do you live here year-around?"

"Just summers. Our permanent home is in Chicago. I attend DePaul University and will start med school this fall." He climbed the steps and held the screen door open for her. The porch had a variety of wicker chairs and rockers. There were couches and canvas lawn chairs. A table and four chairs sat to one side, a chess board with all its pieces graced the center.

"Do you play?" Sarah asked, picking up the black queen.

"I do. You?"

"No, but I always thought it would be fun to learn." She replaced the piece and stepped through the doorway. The main room was filled with vintage furniture, all in beautiful condition and arranged in a neat and orderly fashion. The wood floor was polished to a high shine. On the left, bookcases loaded with hard cover books extended the full length of the wall, interrupted by two windows that stretched floor to ceiling. Near the front door a large grandfather clock with its pendulum swinging, made a loud ticking sound. A massive fieldstone fireplace with a huge bear skin rug in front of it, stood opposite. The mantel was a wood timber that looked to be hand-hewn and above that was a large mounted deer head. Griff disappeared through the archway to the right of the fireplace. She leaned to see where he was going. The room contained a large, ornately carved dining room table with eight high-backed chairs and a matching break front. Through the glass doors, she could see a collection of colorful dishware.

A breeze off the lake reminded her of her wet hair. Goosebumps rose on both arms. The wet towel offered little warmth. Her teeth chattered.

"Here, I found a safety pin. I believe you can find one of everything in our kitchen junk drawer." He handed her the pin.

Her hand shook as she reached for it.

"You're shivering." He took a closer look. "Your lips are purple. Maybe, you should get out of that wet suit." He pointed to the right of the fireplace. "There's the bathroom."

Sarah nodded and hurried off. Being out of the draft made a difference. She let the towel fall to the floor and unbuttoned her blouse. Shaking fingers made it difficult. Once she got her blouse off, she dropped her shorts and kicked them aside. Then, unhooking the one strap that was still attached to her wet suit, she put her thumbs into the sides and pushed it down over her hips and let it fall to her ankles. She picked it up and dropped it in the sink.

A large tan bath towel hung on the bar above the toilet. After a slight hesitation, she threw caution to the wind and took the towel. The warm dry terry felt wonderful. She wiped her arms, her legs, and her back. She gathered it in front of her and held it to her chest. To be dry and warm never felt so good. She wrapped the towel around her waist and looked at herself in the mirror. Her hair was a tangled mess.

Well, I breeched their privacy with the towel, I might as well search for a comb. The first drawer contained two flavors of toothpaste and an assortment of brushes. The second held the motherload, not just a comb, but a hairbrush, too. She brushed the snarls out of her hair. Digging in the drawer, she came up with a rubber band and finished by putting her hair in a ponytail. She looked at herself in the mirror. Beyond her own image, she imagined Dee's smiling face. "I know you think this funny," she said, shaking the hairbrush at the glass. She had to chuckle at her own predicament. *Dear God, I've known the guy for less than six hours and now I am standing here in his bathroom—naked."* Her eye caught a colorful assortment of bottles and small jars on the counter. She opened the largest bottle and sniffed the fragrance. This had to be his. It smelled the same as she remembered when he came to pick her up. The small jar with the pink cloisonné rose bud on the lid was definitely feminine. She put a dab of the smooth cream behind each ear and a little in the cleavage between her breasts.

Unwrapping the towel, she folded it and laid it across the edge of the tub. Picking up the blouse, she put it on and buttoned it. It was still wet, still cold, and worse, it clung to her skin and made it look like she had nothing on. You could see everything, the roundness of her breast, even the dark colored nipples. Worse, the nipples blossomed from the cold and looked like little noses protruding from the cloth. She couldn't face him like this. She looked around. Behind the door was a bright blue bathrobe with a large gold "DBD" monogramed on the chest. She took off the blouse, brought down the robe, and put her arm into the sleeve. It smelled of his cologne. She giggled at seeing her saddle shoes poking out from under the bottom of the robe. She tied the belt and looked at herself in the mirror. *Not my size, but it'll have to do.*

She gathered her blouse and shorts, opened the door part way and poked her head into the room. It was dark. The sun had set. She heard the crackling of a fire and saw shadows dance on the walls and ceiling.

"I thought maybe you went to sleep in there," he said, as she stepped out of the bathroom. He was stoking the fire but stopped when he saw her wrapped in his bathrobe. "Go Demons."

"I'm sorry, but all my clothes are wet. Is there some way to dry them?"

Griff hung the poker. "Sure. Let me get a couple of chairs from the dining room. We can hang them here next to the fire." He brought two chairs, draped her blouse on one and her shorts on the other. "What about your suit?"

"It's still in the bathroom." She turned and scooted off to retrieve it.

He already had another chair in front of the fire. She used the safety pin to fasten the torn strap and hung the suit on the back of the chair.

"I hope you don't mind me using your robe. I didn't have much choice."

"I see your point." If he was going to make some off the cuff remark about her not having any clothes on, he didn't. "Besides," he said. "It looks far better on you than it does on me."

She put her finger on the embroidered monogram. "Is this your school?"

He nodded, "DePaul Blue Demons" He appeared to be waiting for a reaction.

Sarah shrugged. She'd never heard of it. She looked at the staircase to the second floor. "Is anyone else here?"

"Mom and Dad are at a medical seminar in Minneapolis. It's just you and me."

She wasn't sure if that was a good thing or a bad thing. "When you came by Nora and Duke's, you said your folks were holding supper for you." Her voice had an accusatory tone.

"I wasn't up for wieners and beans."

That brought a smile to Sarah's face.

"So, I came home and warmed up a can of soup."

"Not much of a gourmet improvement," she said.

"I guess not." Griff chuckled before grabbing a couple pillows off the couch and tossing them on the big brown rug. "Why don't you cozy up to the fire. I'm going to see if I can scare up something to snack on." He disappeared through the archway.

Sarah dropped to her knees and ran her fingers through the long soft fur. Rolling to her side, she positioned a pillow behind her head, and made sure all her sensitive body parts were covered. Seeing how silly it looked with her shoes on, she quickly removed them and set them aside. The bear fur tickled, as she dug her toes into the long, soft strands. Stretching out, she watched the flames lick up the blackened stones. Bringing the lapels of the robe to her nose, she drew a deep breath and inhaled the lingering smell of his cologne. She closed her eyes. *This can't be real. How did I get from learning to water ski to lying naked…wrapped in his robe…on a bearskin rug…in his house?* "Even you, or your Grandmother Belle, couldn't come up with a story as unlikely as this," she said.

"What did you say?" Griff asked, as he set the tray on the floor. "I don't have much to offer, but I did find some sliced cheddar and Ritz crackers, and one dill pickle." He handed her a large mug. "I also made us some hot tea, spiked with a little peppermint schnapps and lemon."

Sarah perked up. "Is that alcohol? Are you trying to get me drunk?"

"I doubt a tablespoon of schnapps would have that effect. It'll help you warm up inside."

She took in the sweet aroma before taking a sip. The hot liquid and the bite of the spirits had the suggested effect. She felt the warmth all the way down to her stomach. "It's good," she said, putting a piece of cheese on a cracker. "Are you serious, a dill pickle?"

He picked it up and took a crunchy bite. "Outside of breakfast, we eat most of our meals out. The kitchen is pretty bare."

"Doesn't your mom cook?"

"Easter, Thanksgiving and Christmas."

Sarah giggled. "That's a long time between meals."

He chuckled. "Mom and Dad both have time-consuming careers. Mom's a child psychologist and Dad is a heart surgeon, although he does mostly research now. He's hoping to one day transplant a heart from a recently deceased, into someone with a heart defect. That's what they are talking about in Minneapolis."

Sarah took another swallow of tea. "Wow, wouldn't that be something."

"Griff sipped his. "You were saying something when I came into the room. I didn't quite hear what you said."

"It was nothing." *I guess he thinks there's nothing unusual for me to be sitting here naked—wearing his robe—and drinking tea spiked with peppermint schnapps.* "Do you have a girlfriend?" *The real question, how many girls has he had in this situation.*

"No one steady." He got up. "Would you like more tea?"

She looked in her cup and handed it to him. "Have you had a lot of girlfriends?

"A few." He stopped and felt the bathing suit. "It's drying." He touched the sleeve of the blouse. "This, too." He disappeared through the archway.

A doctor's son. Strong and handsome. I'll bet he's had a ton of girlfriends. The tea was working its magic. She loosened the belt and fanned the sides of the robe. Looking down at her body, she took note of the roundness of her breasts, the flatness of her tummy, and the shape of her hips and thighs. She hadn't paid that much attention to how her body was changing, and then all of a sudden, there it was, fully developed. She felt Dee's presence and sensed a strong message. *Girl, you better be careful.* She quickly covered at the sound of his footsteps.

Be careful, it's hot," he said, handing her the mug.

His use of the word *careful* caught her attention. *Is this Dee, trying to warn me?* She took the cup. "Did you say it was just a few?"

A few what?" He said, dropping to his knees and then sitting cross-legged next to her.

"Girlfriends. It's hard to believe a good-looking guy like you, son of a doctor, wouldn't be surrounded by girls."

He seemed to be taken aback by the question. "What about you? I'm sure guys by the dozen are traipsing after you."

She stuck her nose in the mug. *Should I tell him I've only had one actual date—to homecoming, with Freddy Stone.*

"The problem with having girlfriends, is not knowing what they want. Are they interested in me, or just a meal ticket?" He pulled the cup from his lips. "This is a funny question, but, how old are you?"

"Seventeen. My birthday is in October."

He rocked backwards. "Maybe we ought to check and see if your clothes are dry." He rose and set his cup on the mantel. "I think this is dry enough to wear," he said squeezing the top of the suit. "I should be getting you home."

Sarah held the robe closed as she struggled to her feet. The grandfather clock near the front door began chiming. *It's only ten o'clock, but all of a sudden, he seems to be in a hurry.* She grabbed her clothing off the chairs and hurried to the bathroom.

Griff was standing by the front door when she returned. "I'll take you home in the car. It'll be easier."

"What about the boat?"

"I'll clean it up and take it back in the morning." He waited for her to go out the door, then followed, closing the door behind him. He walked to a free-standing garage and opened one of the three doors. Inside stood a black convertible with the top down. He walked ahead and opened the passenger side door.

"Is this yours?"

He nodded.

There was a larger four door sedan in the next stall. She stopped momentarily to read the chrome inscription on the door. *Chrysler New Yorker. Wow.*

"That's Mom's," he said, waiting for her to get in his car. "They took the Cadillac to Minneapolis."

Sarah was confused. His whole demeanor had changed. He didn't sound angry. It was more matter of fact, like listening to a tour guide. She got in and Griff closed the door behind her. He started the car, backed out, and drove out the long driveway. "I can put the top up if it's too breezy."

"It's fine." She pulled the rubber band on her ponytail and let the night air blow through her hair. *It must have been something I said.* "Thank you for taking me skiing. I really had a good time."

"You did well for your first time. I'm glad you weren't hurt taking that nasty tumble."

"Will you take me skiing again some time?"

He paused before answering. "Sure, maybe we can get a bunch together and make it a party."

"Sounds good," Sarah said. *Why do we need a bunch?* She touched the chrome Ford name plate on the dash. "This a nice car. Is it new?"

"It's a Forty-six, two-door coupe. During pre-med, I lived at home and used it to commute to school. Once I get settled this fall, I'll probably look for an apartment close to the school." He turned into Duke's driveway. "Well, here you are. I hope you'll be able to fix your bathing suit."

She gripped the metal clasp through her blouse. "Thank you for the safety pin…and the hot tea." She opened the door. "Will I see you again?"

"I've got a lot going on. I might have to go to Chicago and get some things taken care of for school, but I'm sure we'll run into each other."

Sarah stepped out of the car and closed the door. "Thanks again, I had a good time."

Griff waved, backed out, and drove up the street.

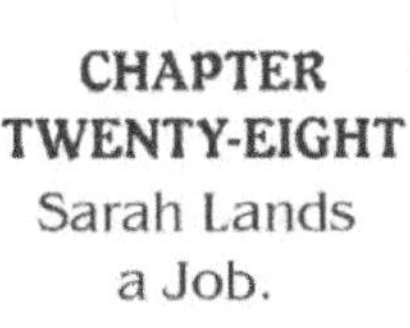

CHAPTER TWENTY-EIGHT
Sarah Lands a Job.

Nora was on the porch when Sarah came up the walk. "I heard the car drive up. Did you have a good time?"

Sarah turned for one last look as the convertible drove down the street. She wiped her eyes on the sleeve of her blouse.

Nora hurried down the steps. "Are you crying? What happened? Are you hurt?"

"It's nothing." Sarah brushed past, went inside, and started up the stairs.

Her sister was right on the girl's heels. "Are you okay? Did he hurt you?"

"Nora, please. Just leave me alone."

"No, I won't leave you alone. You're crying and I want to know why. Did he do something? Did he force himself on you?"

Sarah reached the top of the stairs, turned and faced her sister. "No. He was a perfect gentleman. I practically seduced him, and he never so much as laid a finger on me. There, are you satisfied?" She spun on her heels, went into her room, and closed the door.

Nora, stunned by her sister's outburst, gripped the handrail to maintain her balance. She tapped on the door twice before opening it. Sarah lay face down on the bed. Her body heaved as she sobbed.

Nora sat beside her. "Forgive me," she said, laying a hand on the girl's shoulder. "I had no right to pry. I know I'm not your real sister, but I love you like one. If you're hurting, I hurt, too."

Sarah turned her head to the side. "Dee was right. I'm such a ninny."

"You a ninny? Why would she say that?"

"Because I'm stupid and naïve." Sarah rolled to her side. "We had such a fun time. I learned to ski. I even went out to the side of the boat." Her voice rose with excitement. "I was doing so good. Then this boat came from the other way and I hit its wake and went flying into the air. It flipped me upside down. I did a backwards somersault and dove headfirst into the water"

When Sarah paused, Nora seized the moment to ask, "Were you hurt?"

Sarah's cheek's reddened. A giggle accompanied her answer. "No, but it tore the straps off my bathing suit. If it wasn't for the safety belt I was wearing, I might have lost it altogether. One strap just came out of the loop, but this one tore right through the material." She pressed the fabric of her blouse to show the outline of the safety pin.

Nora took a quick look. "I'm sure we can sew that up."

A long pause followed. Nora knew there was more to the story, and Sarah tried to decide how much of it she was willing to tell. "Here's where the stupid part comes in," she said before acknowledging it was the quest for a safety pin, that set off the chain of events. "I was cold and wet." From there she pretty much gave a running narrative of how the evening played out, extracting any feelings or emotions. Nora also held hers in check, except for a few instances where a slight gasp betrayed her. Sarah finished with describing the quick and quiet ride home. "He probably thinks I'm just another gold-digging female trying to worm her way into his wealthy family." Nora's silence confused her. She finally asked, "Aren't you going to say anything?"

Nora patted the girl's hip. "I'm the last person to be giving advice to anyone on how to conduct their lives. It would take you three lifetimes to make as many mistakes as I have. It probably wasn't the wisest decision to take all your clothes off, but I think it was an innocent one. And don't be upset by the abrupt ride home. He's an educated adult male and you are a minor, I'm sure he had the statuary rape laws in the back of his mind.

"Rape? I never once thought he would try anything like that."

"And it was probably never his intention, but the laws are pretty strict.

Sarah rolled off the bed and unbuttoned her blouse and hung it over the back of the chair. "Like I said, he did nothing wrong. It was just stupidity on my part." She undid the one strap on her bathing suit and unhooked the safety pin. "Do you think we can sew this back together?"

"I'm sure of it," Nora said on her way to the door. "You get a good night's sleep. Like they say in sports, no harm, no foul."

Sarah unbuttoned her shorts and let them fall to the floor. "Well, what's done is done, that's probably the last we'll see of one Griff MacDonald."

Nora was sitting at the kitchen table with a cup of coffee in her hand and her elbow on the newspaper when Sarah walked in. "Good Morning, sleepyhead."

Sarah glanced at the clock. "I think I'm still trying to catch up from all the bus travel." She looked around. "Is Duke gone already."

"Yup, my day off. My turn to loaf around the house. Look, I'm still in my PJ's." She got up and refilled her cup. "Can I fix you something for breakfast?"

Sarah opened the cupboard door. "Do you have cereal?"

"There's a box of corn flakes in the next cupboard. If you like fresh picked blueberries on your cereal, there are some in the frig."

"Just milk and sugar." She opened the refrigerator door. "Oh, can I have some of this orange juice?"

"Help yourself." Nora waited for Sarah to pour some juice, fix her bowl of cereal, and bring it to the table before asking, "Feeling better today?"

"I am. Griff is a nice guy, but the last thing I need right now is a boyfriend."

"There are a lot of fish in the sea and you've got all the time in the world to hook one."

Sarah laughed. "That's if I want to go fishing at all." *Or waterskiing.*

"Do you have plans for today?"

"As a matter of fact, I thought of going down to the Bay Side Restaurant and applying for a job. It'll give me a chance to meet people and make some spending money."

"Do you want me to go too? I can put in a good word for you."

"I'd feel better if I did this on my own."

"Suit yourself. I got plenty of laundry to keep me busy. It wouldn't hurt to mention my name."

Sarah smiled. "If I bring my bathing suit down, do you think you could sew on a new clasp?"

"I'm sure I can figure out something, so you don't have to worry about it falling off…again."

"Did you tell Duke?" Sarah asked.

"Just that you had a good time waterskiing. The rest is between you and me."

Sarah gave Nora a big hug. "I'm sorry I blew up at you last night. I…"

"Sisters don't have to apologize to one another."

*****

Sarah stood on the sidewalk in front of the Bay Side Restaurant. She stepped aside as a group came out the door. With the door being held open, she looked past them into the building. *Geez, they're still pretty busy, maybe I should come back later.* It was probably the thought of Dee laughing and calling her *chicken* that made her enter while the man continued to hold the door for her.

"Thank you," she said with a smile. Once inside Sarah made her way past a counter full of people to the back of the room.

Blanche, the woman that had served them the other evening, rushed out of the kitchen with a tray full of steaming plates on her shoulder. "Take a seat if you can find one," she said. "I'll be with you in a minute."

A busboy, toting a tray of dirty dishes, yelled, "Coming through." As he disappeared through the kitchen door. A waitress came out as the door swung open. She went behind the counter, grabbed the coffee pot and filled the empty cups along the counter. Returning the pot to the warmer, she turned and greeted a couple as they approached the cash register. "Was everything okay?" she asked, taking their money and guest check. The man nodded and motioning with his hand. "Keep the change."

The young waitress smiled, rang up the sale and replied, "Thank you, come again." She put the change in her pocket, cleared the dishes from a spot at the counter, and motioned to Sarah. "There's a seat over here."

Sarah shook her head and waved off the suggestion.

The girl filled two glasses with water, grabbed a couple of menus, and came around the counter. "It'll be a small wait for a table," she said, as she hurried to the dining area.

"I'm waiting to talk to Blanche," Sarah said, unsure if the girl heard or paid any attention to what she said.

"Did you want to see me?" Blanche said, as she passed behind Sarah. "I'm awfully busy."

"I'd like to apply—"

The woman stopped, took one head to toe look and said, "You're Nora's sister, right?"

It was not a time to explain the family connection. "Yes," Sarah answered.

"When can you start?"

Sarah straightened. "Any time—I guess."

"Good, come." Blanche led the way. "Have you ever run a cash register?" she said over her shoulder.

"At a soda fountain," Sarah skipped to keep up.

"Was it anything like this one?" Blanche asked, as she hit the "No Sale" button and caught the drawer as it came out.

Sarah took a quick look. "Yes, it was also a Royal."

The woman pulled money and a guest check from her apron pocket. "See if you can ring this up."

Sarah punched in the amount, put the bills in their proper place in the drawer and counted back the change into Blanche's outstretched hand.

"You're hired," she said. "You are an angel sent from heaven. We'll take care of the other stuff later, but for right now you just handle the till."

An elderly man, sitting on the first stool, yelled as Blanche hurried past, "Where do you find these pretty girls?"

"They just fall out of the sky." She waved her order pad at him. "And don't you be giving her a hard time."

Sarah blushed as the man gave her a big smile. She stuffed her purse under the counter and straightened items around the cash register. *That went easy.*

After ringing up the first few guest checks, her nerves settled and she found herself conversing with the people, thanking them and inviting them to come again.

When Duke and Griff walked through the door it was difficult to determine who was more surprised. "What are you doing here?" Duke asked, stepping to the counter.

"Working," she said.

Duke backhanded Griff in the stomach. "How do you like that, two days in town and already the girl's got herself a job."

Griff forced a smile as he hurried to the far end and took an open seat at the counter.

Sarah was crushed by Griff's lack of interest. *Don't lose it, girl.* She tried to mask her feelings but the look on her face betrayed her. *I guess he has every right to ignore me, but it hurts.* Sarah was happy for the steady stream of people who stepped to the counter to pay their bills. She even made a few sales of her own for candy or gum. In between, to keep her distance from the two, she bused dishes from the counter and wiped the surfaces near her.

"See you at home," Duke said, handing her money and the bill. "This is for the kid and I."

Griff gave a small wave and walked out the door.

Won't he even give me a chance to explain?

It was sometime after four when Blanche patted her on the shoulder. "You did a great job—saved my butt. Grab a soda and come back to the office, let's get you all signed up."

Sarah took a small bottle of coke from the cooler and followed.

The office was closet sized. The small desk, two chairs, and one four-drawer filing cabinet left little space to move around. Blanche took a stack of papers off one of the chairs and motioned Sarah to it. Looking for an empty space on the desk, she finally gave up and laid the stack on top of everything else. She opened the top drawer of the cabinet, pulled sheets from two different folders and handed them to Sarah. "One is the application, the other is for taxes and withholding." She chuckled. "Uncle Sam will want his share." Then looking down at the desk and seeing Sarah searching for a place to fill out the papers, she added, "Take them home and bring them back tomorrow."

The woman sat and swung around to look at a small chalk board on the wall. "What shift would you like, I've got six to one or one to eight?"

"I'm an early riser, I'll do six to one?" *And then I'll have my afternoons and evenings free.*

"Done." Blanche scribble Sarah's name across the board. "I'm marking you in for seven days. If we get more help or you need a day off, just let me know."

"Will I be running the cash register?"

"Oh hell no. We all do everything, serve, bus tables, and seat the people. The only thing I won't ask you to do is cook or mop floors."

Sarah laughed at Blanche's directness. "What should I wear?"

"We're not the Greystone. Dress casual. What you have on is perfectly fine. You might want to have an apron with a pocket. You'll need a place to keep your order pad and it will keep some of the gunk off your clothes. Oh, and a couple of pencils." The woman stood. "That's it. Joanie opens in the morning. Be ready, you'll have fisherman chomping at the bit to get breakfast. I'll leave her a note to let her know you'll be here."

Sarah picked up the papers and led the way out of the office. "Thank you again, for hiring me."

"You might want to hold up on the thank-yous until you've had a few days under your belt," Blanche said. "It can get a little crazy around here."

Sarah grabbed her purse from behind the counter, said her goodbyes, and went out the door. Standing on the sidewalk. She looked up and down the main streets. *So far, I've had three crazy days in Pine Lake, I don't think it can get any crazier*

CHAPTER TWENTY-NINE

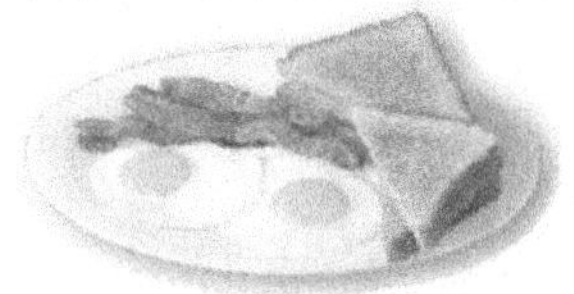

Nothing beats a 59¢ Breakfast Special

"I got a job," Sarah announced as she burst into the kitchen.

Nora turned from the stove. "You're kidding, doing what?"

"You are looking at the newest waitress at the Bay Side Restaurant." She danced in a circle. "Not only that, I already have a half day to my credit. Blanche put me to work cashiering." Sarah sat at the table and spread the papers in front of her. "I have to fill out the application and bring it back in the morning.'"

Nora peeked over the girl's shoulder. "Are you sure you want to go to work right away? You really didn't give yourself much of a chance to enjoy the summer."

"My shift is from six to one. I'll have afternoons and evenings to enjoy whatever I choose to do. Besides, it's important to me to have my own money."

"You have ten thousand dollars in the bank," Nora countered. "From your dad's military insurance."

"But I can't touch it until I'm eighteen, unless Mom okays it."

Nora went back to the stove. "Were having roast beef, mashed potatoes, and creamed peas for supper." She opened the refrigerator door and brought out a quart bottle of milk. She pulled off the paper cap and poured some in the pan. "I'm sure Mom would be happy to let you take some of it."

"I had a good time today. I think working there will be fun." She took a pencil from her purse. "Is it okay if I use your address and phone number?" Taking her billfold from her purse, she took out her social security card and copied the numbers. "Thanks to the man at the bank for helping me apply for this. I guess you can't work unless you have one."

"One what?" Duke asked, as he came strolling into the kitchen.

"Social Security card," Sarah said, waving the card in the air.

"Sarah got herself a job," Nora said, pulling the roast from the oven. "Blanche hired her at the Bay Side."

"Yeah, it surprised the hell out of me to see her behind the counter." He walked behind Nora and planted a kiss on her cheek.

Nora shushed him with the hot pad. "Go wash up, I'm about ready to put supper on the table." Turning to Sarah, she flapped the pad at her. "Save that paperwork for later and set the table."

Sarah quickly obliged. *Geez, I never realized how much Sis is like Mom.*

With everything on the table, Nora took off her apron, hung it on a cupboard door handle, and took a seat. She handed the bowl of potatoes to Duke. "What were you doing at the Bay Side? I thought you took a sack lunch."

Duke scooped a large spoonful of potatoes on his plate. "I took Griff to lunch. I wanted to thank him for his help getting those boats in the water. I certainly couldn't do it by myself."

"Cliff should hire more help," Nora said. "How is the roast? Tender?"

"It's delicious." Sarah passed the platter to Duke. "Did Griff say anything…about me?"

"Just that you did great getting up on skis. Did you know he's studying to become a doctor?"

Sarah stirred gravy into her mashed potatoes. "Yes, he told me."

"There's a lot of money in the family, he'd make a good catch for some lucky young girl."

Yes, but I don't think this fish wants to be caught. Sarah looked at Nora hoping she wouldn't take the bait and reveal details of the previous night.

Nora winked. "I'm sure the young man has any number of girls to choose from," she said. "Are you trying to do a little matchmaking?"

Duke straightened. "I was just saying…I think he's a fine young man."

"Did he say anything else—about me?" Sarah held her breath. *Please say no.*

"It's nothing he says, it's just the way he looks at you. I'd say he thinks you're something special."

Sarah let the air out slowly from her lungs, as the tension released from her chest. *That wasn't the feeling I got.*

"Not to change the subject," Nora said, "have you heard anything more about the break-in at the Liquor Store?"

"No, it had to be kids. Pros wouldn't have stopped at a bottle of Jack Daniels and some cigarettes." Duke stood and walked his empty plate to the sink. "What's for dessert?"

"I picked up a cherry pie from the bakery." Nora looked at Sarah. "Want a piece?"

Sarah pushed her plate forward. "I couldn't eat another bite." *It had to be those three drunk kids I met in the park. I wonder if that broken bottle is still in the rocks by the water.*

*****

Sarah set the alarm for four-thirty but was awake and pressed the button before it went off. Maybe she could fudge the time after this, but she didn't want to be late on the first day. She chose the yellow blouse to go with her tan slacks and pulled her hair into a tight ponytail, tied with a yellow ribbon. Even though her shiner had pretty well faded, she added more of the mortician's special bruise-covering makeup. *It'll save a lot of time and besides, it's none of anyone else's business.*

Sarah was on the bench in front of the restaurant when a gal in her thirties walked up and stuck the key in the door lock. Three men got out of a nearby parked car.

"Good Morning. Are you Jeanie? I'm Sarah."

The woman gave her a puzzled look.

"I'm the new recruit. Blanche said she would leave you a note, but since the note is probably inside, you couldn't have known that."

"Sounds like Blanche. Have you waitressed before?"

"I worked a soda counter in a drug store, but I did the cashiering yesterday, cleaned the counter, poured water—"

"Well, that's better than none. The main thing, don't scribble the order, write so Chuck can read it. He'll have a fit if you don't."

"Chuck?"

"The guy standing behind you. He's a grump, but a darn good cook."

Sarah was startled to see someone behind her. *Where did he—*

The slender man, graying at the temples, nodded and smiled.

The three men approached. "C'mon, Jeanie, shake a leg, we've got some heavy-duty fishin' to do."

The woman turned the key. "Keep your shirt on, Roy. The fish are all still sleeping. The only crazy fools up at this hour are you three, Chuck, me and her."

Jeanie led the way in. "Do you have a pencil?" Chuck light-footed it to the kitchen.

"In my purse," Sarah said, before realizing what she didn't have. "But I forgot to bring an apron."

"Don't sweat it. Blanche has a half dozen laying around." The two walked through the swinging doors. Chuck lit the grill and proceeded to go around the kitchen turning on an assortment of electrical appliances.

The young gal took an apron off the hook and threw it in Sarah's direction. Snatching it from in front of her face, Sarah tied it around her waist. Two school-aged boys, their mouths opened in a collective yawn, came ambling through the door. "Sarah, this is Freddie, our dishwasher and Eric, our number one busboy. They both straightened and threw back their shoulders. Sarah smiled at their obvious attempt to catch her eye.

Jeanie handed her an order pad. "Time to get your feet wet. Take three waters and menus to those *fishermen.* She used her fingers to draw quotation marks in the air. "They're here every Saturday. It'll be three fifty-nine centers, crispy bacon, two with eggs over easy, and one sunny side up. On the toast, two get white—the other wheat. Roy likes milk and the others take coffee—one black, one with cream."

Sarah set the waters on the table and was surprised when they ordered exactly as Jeanie said.

"This gal should give the rest of you girls writing lessons," Chuck said, looking at the order. "I can read every damned word."

Jeanie flapped her hand in the air. "As soon as it gets busy her writing won't look any better than mine."

The woman was right. Once it started, the flow of people about wore the hinges off the front door. And sure enough, Chuck was no longer complimenting her on her penmanship. This led to a few of her orders coming out wrong. Once Sarah explained it was her first day, most customers were super forgiving and kept the food they were served.

Those first couple of hours Sarah wasn't sure if she was on foot or horseback, but she soon fell into a rhythm and found she could save steps and wasted motion by anticipating her next move. A welcomed lull came around eleven. Jeanie was the first to pour herself a cup of coffee and plop her butt on the end stool.

Sarah drew herself a glass of water and leaned on the counter. "How did I do?"

"Girl," Jeanie said lighting a cigarette. "I've worked with a lot of first-timers, but you'd beat the pants off any of them. I even had a couple locals tell me what a sweet girl you are. None have ever said what a sweet girl I am."

Sarah's elbows came off the counter. "Really, they said that?"

"Don't let it go to your head. Words are nice, and we need those townspeople during the winter, but you're lucky if they leave you a quarter or fifty cents. Give me the tourist and lakeshore, they leave the folding money. All I can say is thank heavens for summers. Oh, and while I think of it. There's a jar in the kitchen and we always throw a couple of bucks in it for the boys in back."

A couple of bucks? Sarah hadn't kept track of her tips. She'd just kept stuffing them in her pocket. Putting her hand inside, she did feel a lot of change but there was also a nice wad of paper money. *Criminy, I wonder how much I have in there.*

When a party of six came through the door, Jeanie snuffed her cigarette. "Breaks over. This is probably the start of the lunch crowd." And sure enough, it was back to the races.

Blanche came in at noon. The extra hands and feet were just what they needed to get over the hump.

Mary, a girl Sarah worked with the day before, rushed through the door at the stroke of one. Wrapping her apron on as she scurried. "I'm late. I'm sorry." Blanche, standing by the cash register, pointed to a foursome sitting in the corner booth. "Water, menus, and take their order." Sarah came to ring up a guest check. "Jeanie says you did a bang-up job." Blanche put her hand on Sarah's shoulder. "I guess that means we'll have to keep you around for another day."

Sarah smiled, relishing the compliment.

"Did you bring in your application?" the older woman asked, as she turned and greeted another group of people. "Be with you in a jiffy, staff change."

"I put it on your desk," Sarah rang up the sale, stuck the guest check on the spindle, and put the dollar and change in her pocket.

"Nice tip," Blanche said eyeing the amount. "You must have dazzled the pants off someone." She looked into the dining room. "Was that your last table?"

Sarah nodded. "Did you want me to stay?"

"I think we can handle it from here," Blanche said, taking some dirty dishes and putting them in a bus tray under the counter. "See you tomorrow, okay?"

Sarah reached under the register, pulled out her purse and emptied the contents of her pocket into it. Untying the apron, she folded it and handed it to Blanche "I borrowed your—"

Blanche took the apron. "I almost forgot, Mary has a family picnic tomorrow and asked if you could switch with her and do the one to eight shift?"

"Sure, of course, Sarah said. "I've got nothing planned."

Mary gave her a hug. "You're a doll. It's my husband's mom's birthday and if I didn't show, she'd probably have me drummed out of the family."

Sarah laughed. "We wouldn't want that, would we?"

"Business drops off on Sunday nights," Blanche said. Everyone heads out of town or turns in early. If it's too dead, we'll lock it up early."

Sarah walked into the kitchen, grabbed a handful of change from her purse, and dropped two dollars of it in the jug. "Thanks guys, see you tomorrow at one." She slung her purse over her shoulder and headed for the door with a big smile on her face. *I made it through my first full day.* She slapped the leather bag. *And a profitable one at that.*

A Whole Lot of Moola.

The eight-block walk back to Nora's took less than ten minutes. Sarah wasn't trying to hurry, but her long, quick, strides were fueled by the excitement of finding out how much she had made in tips. She wiped the beads of sweat off her forehead. *Ely was never this warm in June.*

"Anybody here?" she yelled, walking into the kitchen. The Andrews Sister's singing *Near You* on the radio provided the only response. She hummed along with the tune. As she opened the refrigerator door and poured herself a half glass of Kool-Aid. *Duke probably took his lunch and Nora must be held up at the hospital.* She gulped the contents, rinsed the glass, and put it in the dish rack.

Sarah was still humming as she skipped up the stairs two at time. Sitting Indian style on the bed, she dumped the contents of her purse on the blanket. Pushing the billfold, comb, lipstick and hanky aside, she counted three dollars and thirty-five cents in coins. She unfolded each dollar and laid it on a stack. "Nine dollars." She squealed and tossed the bills in the air. "At this rate, I'll be able to buy lots of new clothes for school…maybe even a new bathing suit." She flopped back, rested her head on the pillow, and looked at the ceiling, "What do you think, Dee? Should I get that white two-piece in Penney's window? Wouldn't that be a shocker if I showed up in Ely wearing that?" She snickered at the thought of it.

Sitting up, she scooped up the coins and put them in the change side of her billfold and zippered it shut. Folding the bills, she put them in the opposite side, snapped the flap closed and put the billfold in her purse.

She unbuttoned her blouse. *Whew, I smell like bacon.* She pulled the rubber band from her ponytail, letting her hair fall around her shoulders. Bringing a handful of her chestnut colored locks to her nose, she groaned. *Girl, you need a shower.* It took but a minute to undressed, throw her clothes in a heap, and scampered across the hall to the bathroom.

The hot water felt heavenly and soothed the tightness in her neck. The soap produced mounds of lather and the shampoo smelled of lilac. She stood under the spray for the longest time. Guilt over using so much water finally forced her to shut off the valve. The mirror was completely steamed over. After toweling her hair, she wrapped the terry cloth around herself and strolled back to the bedroom. A breeze sent the curtains aflutter. Stepping to the window, she pulled back the lace fabric and felt the sun's warmth on her face and upper chest. The air was laced with the smell of mowed grass. The backyard looked inviting. *Maybe it's time to do a little tanning."*

Sarah dropped the towel and pulled the blue suit from the drawer and slipped it on. The good strap hooked as it should. The clasp on the one Nora fixed worked but didn't match the original. *My poor suit.* She looked at the pile of clothes on the floor. *I'll sun for a while and then see if I can figure out how to work Nora's washing machine.* She folded the towel, stuck it under her arm and headed downstairs. Passing through the kitchen, she threw a few ice cubes into a glass and filled it from the faucet.

The grass tickled her feet. Looking around, she made sure the house shielded her from anyone seeing her from the street. She spread out the towel. Lying face down, she crossed her arms above her head. The towel was still damp, but the coolness felt good. She fanned out her hair, letting the sun dry it. "Don't need strap lines," she mumbled, as she unfastened both straps, and laying them on the back of her suit.

The sun's warmth left her mesmerized. She closed her eyes and recalled lying on hay bales at the Johnson ranch, listening to Dee ramble on about all the things she wanted to do in life. The schooling, the travel, working for the FBI. It seemed like a hundred years ago. Sarah wiped a tear and rolled onto her back. "I can't tell you how much I miss you," she whispered, as a large cumulus cloud drifted in front of the sun. Sarah took the brief respite to sit up and take a drink of water. She dipped her fingers in the glass and wiped some of the cold water across her forehead. Dipping again, she splashed some on her upper chest.

The cloud passed and once again she was engulfed in the brightness and warmth of the sun. She straightened the towel and flopped on her back. Reaching down, she pulled the bottom of her suit up so the top of her legs could get more sun. She also wiggled the top down to just above her nipples, exposing the top of her breasts. She closed her eyes and relished the intoxicating warmth.

"Hi."

The words came out of nowhere. Sarah jumped to her side, knocking over the glass of water. She grabbed for her top as the cold liquid rolled under her neck and shoulder. "Oowee." She came up, pulling on the suit top and brushing away the water at the same time. "Who is it?" She blinked, waiting for her eyes to adjust to the light. Extending her hand to block the sun she was finally able to recognize the visitor. "What are you doing here?"

Griff backed up a step. "I'm sorry I didn't mean to startle you."

By this time Sarah was on her feet, wrapping the towel around herself. "You've got a lot of nerve—sneaking up—scaring me half to death."

"I'm sorry," he stammered. "I knocked on the front door. Nora said you were out back."

Sarah looked at the house. "Oh, I didn't know she was home." Reaching behind, she grabbed the one strap, brought it over her shoulder and hooked the clasp to the loop. "You could have whistled, or yelled, to let me know you were coming—giving me a chance—"

"To cover up."

"Yes, smarty pants." She hooked the other strap. "A person can't even sunbathe in their own backyard without someone sneaking up to get a peek."

Griff chuckled. "I'm sorry. I didn't mean to sneak up on you and what did I see? A little cleavage. If you'll recall, I saw your whole breast when you were getting in the boat."

"That was an accident. My strap broke—and if you were a gentleman, you'd never mention that again." She picked up the glass. "What are you doing here, anyway."

"Are you done being angry?" he asked.

If looks could kill, he'd be mortally wounded. *Why is it, whenever he's around, I'm naked, half dressed, or exposing my body parts?* "I'll let you know when I'm done being angry."

"I came to apologize for the other night."

"Why, you didn't do anything. I'm the one who should apologize," she said

"I got spooked. When I found out you were…seventeen…"

"And you thought I was trying to trap you, right."

He let the accusation pass. Brushing several strands of hair from her face. "I've thought a lot about you these past few days…in fact, I can't seem to get you out of my mind."

Out of his mind? Sarah re-wrapped the towel. "Why are you telling me this?"

"I have to drive down to Chicago in the morning. I've got to square up some things with Med School and I didn't want to leave you thinking I didn't care."

"Care about what?"

"About you." He reached for her hand. "I think you're special. I've come to ask—"

Ask! "Ask what/"

Neither had seen Nora approaching. "You guys want to come in the house and have some Kool-Aid?"

"I'd love some," Sarah said abruptly, starting for the house. "How about you?"

"Yeah, sure." Griff smiled and followed along.

"I'm going to run upstairs and change," Sarah said, holding the back door for him. "Enjoy some Kool-Aid, I'll be back in a flash."

"Hold on," Nora said. "I picked the clothes off your floor, if you have more that need washing, bring them down."

"I'll check." Sarah waved and sped off.

Griff took a seat at the table.

Nora poured a glass of the red colored drink and set it in front of him. "Sarah said she had a good time waterskiing."

Griff thanked her for the drink. "She did a really good job for her first time. I was afraid she hurt herself when she took the tumble."

"And tore her suit."

Griff's face immediately glowed red. "She told you?"

"Maybe not all, but be warned, she's my baby sister and woe to anyone who hurts her."

"I wouldn't—"

"How old are you?" Nora asked, putting down her glass and taking a seat.

"Twenty-two."

"A grown man, and she's seventeen. I guess I don't have to remind you of the trouble you could get yourself into if you try to take advantage of her."

"I would never—"

"Never what?" Sarah asked as she walked into the room with an armload of clothes.

Griff stood. "Take advantage of you."

Sarah gave Nora a cross look. "Has she been giving you the third degree?"

"Just clearing the air." Nora said taking the clothes. "I believe we have an understanding, don't we?" She eyed Griff before heading to the laundry room.

Sarah shook her head, took her glass of Kool-Aid from the counter, and sat at the table. "I do apologize for the other night. It probably would have been best if we would have just gone back to the boat dock and not stopped at your place on the lake."

"Yes, I suppose, but regardless of the serious implications of the situation, I enjoyed being with you. You're so…so genuine. Most girls are such phonies." Griff stifled a laugh. "When I think about you, lying on the rug, wearing my bathrobe…" he chuckled. "To you there was nothing wrong, you were wet, cold, and that was just the sensible thing to do."

It was Sarah's turn to blush. "All I thought about on the way home is what would have happened if your mom and dad had walked in. How would I explain the situation to them? Maybe we need to forget that ever happened and start over."

Speaking of my folks, that's the reason I came. I'm meeting them at Greystone for dinner and wonder if you'd like to join us? I told them about you, and they'd anxious to meet you."

Sarah slid back in her chair. *All she could imagine was Dee wagging her finger. Meeting a guy's folks is serious business. What would I wear?* She did a quick mental inventory of her available wardrobe. "I couldn't. I don't have anything decent to wear."

"Come as you are."

Sarah looked down at her new tan slacks and touched the collar of the Penney's yellow blouse. She looked nice, but hardly appropriate for evening dinning. "Don't they have a dress code?"

Nora came out of the laundry room. Seeing Sarah's perplexed look, "Is there a problem?"

"Griff wants to take me to Greystone…to meet his parents."

"So." Nora said. "What's the problem?"

"Like this?" Sarah stood and posed.

"Well, I'm not your fairy Godmother, but I'm sure we could scare up something from my closet." Then turning to Griff. "What time did you want to pick her up?"

Griff looked at his watch. "Five?"

"She'll be ready," Nora said.

"Super deluxe," he said as he turned to leave. "I'll be back at five."

CHAPTER THIRTY-ONE
"Wow, that dress never looked that good on me."

Nora reacted with a "no, ank ank, nope, or won't do," as she moved each hanger along the bar in her closet. "Wait," she squealed as she brought out a black sheath. "Here, try this on."

Sarah took the dress off the hanger, laid it on the bed, and unbuttoned her blouse. "It's beautiful. Are you sure you want me…?"

"It's from my thin days, right after I got out of the Army." She waited for Sarah to drop her shorts before helping her slip the dress over her head. "I only wore it once or twice. I doubt it would go over these." She patted her hips.

Sarah straightened the shoulder strap while looking at herself in the mirror. "I love it." she said as she turned and looked at herself from all sides.

"Holy palooka," Nora said. "That dress never looked that good on me." She turned and began moving bottles on her dresser. "Want to do your nails?"

Sarah looked at her hands. "I don't think so. I keep them clipped short."

Feel free to use any of this makeup," Nora said, waving a hand over the dressing table.

Sarah shook her head. "I'm fine, I just needed a dress." She did a few more turns in front of the looking glass.

Nora handed her a pair of black flats. "They're seven and a half? They ain't glass slippers but go good with the dress."

Sarah sat and slipped them on. Jumping up, she twirled on her toes. "I've never felt so grown up."

Nora blinked back the moisture in her eyes. "That's for sure. You've grown up right before our eyes."

Griff rang the doorbell a few minutes before five. Sarah made one last pass through her hair with the comb. Loose natural curls lay on her shoulders. She straightened the dress, smacked her lips, and wiped a smudge from the corner of her mouth.

Nora had already let her date in when Sarah began her descent down the stairs. Her first two steps were fast. *Slow down girl. You don't want to go skipping down like some nincompoop.*

Griff watched each deliberate step. Moving forward he extended his hand as she stepped to the floor. "Wow. You look terrific."

Sarah couldn't help herself. She twirled around. "Isn't this dress pretty? It's Nora's. She's letting me wear it."

Griff gave Nora a slight head bow. "Allow me to add my thanks."

Nora draped a long black silk scarf over Sarah's shoulders. "It may get chilly later." She also handed her a small beaded purse. "Girl things," she said. Then, letting that sink in, she pushed the young man toward the door. "You guys go. Have fun. Enjoy your dinner."

Sarah tucked the purse under her arm and threw one length of the scarf over her shoulder. She giggled as she walked ahead of Griff. "That's the way they do it in the movies."

The MacDonald's were already at the table when Griff and Sarah arrived. Sarah felt a roomful of eyes on her as she nervously looked about. The lights were dim. Candles flickered on each table. Soft music muffled the chatter of voices, but the finger pointing at them was totally uncloaked. She couldn't get over the transformation between the casualness of the lunch time waitresses and how the tuxedo-clad waiters attended to the well-dressed evening patrons.

Dr. MacDonald rose when Griff ushered Sarah to the table. The man seemed authentically enthused to shake Sarah's hand. Griff's mom remained seated, smiled pleasantly while her eyes darted, taking inventory of the young girl. "I'm John," the man said, "and this is Eleanor."

Griff held Sarah's chair. "Mom, Dad, I want you to meet Sarah Jean Connolly."

Mrs. MacDonald perked up. "Are you related to the Connolly's in Chicago?"

"I don't think so," Sarah said, resting her hands in her lap. "I grew up in Danville, Indiana."

"A shame," the woman said. "Dexter Connolly is a very respected doctor and large contributor to DePaul University. That's where Griffin will be studying medicine."

Griffin? Sarah waited for the server to pour water in her glass and took a drink.

Griff has told us a lot about you," the father said. "You've seemed to have caught his eye."

I'll bet he didn't tell you about me being naked, wrapped in his robe and laying on that big bear rug in front of your fireplace. Sarah forced a smile

"Yes," his mother said. "He was quite impressed by how quickly you learned to waterski."

Taking a big dump and tearing my suit. "Your son is a very good teacher." She looked at Griff. *I can use some help here. Feel free to jump in any time.*

Griff opened the menu. "Would you like an appetizer? Their escargot is wonderful."

Sarah peeked past her menu, "I don't know what S—car—go is."

The elder MacDonald chuckled. "They're snails, cooked with parmesan and garlic butter."

Sarah's eyes grew big. "Are you serious?" she blurted. "You eat snails." She quickly covered her mouth and wished she hadn't said it so loud.

Griff closed his menu. "Maybe a shrimp cocktail would be a better choice." He turned to Sarah. "Is that okay with you?"

"I've never had shrimp either."

He turned to his dad. "Just order us one. She can try one to see if she likes them."

His father nodded. "Your mother and I are having their special, Beef Wellington. What would you and Sarah Jean like?"

Griff pursed his lips. "That's with liver pate', right? He turned to Sarah. "Do you like steak? They have a nice six-ounce Filet."

Sarah nodded and closed the menu.

Griff order them each a Filet Mignon, baked potato, and Caesar salad.

"Did you want a glass of Chardonnay" his mother asked, lifting her glass.

"Water will be fine," Griff said.

The woman snickered. "Oh. Of course, how silly of me, Sarah isn't old enough, is she."

Was that some kind of put down? Sarah forced a thin smile.

"Griff tells us you just graduated from high school," John said. "Are you planning on college?"

"I have a scholarship to the University of Nevada."

"In Las Vegas?" Eleanor questioned. "It's not in one of those casinos, is it?"

"No. It's in Reno." *Mrs. Uppity-up is getting on my nerves.* "It's very well-respected—established in 1875." Sarah broke eye contact and leaned back as the waiter set a leafy salad in front of her. "It has a very nice campus." She studied the two forks resting on her napkin. *Why two?*

Mrs. MacDonald reached over, picked up the smaller one and handed it to Sarah. "This is your salad fork."

Sarah accepted the fork and poked at her salad. Leaning to Griff, she whispered, "Why does it smell like fish?"

"It's the anchovy," he said.

Sarah felt her stomach roll. *I don't think I can eat that.* She stood. "Would you please excuse me. I'll be right back." She was gone before either man had a chance to rise from their chairs. She caught a waiter's eye. "Restroom?" She asked.

Standing in front of Ladies Room mirror she wiped the moisture from her eyes. *Dee, what have I gotten myself into? I don't belong here—with them. Snails, shrimp, liver, fish in the salad, and why do I need two forks? I've always eaten everything with one.* She tossed the tissue in the basket and left the room. Looking towards the dining room, she instead went to the hostess stand. "Is there any way you can get me a ride into town?"

The young lady looked puzzled.

"Please, can you?" Sarah looked over her shoulder. "I really need to get out of here."

"We have a shuttle." The hostess hesitated a moment and then grabbed Sarah's arm. "Come this way." The girl led Sarah through the kitchen and out the back door.

A guy in his late teens, leaning against a black car, jumped to attention.

"Barry, can you drive her into town?" The hostess glanced over her shoulder.

"Sure." He opened the car door and raised an eyebrow to the woman.

Sarah quickly ducked into the back seat. She watched as the hostess retreated into the kitchen and close the door. Her heart skipped a few beats waiting to see if anyone had followed them.

The young man got behind the wheel. "Any place special?"

"Just get me out of here—now!"

The lad wasted no time. The tires squealed as he sped up the driveway. "You didn't kill anyone, did you?" He chuckled half-jokingly."

"Just a chance to be a doctor's wife."

The guy's face twisted with confusion. "Seriously?"

"Nothing serious. Just in over my head," she said, breathing a sigh and resting against the seat back. She turned her head and looked at a sky full of stars. *Shoot I know we're just small-town girls from Ely, but we've never pretended to be something we're not.* "And I'm certainly not going to start now." The words came out unexpectantly.

"You talking to me?" He asked.

"The man in the moon." *Sorry Dee now is not a good time to try to explain the you and me thing.*

The driver pulled onto the main drag. "Just tell me when to stop."

"Do you know where Duke Brady lives?"

The guy laughed. "I live three doors down the street."

"Nora's my sister. If you could drop me off there it would be great." She fumbled in her purse. "I'm sorry, I don't have any money for a tip."

"Don't worry about it. Duke would have my hide if I took money from you."

The young man pulled into the driveway. He leaned over the seat. "Are you going to be in town long."

"The summer," she said as she opened the door. "I have a job at the Bay Side."

"I have Monday nights off. Would you like to take in a movie over in Middletown?"

Sarah smiled. "Let me think about it." *Geesh, am I the only available girl in this whole town?*

CHAPTER THIRTY-TWO

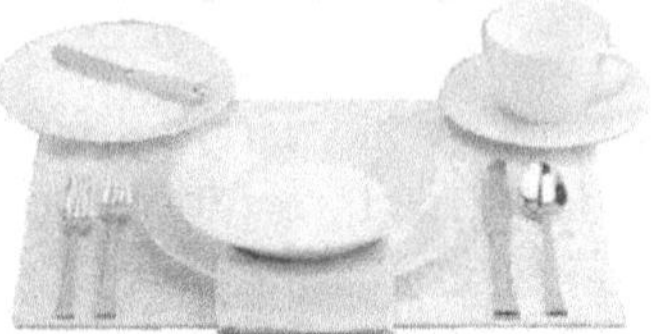

A Fork just for Salad?

Nora held out the phone as Sarah came through the front door. "Just a minute, she just walked in the door." She pointed to the receiver. "It's Griff. He's wondering if you're alright?"

Sarah waved her hand and headed straight for the stairs.

"What should I tell him?" Nora asked, holding her hand over the mouthpiece.

Without stopping, Sarah blurted, "Tell him I went to bed." She entered her room and slammed the door. "Tell him it's been nice knowing you." Her angry voice echoed in the empty room. She unzipped the back and stepped out of the black sheath.

Nora knocked before coming in. "Is everything—"

Sarah ignored the obvious question. "Thank you for letting me wear the dress," she said, positioning it on the hanger. "I felt very special." she held it to herself a final time before handing the hanger to Nora.

"That dress was made for you. It's yours." Nora hung it in Sarah's closet.

Sarah sat on the bed. "I don't belong with them. They are way out of my league." She squeezed her lips determined not to break down. "Since when do I need a special fork to eat a salad—and why put in stinky fish? It tasted awful, made me gag." Tears arrived against her will.

Nora sat beside her. "Did Griff make you feel uncomfortable?"

"No," she sniveled. "He and his Dad were nice. It was his mom…and maybe I just let her get under my skin. Did you know about salad forks, or that people eat snails?"

"The latest is chocolate covered grasshoppers." Nora exaggerated a bitter swallow. Some people have funny tastes and find silly things to spend their money on." The doorbell interrupted their laughter. Nora walked to the window. "If Griff drives a black convertible, I'm assuming that's him at the front door."

"Please, I don't want to face him," Sarah said. "Tell him I'm sick—I'm puking my guts out."

"Stay here. I'll handle this."

Duke and Griff were standing in the doorway when Nora came down the stairs. "Griff is wondering if Sarah is okay?"

"A mild upset tummy." Nora said. "A bad case of nerves."

Griff was quick to respond. "It was my mother, right?"

Nora's eyes darted to the side. "It was probably the excitement of the dress and going out to dinner that got to her. She'll be better in the morning."

"Can I see her?" The young man took a step forward. "I'd like to apologize…"

Nora held up her hand. "Why don't you call tomorrow. I'm sure she'll feel better."

Griff backed onto the porch. "I'm leaving for Chicago at six in the morning—got school things to take care of. Tell her I'm sorry. I'll call when I return."

"See ya," Duke yelled, watching his young friend trot down the steps. He closed the door and turned to Nora, "What was that all about?"

"I guess Mrs. MacDonald gave Sarah one of those 'I'm looking down my nose at you, welcomes' and Sarah up and left."

"That must be a Jensen thing. I can see you doing the same." When her hand came up, he made a quick retreat to the kitchen

Nora chased after him. "Wrong, smarty-pants," she said as she swatted him on the back. "I would have stayed and accidently knocked a glass of water into her lap."

He turned, took her in his arms and kissed her. Holding her, he laughed. "Yeah, I can see you doing that. Oh well, they'll have to work that out themselves."

Nora pushed him away. "And maybe it's not a workable situation."

Sarah woke to a room full of sunshine. Her curtains fluttered. A cool breeze filled the space with fresh, pine-scented air. She put the extra pillow behind her head… and thought of Dee. *Well, Miss Johnson, what do you think? Dumb move, huh? I embarrassed him and I embarrassed myself. I wish I hadn't acted that way, but dang it, his mother was not very nice.* She rolled out from under the covers, walked to the window, and took in a deep breath. *Oh well, that's probably the last I'll see of one Griff MacDonald.*

Hearing a noise in back of the house, she watched Duke roll the motorcycle out from the garage. He put down the kickstand, took a rag from his back pocket, and began polishing the gas tank.

She looked at the beautiful blue sky. *A great day for a ride.* Sarah let go of the curtain and picked up a hairbrush from the nightstand. She hummed as she made several passes through her hair. Closing her eyes, she recaptured snippets of the day she spent with him, driving the boat, getting up on skis, lying in front of the fire wrapped in his bathrobe. They all brought a smile to her face. The corners of her mouth suddenly turned down. "Ugh." She tossed the brush on the bed, grabbed shorts and a clean blouse and headed for the bathroom. "Oh well, it was fun while it lasted." She said.

It was close to ten o'clock before she ambled into the kitchen, tying the second knot in the scarf around the pin curlers.

Nora turned from the kettle she was stirring. "Feeling better?"

"I guess." Sarah took a cookie off the platter and took a bit into it, "I'm such a bone-head."

Nora let the remark pass. "I made chicken soup for supper. Will you be here?"

Sarah opened the refrigerator and brought out a quart of milk. "I work two to closing. I'll probably just grab a sandwich or something." She filled a glass with milk. "He must think I'm some kind of nut case."

"Are we talking about Griff?"

Sarah dunked her cookie in the milk. "He's a nice guy, but..."

"He left for Chicago early this morning...said he'd call when he got back." The slamming screen door caused both girls to turn.

"Alright," Duke announced. "Which of you beautiful ladies want to go for a bike ride?"

Nora looked down at her house dress and apron and then at Sarah, with her hair in curlers. They both laughed. "Don't look at me," Nora said. I've got laundry to do, unless you won't mind going without clean underwear." Seeing Duke's eyebrows raise, Nora quickly waved her wooden spoon at him. "Don't you dare say it."

"If you don't mind me going like this," Sarah said, "I'd love to go."

Nora pointed the spoon in Duke's face. "Don't you go driving like a crazy fool. If anything happens to her, I'll break your neck."

Duke laughed, held Nora's spoon hand and gave her a peck on the cheek. "I thought we'd take a spin around the lake. She's seen it from the water. This will give her a look from the landside."

"Just be careful, okay?" She turned to Sarah. "Better grab a jacket from the closet. It could be a chilly ride."

Sarah hugged Nora. "Are you sure you don't want to go?

"No. You go. Have fun...and if he' driving too fast poke him in the ribs."

Duke's 1945 Army Issue Harley-Davidson
Going for a Ride

Sarah waited anxiously while Duke kick-started the bike and settled on the seat. The knucklehead engine came to life, backfired and began to sputter. He feathered the throttle until the motor settled to a mild roar. "Too much choke," he said, apologizing for the ragged start. "Come, hop on."

Sarah put her foot on the bar and swung her leg over the seat. She grabbed his waist as he put it in gear and released the clutch. The cycle leaped forward, and they headed down the driveway.

Nora stood by the backdoor and shook her spoon as they drove by. "Slow down," she yelled. "Darn him anyway," she muttered, shaking her head as she went back into the house.

Duke cruised through town, nodding to the waves and smiles from friends before turning onto Chicago Avenue and heading for the highway. Cabins and cottages lined the property bordering the lake, everything on the opposite side of the road was woods and farmland. Sarah coughed as the air changed from the pleasant scent of pine to the stomach-turning stench of cow manure. Relief came when they left the highway and began riding the county roads along the shoreline. The tall pines, for which the lake was named, provided a pleasant Christmas tree smell as the sunshine flashing through the branches made the landscape sparkle. Unlike their first ride, where Duke fed his need for speed and nearly scared the pants off her, today he was content to cruise along and soak up the scenery.

Every now and then, he would poke his head to the side and point out a landmark, or the home of an acquaintance. After more than an hour, they came to an intersection. Duke turned right and followed the road up a long hill. At the top, Duke maneuvered onto a dirt path and weaved his way through the brush and undergrowth.

"Ouch! Ouch!" Sarah wished she had worn long pants as the branches poked and scratched her bare legs.

"Sorry," he said as they came into a clearing. He drove to the top of a knoll, stopped, and turned off the engine. "Want to get off and stretch a little"

Sarah slid off the back of the seat and stood for a minute. The view was breathtaking. They were hundreds of feet above the lake and she could see it from end to end.

Duke dismounted and put down the stand. "Sorry about the branches, but I wanted you to see this," he said, as he walked ahead to a large stone outcropping.

Sarah scooted to catch up. "Where are we? What a beautiful view."

"Sandstone Bluff." He reached and pointed to the right. "That's the inlet down there." The sunlight reflecting off the water sparkled like a million gemstones. A sailboat passed below, its sails billowing in the wind. Farther out, a pontoon boat of fishermen, with their trolling poles bent, seemed locked in place. "That's town over there," he said, pointing directly across from where they were standing.

Sarah was still looking right. "The inlet—that's where Griff and I waterskied." Sarah continued looking, trying to locate about where they had been. She wiped the corner of her eye before turning and looking across the lake. "Oh yes, I can see the roof of the courthouse."

"I don't know what the big hubbub was all about last night," Duke said, "but I've known Griff since he was fourteen-years-old. He's a great kid and I get the feeling he thinks the world of you."

"I doubt his mother shares that opinion." She kept her eyes focused on what she could see of the town. "It's not him. It's me.

I seem to have poor luck when it comes to boys. First, it's a sailor who wants me to become a farmer's wife. Then that dirtbag in Chicago tries to rape me. And now, I totally screwed up everything with the one decent guy in the bunch."

"All I'm saying, is give him a chance—and his mother, too. I've known the MacDonald's for years. They're good people. Maybe you and the misses just got off on the wrong foot."

Sarah picked up a stone and threw it over the side of the bluff. "The problem is we live in two different worlds. He's steak and caviar and I'm pot roast and mashed potatoes. I just don't see me fitting into his world."

"Don't put yourself down. You're just like Nora, smart and self-assured.

Doubling over, she giggled. "Me? Self-assured? More of a dithering klutz tripping over childish emotions."

"Nothing says you have to be perfect—all of the time. Give yourself some slack. If things are meant to be, they'll be."

Sarah climbed and sat on the huge rock. "Since we're getting personal, why haven't you and Nora married? If ever two people were meant for each other it's you two."

Duke looked out over the water. "Normally, I don't talk about that, but I guess you deserve an explanation. Nothing says we can't—or won't get married sometime, but for now, we don't need a piece of paper to validate our commitment to each other. Nor do we need the acceptance of others. When she went through that Molar pregnancy, she came within a heartbeat of dying. And then, to be told she could never have children…" He took a moment to compose himself. "Neither of us could think, much less decide, how to move forward. She didn't believe I could love her if she couldn't give me children. I was afraid of losing her altogether. We just held onto each other and have taken it one day at a time since. Who knows, maybe we'll tie the knot someday, but for now, just being together works for us. And, as I said earlier, what will be, will be."

Sarah jumped down from her perch. Touching his sleeve, "I'm sorry," she said, "I had no right to pry."

He forced a smile. "That's okay." Then, gathering himself, he waved his arm in the direction of the cycle. "Come, let's finish our ride."

It was well past noon before they got back to the house. Nora came out to greet them as Duke pushed the cycle into the garage. "I was hoping you'd get back. I made chicken salad sandwiches for lunch."

"Sounds good," Duke said, putting his arm around Nora's shoulders and kissing the top of her head. "It was a good ride. We circled the lake." Without removing his arm, he walked her towards the house. "Chicken salad sounds good."

Sarah untied the knot in the handkerchief covering her curlers and danced in front of them. "We stopped on—" She waited for Duke to say Sandstone Bluff. "It was so beautiful; you can see the whole lake from up there."

Nora poked him in the ribs. "Duke always says, Pine Lake is so beautiful we must live in God's pocket.

CHAPTER THIRTY-FOUR

Rule #1, Preserve the Evidence

Blanche was happy to see Sarah walk through the Bay Side's front door. Without so much as hello, or how do you do, she handed the girl menus. "Tables six and ten need water and their orders taken."

Sarah hustled behind the counter, threw her purse on the shelf below the cash register and began filling a tray of glasses with water.

Mary came from the other direction. "Of all the days to get slammed, it has to be the one I'm supposed to be at a family picnic." She took off her apron and tossed it under the counter. "My husband will kill me if I make us late." She spread out a few guest checks next to the register. "I'm sorry to leave you guys in the middle of this mess. These are my last three tables. You'll have to see if they want dessert."

"Don't worry," Sarah said, handing Mary her purse. "we'll handle it. Have fun."

"Oh right, with *his* family." She pointed her finger to her mouth and made a gagging gesture.

Sarah chuckled and waved as Mary rushed for the door.

"C'mon girl, get a move on." Blanche said, as she charged out of the kitchen, her arms loaded with plates of food.

Sarah tucked a stack of menus under her arm, picked up the water tray and rushed to the dining room. Setting the tray on a folding stand, she grabbed two glasses and plopped them in front of two young men sitting at table six. She pulled out the menus and put them down before serving the third man his water. "I'll be right back to take your order," she said as she scooted off toward table ten.

Her arms now empty she returned to take their order. Sarah took a stutter-step when she noticed the strawberry shaped birthmark on the curly-headed blond's neck. Her mind flashed back to that first night in the park. Sizing up the other two, she was sure these were the drunken hoodlums that had roughed her up. Her face colored as she fumbled to get the order pad out of her apron pocket. *Do they know it's me?* She pulled a pencil from behind her ear and asked for their order, her voice cracked and pitched two octaves higher than normal.

The guy with the neck decoration and the obvious leader of the pack, looked up. "Double cheeseburger, fries, and a chocolate malt." He eyed Sarah, but showed no sign of recognition. The other two ordered the same.

Sarah avoided eye-contact as she scooped up the menus and hurried to the other table. She took the second order, and glanced toward table six as she hurried to the kitchen. None of the boys looked her way. *Maybe you don't recognize me, but I recognize you.*

While waiting for her orders to come up, she served desserts to Mary's tables. She held her breath each time she passed table six. To Sarah's relief, the three were involved with each other and hadn't made the connection to her and the night in the park.

Their eyes were glued on the burgers as she set the food in front of them. Even as she reached across the table to refill their water glasses, they showed no sign of recognizing her. It wasn't until they came to the counter to pay that one of the younger guys kicked the blond one in the ankle and nodded in Sarah's direction. "What's your problem?" he barked to his friend as he picked up his change.

Sarah watched them leave before putting the money in the cash drawer. The three no sooner reached the sidewalk when the kicker feverishly pointed back to the restaurant. Blondie, narrowed his eyes and glared through the window. Sarah's stomach clutched as she watched his birthmark turn purple. The three took off running.

Business slowed as the afternoon wore on. A small run of customers came in around suppertime, but by seven the place had pretty much emptied. Sarah straightened place settings, filled salt and pepper shakers, and folded napkins for the following day. She kept one eye peeled outside. She never saw them, but was sure her nemesis' were out there—somewhere—cooking up something. It took forever for the minute hand to make it to eight o'clock.

Sarah stood on the sidewalk and waited as Blanche locked the front door. She glanced in each direction. "There's not a soul left on the street."

"That's Pine Lake for you," Blanche said. "Come eight o'clock Sunday night and they might as well turn out the streetlights and roll up the sidewalks." They both chuckled. "You're back at six in the morning, right?"

Sarah nodded. "Wouldn't miss it."

The sarcasm stopped Blanche in her tracks, another chuckle. "Want a ride home?" she asked, opening her car door.

"Nah, I'll walk. It's a beautiful evening." A ride would have been nice, but she had a pressing matter to attend to. She waited until the woman drove off before heading to the park. *I should have done this before. Dee's rule number one, preserve the evidence. It's not much to go on but it might prove the case.* She moved quickly, constantly checking for any sign of the fearsome threesome.

Heavy clouds had rolled in and with them a premature end to the day. A curtain of darkness was dropping fast. It was too early for the streetlights to come on but the illuminated windows of shuttered stores cast an eery glow and lighted her way as she hurried along. By the time she reached the park she was in a dead run. Using the Starlight Stage to get her bearings, she recalled the confrontation happened at the water's edge. The parking lot light from the nearby boat dock provided another reference point and enough light to locate the park bench she sat on. The air was moist, delivering an overpowering smell of fish, algae, and wet grass. She stopped to catch her breath.

It wasn't like the thought of Dee just popped into her head, she had been talking to her the whole way. Not just in her mind but out loud. "I know, I know, the first thing is to preserve the evidence." She walked along the waterfront, searching between the rocks. "It's got to be here." A thousand thoughts raced through her mind. *Was this the right place? Did someone move the park bench? Maybe a groundskeeper picked up the pieces. Or, could THEY have come back for them?* She continued searching the rocks. "The bandshell is too close," she said. "I'm too far left. It should be more to the right." She retraced her steps. Ahead, she caught a sparkle of light in the water between two large rocks. Kneeling, she picked up the neck of a broken bottle. She looked for more, but the other pieces were small. "Dammit," Sarah exclaimed in frustration. The rest of the bottle was missing, especially any that included the label. *Duke said they took Jack Daniels. There's no way to prove any thing with what's here.*

Sarah stood. By now the park was shrouded in darkness, cricket chirps the only sound. On a slow turn, she strained her eyes watching for any kind of movement. *Mea culpa Dee, I never checked to see if they followed me?* "Yipes!" A loud splash behind her brought her heart to her throat. She gulped for air and muttered, "Stupid damn fish."

"It'about time," she griped, as the streetlights came on and shed a comforting glow over the whole town. She breathed a sigh as she threw the broken bottle neck in a nearby trash can. A chill raised goosebumps on her arms. She still had a long walk back to Nora's.

Happy to be out of the park, she made it back to Bay Side. Standing on the corner, she searched the streets in both directions and saw no one. "This town is deserted." It sounded more like a warning than a statement. She stepped off the curb and hurried across the street. Her fast walk turned into a jog, slowing only when she approached a dark alley or unlit store front. She still had eight to ten blocks to go as she left the downtown area. The distance between street lights left long stretches in near-total darkness. Her breaths came in shallow pants as fear gripped her body. She fanticized someone lurking behind every tree, peering over every wall and around every bush. She ran through the dark segments, faster than she and Dee had ever run in their many foot races. Winded, she stopped under a street light. "I'm half way," she huffed. The words were barely audible as she bent, gasped for breath, and studied what lay ahead of her. She checked behind her. It was totally quiet. She felt relieved when nothing moved. *Those boys are probably more afraid of me than I am of them.*

"Looky here," the voice came from behind. "It's little Miss Buttinski."

Sarah spun on her heels. "What!"

Three figures came out of the shadows, led by the Blond with the birthmark. "I think you and I need to have a little talk," he said snidely, closing in on her.

"About what?" She went with her first thought, turned, and started to walk away.

The boy jumped in front of her. "About what you didn't see in the park the other night." The other two joined their friend and further blocked her escape.

She stepped into the street to go around them, but they cut her off. *Three against one. Got to take away their advantage.* She reshouldered her purse, using her arm to press it tight to her side. *Get them offbalance.* "Are you saying I didn't see the three of you. Or, that I didn't see the bottle of Jack Daniels whiskey and the cigarettes?"

"Both." He pounded his fist into his other hand. "If you know what's good for you, you'll forget you ever saw us." He pushed his face close to hers. "We wouldn't want anything bad to happen to you."

It was Dee whispering in her ear. *Time to divide and conquer.* "Seeing the three of you drinking whiskey, and smoking cigarettes on the night of the liquor store breakin…I'm thinking you guys must be the guilty culprits."

"That is no concern of yours." He shook his fist. "You need to keep your nose out of this—or else"

"Or what? You'll beat me up?" She looked the smallest one in the face and shouted. "What do you have in mind? You gonna tear off my clothes?" She grabbed a handful of blouse covering her chest and shook it. "You gonna squeeze on my breast?"

The would-be thug dropped his head and stepped behind his leader.

Sarah turned to the one on the other side. "What about you? You gonna beat me up, rape me?" He too, retreated behind number one.

Confronting the mouthpiece, she looked at him dead on. "Here's a suggestion. I think you ought to go to the sheriff's office right now and turn yourselves in. Say you're sorry, pay for what you took, and they might let you off with a slap on the hand."

"Hah, why should we do that?" The mouthy kid spit on the ground. "You can't prove a thing."

Sarah, being a half a head taller, leaned into him. "You should've come back and destroyed the evidence." She took a big gamble but he took the bait.

"What evidence?"

"The Jack Daniels bottle with all your fingerprints on it."

The boy hesitated. His brain had to be going a hundred miles an hour. "That's crazy, It hit the rocks and busted in a million pieces."

"Except for the one large piece," she allowed for a dramatic pause, "the one with the label on it."

The boy grabbed her arm, swung it around, and pressed it up her spine. He cupped the other arm around her neck. Her purse dropped to the sidewalk spilling coins and dollar bills. "Johnny, check her purse. See if that piece of glass is in there."

"Touch that purse and you can add a charge of attempted robbery," she sneered. "You could be looking at six months of jail time." The boy stopped short of picking up the bag.

"Don't listen to her. Check the bag."

Johnny backed away. "Bullshit! I don't wanna go to jail."

"Would I be foolish enough to keep it with me." Sarah said. "I hid it in the park. You'll never find it in a million years."

Blondie pushed her arm further up her back. "Where? Where in the park."

Sarah groaned in pain. "If you break my arm, it's assault to do bodily harm, could get you three to five years." She looked at the smallest one. "You're an accessory. You'll get the same."

"C'mon Danny," the young boy said, his eyes tearing up. "Let her go. Let's get out of here."
Without another word he turned and ran into the dark.

"That's it Danny," Johnny said. "I want no part of this." He tripped and stumbled his way in the opposite direction.

Sarah waited, unsure how the bully holding her would react to his cohorts deserting him. *He needs a little nudge.* "Have you ever been in jail? Do you know what those lifers do to good looking young guys like you?" She felt him slowly release the pressure on her arm. His other arm loosened from around her neck. Before letting go, he spun her around, pushed a shaky finger in her face, and yelled, "You haven't heard the last from me. You'd better keep your mouth shut if you know what's good for you." With that, he dropped his grip and disapeared into the night.

Just as I thought, he's a big sissy when he doesn't have the other two backing him up. Sarah rubbed feeling back into her arm, gathered her tip money off the sidewalk, and picked up her purse. A smile of satisfaction crept across her face as she strolled leisurely up the sidewalk.

"Did you see that?" She squealed, knowing Dee would appreciate the fine piece of detective work. "I bluffed them. They think I have the label with their fingerprints on it. They fell for it and basically admitted to breaking into the liquor store."

She no longer feared the night, in fact, a warm breeze and the smell of lilacs lifted her spirits. Feeling Dee's presence, she continued replaying the chain of events in her mind. Sarah stopped suddenly. "I don't know," she said. The outburst appeared to answer a question. "We'll just have to wait and see what they do. One things is for sure. I'm not afraid of them, especially not the pee-brain with the birthmark. He showed himself a coward as soon as the other two took off. I have a feeling they'll steer clear of me." She climbed Nora's porch steps before finishing her thought. "They aren't going to do anything stupid as long as they think I have the label from the mysteriously missing bottle of Jack Daniels.

Duke was sitting in the front room with a book in his lap. He looked at his watch. "Did you have to work late?"

Sarah stopped at the bottom of the stairs. "Nah, It was such a beautiful night, I strolled through town and took my time walking home."

"Nora went to bed," he said. "She's has three early surgeries in the morning."

"I'm heading there myself. I have to be back to work at six."

He switched off his light. "That makes three of us. We'll see you in the morning."

Sarah hummed an Andrews Sisters tune as she climbed the stairs.

CHAPTER THIRTY-FIVE

A Town in an Uproar

Sarah's alarm clock woke her from a dead sleep. Wiping the grit from her eyes she lay for a moment deciding if the encounter with the three boys actually happened or was a lingering memory of a nightmare. A smile crossed her face as she threw the covers back and sat up. *That was no dream.* She gathered a fresh set of clothes and made a dash across the hall to the bathroom. She threw her pajamas over the shower bar, dressed, and did a hurry-up face wash. A dozen strokes with the tooth brush and a like number with the comb, resulted in two pigtails tied with red ribbons, and she was skipping her way down the stairs.

Duke sat at the breakfast bar while Nora stood across from him nursing a cup of coffee. "I'm sorry I didn't wait up for you last night," she said as Sarah walked into the kitchen. "We've got a C-section birth and a double hernia to take care of this morning. There's still a little coffee left in the pot."

Sarah reached into the refrigerator. "Orange juice will be fine. I'll probaly grab a sweet roll when I get to work."

"Duke said it was after nine when you got home. Did you have a busy day?"

"It was crazy when I got there," Sarah said. "Mary had this picnic to go to so Blanche and I ran our butts off. It slowed in late afternoon, but I was surprised how the town dies on Sunday night."

"Chicago people have to head back to the city and the locals have to work on Monday mornings," Duke said. "Which includes the three of us." He stepped to the sink and dumped the last swallow of coffee.

Nora did the same. Then, opening a lower cupboard door, she pulled her purse, set it on the counter, and dug out her car keys. "Will we all be here for supper? I'm thinking we should have something light. Maybe bacon, lettuce and totmato sandwiches"

"We sell a lot of BLTs at the Bay Side," Sarah added. "I've never had one but they look and smell delicious."

Duke pecked Nora on the cheek. "We have plenty of lettuce and tomatoes, I'll swing by the market and pick up some bacon on my way home."

"And Miracle Whip." Nora said throwing the purse strap over her shoulder. The phone rang interrupting her walk to the door. "You want to get that, Duke? I have to go."

Duke picked up the receiver. "Hello." He listened for a moment and then turned to Sarah. "They got the kids that broke into the liquor store," he said, cupping his hand over the mouthpiece.

Sarah choked and spit a mouthful of juice into the sink.

Duke hung up the phone. "That was one of my bowling buddies. He dosen't have a lot of details, but a lakeshore kid showed up with his dad at the sheriff's office last night and confessed. Dang, can you believe that?"

"That is hard to believe," she said through a forced smile. *It had to be the small one of the three*

"Those lakeshore kids have everything," he said. "Why would any of them do something as stupid as that?"

Sarah shrugged. *All it takes is one bad apple.* She grabbed her purse and headed for the door. "See you tonight."

"Don't you want a ride? I can drop you off."

"No, that's okay. I'm a little early and the walk is good exercise." *Plus, I have to digest whether my name was brought up and if this affects me?*

Duke called after her, "See ya," as she walked out the back door.

Sarah was surprised to find a half dozen people already sitting at the counter when she got to the Bay Side. *Blanche must have opened early.* The buzz at the counter quieted as she walked through the front door, all eyes turned her way. *uh-oh, this is not good.* She stepped behind and put her purse under the register. She came up tying her apron strings behind her back.

"Have you heard the news about the liquor store break-in?" asked the elderly gentlemen sitting on the first stool.

Sarah shook her head. "No, what about it?"

"One kid confessed and blew the whistle on the other two."

Sarah grabbed the coffee carafe and filled the man's cup. *Play dumb. They might not have mentioned me.*

"Yep," the man said, picking up the sugar jar. He poured a long stream in his cup and began stirring. "The sheriff's office is trying to keep the whole thing hush hush. Ol' Harley doesn't want to create bad blood between us and the lakeshore folks."

"Sensible," Sarah replied. *What does he mean, bad blood?*

"But the rumors have already started," he said, through a missing tooth smile.

"Rumors?" Sarah took his breakfast plate and put it in the dish tray under the counter. She used a dish rag to wipe the counter. "What have you heard?"

"Supposedly," he used his fingers to put the word in air quotes, "some girl had evidence linking them to the crime and threatened to turn them in. The one kid came clean to his parents and the dad brought him to the sheriff. The families offered to pay for what the kids stole and any damages. The people at the liquor store don't want the bottle of Jack and a couple packs of cigarettes to become an issue. Lakeshore people buy a lot of top shelf whiskey.

Blanche came out of the kitchen at the same time Sheriff Harley Durham walked through the front door. The sheriff and his wife came over from the jail once or twice a week for supper, but this was the first she could remember him coming in at breakfast time.

The elderly gent at the counter swung around on his stool and waited for the sheriff to sit. "Congratulations, Harley, I hear you nabbed the kids that broke into the liquor store."

Blanche slid a glass of water in front of the officer. "Want to see a menu?"

The Sheriff waved a finger and gave a slight head shake. Leaning forward, he whispered, "Can we talk in your office.?"

Blanche nodded towards the kitchen door.

The man glanced at Sarah as he followed Blanche.

The old fellow pushed two dollars and his food bill in Sarah's direction. "Tell Blanche to keep the change." He waited to let four men come in before waving and making his way out the door.

Sarah responded with a weak smile and put the money and bill next to the cash register. She had a bad feeling about the way the sheriff had looked at her. *Can't worry about that now.* She grabbed menus and followed the men into the dining room. "Coffee all around?" she asked, handing each a menu. Four heads nodded. Returning to the counter, she poured four cups of coffee and filled four glasses with water. She was about to pick up the tray when Blanche touched her arm.

"The Sheriff would like you to go with him over to the courthouse."

Sarah glanced at the tray. "Should I serve this first?"

"You go," Blanche said. "I'll handle things until you get back."

The sheriff waited by the front door. Sarah took off her apron, grabbed her purse and followed him out.

The courthouse was catty corner from the Bay Side. The jail, the sheriff's office, and his living quarters took the entire west wing. He offered her a chair before excusing himself and stepping out of the room. Sarah looked around. The desk was cluttered in paper. Wanted posters filled most of one wall. Heavy steel bars hung on the outside of the windows. The rust and chipped paint showed they had been there for years. The place smelled like the men's locker room at school. The arms of her chair were black and greasy and needed a good scrubbing. She drew her arms to her side. *Eck. This whole place is disgusting.*

The sheriff returned a few minutes later. A buxom woman followed him into the office. "This is my wife, Tess," he said. "She's also the undersheriff for Marshall County. She sits in when I'm interrogating females."

Sarah came to the edge of her seat. "You're interrogating me?"

"Geez, Harley," the woman said, "you're going to scare the dickens out of the poor girl." She patted Sarah on the knee. "He just wants to ask you a few questions."

The sheriff raised his hand to shush the woman. "I'd like to ask what you know about the liquor store being broken into a short time ago," he asked.

"I don't know anything about the break in."

"Nothing?" The man scowled as he leaned back in his chair. "Do you know Danny Scofield, Johnny Pearson, and Andrew Cousins?"

"No sir."

The man pounded his desk. "They know you. They said they talked to you last night."

His wife admonished him. "Take it easy, Harley, you'll blow a gasket."

He leaned forward and lowered his voice. "Are you telling me you didn't talk to them last night?"

"I don't know them by name."

"So you did talk to them?"

"Yes, If they are the ones that tried to stop me from going home last night.

The sheriff curled his brow. "They seem to feel you have evidence that connects them to the break in.

Sarah reamained silect.

The man's face reddened. "You know it's against the law to withhold evidence."

"Yes sir."

The sheriff stood and wagged a finger. "Let's stop playing games. Do you have a Jack Daniel's label with those boy's fingerprints?"

"No, sir."

Andrew Cousins came in here last night with his dad, confessed to the break in, and said you had this piece of glass with their fingerprints on it."

"That's true. I did tell them that, but I was only bluffing, so they'd let me go."

"Bluffing?" The word shot from the woman's mouth. "There has got to be a lot more to this story. Would you care to share it with us?"

Sarah told them about going to the Bay Side for pie and then taking a walk in the park.The three boys stumbled out of the darkness, smoking, and drinking out of a bottle of Jack Daniels. The one smarted off, the bottle went flying, and broke when it hit the rocks.

"So you don't have anything with their fingerprints on it?" the sheriff asked.

"I hoped I would. That's why I went to the park looking for the broken bottle, but someone must have picked up the pieces before I got there. I thought having the label would connect them to the crime. When they confronted me last night, I told them I had it…just to scare them off. Is Andrew the shortest one?"

The woman nodded. "He thought for sure he was going to jail."

The man scratched his head. "It was all a bluff?" He leaned back in his chair. "That's the dangedest thing I ever heard."

"Am I free to go?" Sarah asked.

The woman stood first. "Since we already have a confession, I guess we won't be needing your non-existent evidence. That is so funny." She laughed on her way out of the room.

"Is everything alright?' Blanche asked, when Sarah got back to the restaurant.

"Yeah, sure." Sarah tossed her purse under the register, put her apron around and tied the strings behind her back. "Let's hope that's the end of that."

The restaurant was unusually busy. Even Blanche commented on it. The break-in was all people talked about. Sarah avoided being drawn into the conversations. By midday, the gossip-mill had identified her as the girl who sucker-punched the boys into giving themselves up. Most people were supportive, but she caught some accusing glances and a few fingers pointing her way. Sarah knew she was over-reacting, but burst through the kitchen door when she could no longer hold back tears. Blanche handed her a paper napkin. "Mary is coming in early. Why don't you leave. Tomorrow this will all be old news and we can all get back to normal."

"Thank you," Sarah said. She asked one of the busboys to retrieve her purse from under the counter. "If it's okay, I'll leave by the back door."

Blanche nodded. "That's fine. We'll see you tomorrow."

CHAPTER THIRTY-SIX

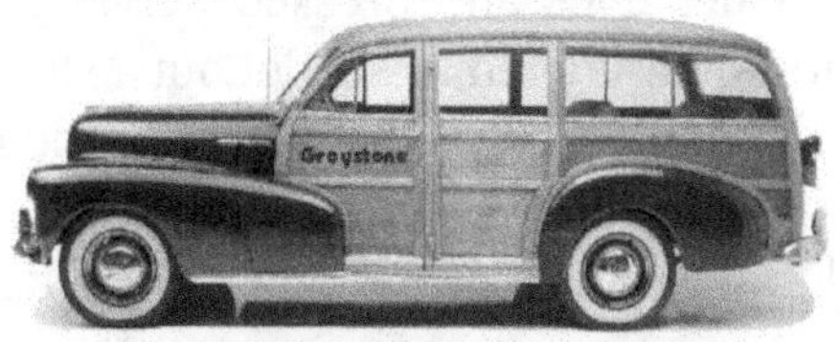

When You Need A Friend

Sarah kept her head down and walked briskly back to Nora's. Cars drove past, but she was thankful to not have encountered anyone on the sidewalk. *I should never have gotten involved. No, I had to play detective, now everyone is upset with me.* She was so deep in thought, she never heard the young man call to her, shut off his lawnmower, or see him running toward her. It wasn't until he touched her shoulder that she realized someone was standing next to her. She turned abruptly. "What do you want?" Her voice was curt.

The man took a step back and stammered. "I…I just wanted to say hi."

The man's face was familiar, but Sarah couldn't remember where or when they met. "I'm sorry, I don't…"

"I drove you home the other night…from the Greystone."

Sarah drew a half smile, not knowing if he too wanted to discuss her part in solving the liquor store breakin. "It's Teddy right," Sarah said as she continued walking.

"I was hoping to have a chance…" He quickly stepped in front of her, "to see you again."

She stopped, put her hands on her hips, and glared. "For what reason?"

He stepped aside. "Reason?" His eyebrows knitted together and he looked stumped. "I just…thought…we could get to know one another…that's all."

Sarah closed her eyes and pressed her fingers against her temples. Her shoulders sagged as she let out a stream of air. "I'm sorry," she said. "I don't mean to be rude. It's been a trying day."

"I've heard the gossip. That Scofield kid is a spoiled dipshit. Someone should take him to the woodshed and beat the crap out of him."

"The blond? Curly hair?" Sarah gazed into the distance not wanting this Ted to see her watery eyes.

"He's nothing but nine miles of bad road," he said, taking off his gloves and wiping the sweat from his brow. "Are you going to be okay?"

"I'll be fine. I just need time to shake free of this whole mess." She looked at Duke and Nora's place, three doors up. "I was hoping there'd be a shoulder to cry on but I doubt if anyone is home."

"I'm a good listener."

She laughed. "You seem to be there every time my life is upside down."

"C'mon, want to sit on the porch. I think we've got lemonade in the refrigerator." He took her hand and pulled her toward the house.

"You need to finish cutting the grass," she said, casting for an excuse.

He threw his gloves on the idled machine. "It can wait."

Sarah followed him up the steps. The covered porch stretched the length of the house. An assortment of metal chairs sat on either side of a large three seat glider. The support posts were lathe cut round with ball shapes and curvesfrom top to bottom. The front rail had matching white spindles.

"Have a seat. I'll fetch the lemonade," he said, before disappearing into the house.

Sarah dragged her hand along the railing as she walked the length of the porch. She expected Dee to invade her thoughts, to make fun of the situation or even offer encouraging advice. From the far end she could see the front of her sister's house. *I hope I haven't caused them a problem. Maybe the best thing I could do is jump on a bus and head back to Ely.* The humidity and the midday temperature felt oppresive. She wiped a bead of sweat from behind her ear and opened the top button of her blouse. Watching the trees and lilac bushes sway in the gentle breeze lulled her to momentarily forget her troubles.

"Here's the lemonade," he said, holding out a glass.

"Oh!" His voice startled her. She was surprised to see he had taken the time to wash up, comb his hair, and put on a change of clothes. She caught a wiff of men's cologne. He pointed to the glider. "Want to sit?"

Sarah took the glass. "I guess you no longer intend to finish mowing the grass." She smiled broadly as she walked passed him.

His face reddened. "You said you needed to talk."

She sat on the edge of the glider. Looking over her shoulder, she asked, "Are your folks at home?

"Working. They'll be home at five."

A car drove by. A man with his arm out the window, honked and waved a finger at them.

Sarah took a sip of lemonade and let her head rest on the seat back. "I suppose that was meant for me. I seem to be caught in a bad situation and have somehow managed to make things worse."

His offer to go inside set off warning bells. A presummed cackle from Dee also confirmed her negative response. She definitely wanted to escape, to hide from prying eyes, but where, how? The wood-paneled car sitting in the driveway, the one with the Greystone lettering on the door, offered a glimmer of hope. "Can we go for a ride?" she asked.

The young man hesitated. "I'm only suppose to use the car to get back and forth to work and shuttle guests to and from the restaurant."

"I ate there twice," she said, trying to make her case. "And, you did shuttle me the other night."

"We'd have to stay off the highway and away from town. Maybe it would be alright if we just cruise around on the back roads."

"That would be perfect," she offered. "Just until Duke or Nora gets home."

He opened the passenger side door."Maybe you could scooch down so no one can see you…just until we get out of town."

Sarah obliged, her head barely reached the top of the seat. He got in, turned the key, and pressed the starter button.

She rubbed along the wooden arm rest on the inside of the door. "What kind of car is this?"

"It's a forty-six Oldsmobile wagon."

Looking up, the ceiling had wood support struts and varnished veneer panels. "Is this made entirely of wood?"

He laughed. "It's called a woody. During the war when so much steel went to making tanks and airplanes, they reverted back to early car construction and began using more wood. I think it gives the car a distinctive look."

"I guess I didn't pay much attention when you gave me a ride home the other night." She watched as he shifted through the gears. She mimicked the synchronization of his hands and feet with hers. "Is it hard to learn?" she asked.

"To do what?" He turned the corner and shifted into second.

"I'd love to know how to drive."

"It's not that hard. Shifting is a little tricky, but once you master that, the rest is easy."

Sarah quickly identified the brake pedal and accelerator. She didn't know what to call it, but reasoned that the pedal on the left worked in conjunction with the shifting lever.

"That's the clutch," he said, in answer to her question. "You push it down each time you shift gears." She continued watching and matched slight hand and foot movements to his as the car went through a series of turns and long stretches of going straight. Slowing, he turned his head, first to the right and then left. "I think we're far enough out from town…it's probably okay to sit up now."

Sarah raised up and looked around. They were definitely no longer in town. Fields of knee high corn, interrupted by patches of woods and an occasional farm dotted the narrow roadway. She rolled down the window and drew in a breath of air. "The land here is so much more productive than what we have in Ely. We grow some hay, but it's mostly high desert and mountains."

"Is that in Nevada? I've never been west of the Mississippi," he added. "I'd love to see the Rockies, and maybe go on to California."

"I've seen a lot of America between here and Nevada, but it's been mostly from looking out a bus window."

"Are you thirsty?" he asked, pulling to the side of the road. He turned off the engine and got out. "C'mon."

Sarah opened her door and slid off the seat. She looked around. The only building was a small concrete cubicle sitting at the base of a multi-blade windmill perched high on a metal framework. Teddy opened the gate and waved for her to come.

"What are you doing?" she asked. "Isn't this private property?"

"It belongs to one of these farms around here. They use the well to water their cows." He walked around the building and pushed open the door. The room smelled dank. In the middle of the floor stood a hand pump. Teddy grabbed the handle and began moving it up and down. A half-dozen strokes and water streamed from the spout. "Grab that cup hanging on the wall. This is the best tasting and coldest water you'll ever have." Sarah filled the cup and took a big mouthful.

"That is good." She dumped the rest in the drain, refilled the cup and handed it to him. "Does anyone mind you coming in here?" She washed her hands as the stream slowed to a trickle. Wiping some of the cold water across her forehead, she looked around the room. Above the pump, a metal bar continued to go up and down. "What does that do?"

Teddy laughed. It's from the windmill. When you hook it to the pump, it does the work for you." He swung a pipe with a bowl beneath the spout. "This catches the water and sends it out to the water tank in back. The cows get watered and the farmer saves time and a lot of hand pumping."

"How do you know about this place?"

"As kids, we'd ride our bikes to Middletown for a Saturday movie matinee. This was a stopping point to get a drink."

"Are we close to Middletown? she asked.

"About three miles."

"Can we go there? Please, can we?"

Teddy took a moment to weigh the requests. "Why do you want to go there? We risk being seen."

I'd like to go to Penney's. I ruined my bathing suit and would love to get another. I know exactly what I'm looking for, it would only take me a few minutes. Please, can we?"

Teddy's resistance melted away in the pool of her baby blue eyes.

"I'll park in back of the store," he said, as they approached the town. "I'll wait in the car." He avoided the main drag, driving the side streets before pulling behind a large tan brick building "You be quick about it, okay."

Sarah hurried around the building while fumbling in her purse for her sunglasses. "My God, Dee," she mumbled under her breath, "I feel like Bonnie and Clyde coming into town to rob a bank." She plunked on the glasses and ducked through the front door.

In outlaw fashion, Teddy had the car turned around and ready for a quick getaway. As soon she opened the door, tossed her package on the seat and jumped in, he hit the gas and sped off. They giggled as if they had pulled off a heist. In minutes they were back in the rural countryside.

"How do you know what gear you're in," she asked, as he made another shift.

"You have to think of the transmission in the form of an 'H.' On the left leg you have reverse on top and first gear on the bottom. The crossbar is neutral. On the right leg, second is on top and third is down here, on the bottom. You only use first gear to get started. Once you're moving you only use second and third."

He slowed and pulled to the side of the road. "Slide over by me." He shifted into neutral. "Now put your hand over mine and move it with me." He pulled the shifter down into first and released the clutch. The car moved forward and he steered back onto the pavement. "Once you're going ten to fifteen miles per hour, it's time to shift into second. You step down the clutch, bring the lever up, use a little forward pressure to move through neutral…and up into second."

Sarah gigled with excitement. "Can we stop and do that again?"

Ted brought the car to a stop and shifted to neutral. "Let's see if you've been paying attention, put it in reverse."

Without hesitation Sarah pulled the lever and pushed it up. She waited for a look of approval.

"Good job," he said, easing off the clutch and allowing the car to move back a few feet. He reengaged the clutch, "Okay, let's see if you can ace your driving test. I'll do the footwork, and you take it through the gears."

Sarah brought the shifter straight down, and waited for him to accelerate. Listening to the engine and waiting for him to depress the clutch, she made a smooth shift to second and then another into third.

"Give the lady an A and a gold star," he said. "See, that's all there is to it."

"Except, can I do the hand thing and the foot thing at the same time?" She looked at him. Her eyes posed the question.

"No," he said straightening up. "I can't let you drive this car. My head would be in a noose if you wrecked it."

Sarah was disappointed, but, considering how her luck was going, she knew something bad was bound to happen if she tried. "How long have you worked at Greystone?"

"Four summers. Freshman and Sophomore years I busboyed. Last two driving shuttle."

"Got a girl friend?"

He did a double take before answering. "Yes and No, I like her, but she doesn't know it."

She tried to read his broad smile. Still unsure, she asked, "You don't mean me, do you?"

He laughed. "Would you want it to be?" He didn't give her a chance to answer. "Nah, it's a girl I went all through school with. She's a cheerleader, class president, way out of my league."

"What's the big deal? When are you going to tell her how you feel?" *You're a fine one to talk.* Her thoughts immediately shifted to Griff. *Oh boy, I know the feeling.*

Maybe someday." He looked at his watch. "Unless you're in a hurry, there *is* one place I'd like to show you before we head back to Pine Lake." He shifted into second, put his arm out the window to signal, and made a left turn.

Sarah's question was the same as the one Dee posed. *What is this all about?*

CHAPTER THIRTY-SEVEN

Teddy drove down a narrow, winding, country road. The terrain provided a roller coaster ride where Sarah's stomach floated as they crested each hill. He slowed when the pavement changed to gravel. "We're almost there," he said.

Sarah looked ahead. The road appeared to run right into the side a large hill. She leaned forward to see how far it rose. "It's huge. What is it?"

"Mount Tom. It's the highest point in the county. Are you ready to do a little hiking?"

She pointed. "You mean to the top?"

"The view is spectacular. You can see for miles." He pulled the car to the side of the road.

"Is this more private property?" she asked. "We won't get in trouble, will we?"

"I have no idea who owns it, but as kids, we played up there all the time." He walked across the road. "C'mon, we're probably five to six miles, as the crow flies, from the lake, but you can see just about all of it."

The path to the top was visible through the trees. The incline was manageable at the start but became steeper the farther they went. Soon they could no longer go straight but had to crisscross the hillside. Teddy moved at a steady pace as if retracing steps he had taken many times. Sarah struggled to keep up.

"Wait," she called out, as she plopped down on a large stone. "How much farther do we have to go?"

He came back to her. "We're more than halfway. There is an easier way. We can circle around and come up the back side."

"Yes please, I vote we take the easier way." She pushed herself up off the rock. The back way proved to be much easier and they soon broke into a clearing. They were still the length of a football field from the top.

Teddy grabbed her hand. "Let me help you, we're almost there."

Reaching the crest, Sarah stood silent as she gazed at the countryside that lay before them. Although they had climbed up through trees, the face on front side was a cliff that dropped a couple hundred feet. She had an unobstructed view and could see for miles. A glance in any direction blended multiple shades of green, as trees and the rolling landscape produced a setting worthy of an artist's brush. The lake shimmered as the sunlight danced across the deep blue water. Boats looked like tiny toys

"Isn't that a sight?" he said, picking up a stone and tossing it into the abyss.

Sarah eased herself to the grass and brought her knees to her chin. "What did you call this place?"

"Mount Tom," he said, dropping to one knee. "This part of Wisconsin is hilly, but no one knows how this huge mound shot up from nowhere."

"It feels like you could touch heaven," she said, looking to the clouded sky.

Teddy flopped to his back. "I know what you mean." There was a long silence.

"Remember the other night when you drove me home," she said, without looking his way. "When you heard me talking in the back seat, you asked if I was speaking to you, and I said I was talking to the man in the moon."

Teddy came up to face her. Resting on his forearm, he nodded.

"I know this sounds crazy." She paused, not sure if she should continue. "I was talking to my best friend…who died in a riding accident…three days before graduation." She glanced to see his reaction. His face remained stoic. "I talk to her, sometimes in my head and sometimes out loud." Another glance, still nothing. "I swear to God, I hear her, feel her presence, and see her responding to me." This time she fully expected him to say something…anything. His silence confused her. She watched as he rolled and got to his feet. He turned and stared at the trees. His shoulders were slumped, and his fingers pinched his lips.

"It's funny you should tell me that," he finally said, "especially here." He continued to look off in the distance. "My best friend Joey drowned nine years ago."

As he turned to her, she saw the anguish on his face. "How did—?"

"There was a cold snap. The pond froze—perfect for skating—it was stupid. We tried to go under the causeway bridge. We didn't know—the movement of the water kept ice from forming. It was barely an inch thick. We broke through. I was lucky. I grabbed one of the girders…Joey went under the water and never came up. I still see the look on his face." Ted turned and buried his face in his hands.

Sarah stood and put a hand on his shoulder. "I know, you feel so helpless. I watched as my friend and her horse slipped off the ledge. That moment is indelibly etched in my mind."

"All of us third grade boys were pallbearers." He spread his arms. "This was our mountain. We built a cardboard fort over there in the woods." Teddy chuckled as he pointed to a stand of trees. "We were going to quit school and live up here." He wiped his eyes with his fist. "In the spring, I'd come up here, either after school or on Saturdays, and he'd be here waiting for me. We'd talk for hours." He cleared his throat. "I guess it was me doing all the talking." He reached down and pulled out a handful of grass. Tossing it in the air, he said, "I haven't been up here in years."

Sarah broke the silence. "Is he here now?"

Teddy straightened. "He could be. I don't believe he's ever too far off."

"When did you stop talking…to Joey?"

"That summer I went to stay with my grandparents on the farm in Appleton. Grandpa caught me crying in the hay loft. When I told him about Joey, he said I should stop feeling sorry for him because Joey was in heaven having a life, we all dream of. And, if I was feeling sorry for myself, I should be happy because now I had this extra angel who would help guide me through life. It was never the same after that."

Sarah walked to the edge of the cliff. *Who am I feeling sorry for? Being in heaven has to be better than what's going on down here. It would be wonderful to think of Dee as being my special angel.* "I guess I didn't want to accept Dee's death. I thought if I talked to her and kept her in my thoughts, she'd somehow come back to life."

"Yup, I did the same thing. I begged him to come back." He looked at his watch. "It's past five. We'd better get back to town."

"How long did it take for the ache in your heart to leave?"

"It never goes away completely, but one day, you realize the life you had with that person is over, and it's time to move on." He held out his hand to help her up.

She gave it an extra squeeze. "Thank you for sharing…about you and Joey. It'll help me as I sort out my feelings for Dee."

At first, they walked slowly down the back slope. After a short distance, the pace quickened. They laughed and raced toward the trees. Teddy opened a lead, but when he turned to check her position he tripped and went tumbling head over heels on the grass. Sarah, propelled by her momentum, crashed on top of him. Entwined, they rolled a few times, before he ended on his back and she, across his chest. They laughed for a moment. Their eyes locked and she felt drawn. Lowering her head, their lips met, barely touching at first, then, like melting wax, their mouths pressed together. Suddenly, everything felt wrong. She pushed herself to the side. *What am I doing? I barely know this guy. I don't even know his last name and I doubt he knows mine.* It felt strange not to have Dee adding her two cents. "I'm sorry," she said. "That probably shouldn't have happened." She felt like a wanton woman, having betrayed the unnamed girl of his dreams.

He got up and brushed the grass off his pants. "I sorta liked it."

Saying that made her feel worse. She scrambled to her feet. "We'd better get back to town." She pushed him to lead the way. "I wouldn't wait," she said.

"Wait for what?"

"To tell that girl how you feel."

He laughed. "Yeah, you're probably right."

"And another thing, do you know my last name?"

"I heard someone say Conway or Conroy.

She laughed. "It's Connolly, Sarah Jean Connolly. Now that you know who I am, would you mind telling me yours?"

"Teddy…er, Ted Dobrinski."

"Which do you prefer?"

"I guess Ted sounds more grownup."

"Well, Ted Dobrinski, thank you for a wonderful afternoon, but we really should get back to town.

Both were silent on the ride to Pine Lake. She wasn't sure if his smile came from thoughts of the girl, or if he might be savoring that kiss. No matter. Her concern was what tomorrow would bring in the saga of the three boys and the liquor store break-in.

A small crowd of people were moving about when Teddy turned down their street.

Sarah pointed ahead. "That looks like Duke and Nora—"

"Talking to my folks." He took his foot off the accelerator and softly pressed on the brake. "Somethings up, and it doesn't look good."

His folks and Duke and Nora separated to allow Teddy to pull into the driveway. With his mom screaming at him through his window and Nora shouting questions through Sarah's, it was total bedlam. Nora didn't wait for answers, she opened Sarah's door and literally pulled the girl out of the car. "Come, let's get you home. We can sort out this whole mess when we get there."

What mess? Sarah was totally confused.

Duke grabbed Sarah's other hand and the three of them broke through the crowd and hurried up the street.

Sarah turned and caught a glimpse of Teddy's folks dragging him into their house. *What's going on?*

"Where were you? Nora shrieked, as Duke closed the door behind them. "You had us worried sick."

"We just took a ride." Sarah said, still bewildered by the commotion. "We stopped in Middletown. I bought another swimming suit at Penney's, and he showed me Mount Tom."

"Why would you do that? Nora looked to Duke for support. "Why would you leave town without letting one of us know? I was ready to call the sheriff and report you missing."

Sarah backed her way to the kitchen. "I'm sorry. Things got a little out of hand at the Bay Side. The sheriff questioned me about the liquor store break-in and now it seems I have both the locals and lakeshore upset with me." She turned and moved to the other side of the island counter, keeping some distance between them. "I felt trapped. Taking a ride out of town seemed like a good idea, but you're right, I should have left you a note."

Nora was about to pepper the girl with more questions when Duke came from behind and grabbed his mate by the shoulders. "Let's calm down. Sarah is safe. There's no harm done." He turned to Sarah. "What did you do on Mount Tom?"

"Nothing, we just talked."

"Nothing?" The inflection in his voice suggested doubt.

Sarah stared at the countertop. *Oh great, they think we were messing around. The gossip ladies are probably having a field day with this.*

Nora elbowed Duke. The look suggested it was time for him to butt out. Coming around the counter, she put her arms around Sarah and hugged her tight. "I'm sorry for getting so excited, but Blanche called me at the hospital and told me about the commotion at the restaurant. I called Duke. We checked the house and then searched the whole town. When we learned that Teddy and the Greystone car were gone too, every scary thought raced through my mind."

"I'm sorry," Sarah said. "I just wanted to get away…at least until you got home."

Duke stepped up and hugged both of them. "Let's be happy that nothing happened, and it was all a big misunderstanding. You both may think it's crazy, but I think we should go to the Bay Side for supper. I'm hungry and think the best thing is to face this brouhaha before it gets out of hand."

"Are you sure?" Nora asked. "Maybe we should let things die down and deal with it in the morning."

"After all of this, I won't be able to sleep a wink," Sarah said. "I agree with Duke."

On the drive to the restaurant, Sarah sat in the back seat and took a mental journey back through the day. She thought about Duke's question. *Nothing did happen. Well, almost nothing. It was just that one kiss.*

CHAPTER THIRTY-EIGHT

"You don't want
to miss the big
Fourth of July
celebration,
do you?

Blanche came around the counter as Duke, Nora and Sarah entered the Bay Side. She went straight to Sarah. "I'm glad you're alright. We heard you were missing."

"There's no big mystery. She and Teddy Dobrinski drove over to Middletown," Nora interjected, "to do a little shopping."

Blanche grabbed a handful of menus. "We've had a pretty interesting day ourselves." She laid the menus on the table. "We've found ourselves in quite a dilemma."

"Because of me?" Sarah asked. "Why?"

Blanche stepped aside as Mary, the other waitress, set down three glasses of water. "Nobody wants this break-in thing to get out of hand. Not the boys' families, and certainly not the local business community."

"So, they are going to sweep it all under the rug?" Nora's tone was sharp.

Blanche leaned over the empty chair. "The DA is not going to press charges but instructed the boys to stay away from Sarah."

"And that's a good thing," Duke interjected.

"But therein lies the problem." Blanche straightened. "These families are really good customers. They eat a lot of meals here."

Duke was quick to pick up on the meaning. "And if their boys can't be around Sarah…"

"They won't come in." Mary said.

"And worse," Blanche added, "a few locals have expressed concern that this whole thing could have a souring effect on our business relationship with the lakeshore families." She looked at Sarah. "I hate doing this, but I have to let you go."

Nora jumped to her feet. "That's not fair. All she did was tell the truth."

"Don't you think I know that," Blanche said. Then looking at Sarah. "You're a great kid, a quick learner, and did a fantastic job on the few days you worked. I hope you won't be too upset, but I have to think about the business."

Nora was about to speak when Sarah grabbed her arm. "It's okay." She walked around the table and gave Blanche a big hug. "I understand. There isn't much else you can do. I enjoyed working here and I want to thank you for giving me a chance."

Mary hugged Sarah. "This stinks the way it turned out, but I'm a single Mom with a small mouth to feed. We can't live without the lakeshore business."

Sarah gave her a big smile. "And I don't want to stand in your way."

"Swing by tomorrow and I'll have a final check for you," Blanche said. She turned and used her apron to wipe her eyes as she walked away.

The four stood for a moment. Mary was the first to speak. "Are you ready to order?"

Nora looked to Duke and then to Sarah. "That's okay, I think we've lost our appetite. We'll take a pass tonight but will come again…soon."

"I guess the only loser here is Sarah," Nora said, as they got to the car. "Those boys get their hands slapped and she loses her job. What a fine kettle of fish that is."

"A lot of livelihoods hang on our lakeshore friends," Duke said, "including mine. I don't agree with how this all played out, but we can't blame Blanche. Her hands are tied."

Nora stumped her foot on the running board. "It's just not right. Where's the justice?"

"I'm not a loser," Sarah said softly. "I did the right thing. Those boys will have to live here the rest of their lives, and sadly, will be remembered as the thieves who broke into the liquor store."

"And I have a feeling," Duke said. "You'll be remembered as the girl that outsmarted them."

"I'm thinking of going back to Ely." Sarah's announcement shocked Nora.

"Why? You've only been here a few days."

"I know and look at the trouble I've caused." Sarah let a slight giggle escape. "If I stay much longer, I'm liable to bring down the whole town."

"Stay at least over the fourth," Nora pleaded. "Gladys will be back in town. We'll have a picnic. It'll be a lot of fun."

"It's only two days away," Duke said. "There's going to be a corn roast in the park, and I heard they have a huge pile of fireworks to shoot off."

"I certainly don't want to miss that," Sarah said, in an over-the-top response. She moved to a serious tone. "I'll call Mom and Dad and tell them I'm leaving on the fifth. That should put me back in Ely on the eighth."

Nora swallowed hard. "Darn, I so wanted us to have wonderful summer together."

"I know it's been short," Sarah offered, "but, even with all the commotion, I've had a really good time. Maybe we can plan something for next summer."

"Maybe we can." Nora's voice lacked conviction.

"I don't know about anyone else," Duke said, "but I'm still hungry. What say we drive to the west end and grab a burger at Harvey's Tavern."

"I think we've had enough excitement for one day," Nora said. "Let's just go home. I've got sliced ham and fresh buns from the bakery."

Sarah concurred. "A quick bite and I think I'll be ready for bed." She watched as they passed Teddy's house. *I wonder how much trouble I caused him.*

Having gone to bed a little after nine, Sarah was not surprised her eyes flew open a little past five. It was still an hour before daybreak. She stared into the darkness. *Maybe I'm being foolish. With Dee gone, there's no reason to hurry back to Ely. Is this my life's pattern? To run at the first sign of trouble. I ran from Ely because I didn't want to face dealing with Dee's death, and now I'm running back to Ely because I've upset a few people and don't want to face them. Arrrgh! How do I get myself into these situations?*

She got out of bed and opened the armoire. Bringing out her package from Penney's, she tore away the paper, and held the top of the bright red, two-piece bathing suit in front of her. *Sarah Jean, are you a glutton for punishment? Tongues will really wag if you wear this in public.* With a glint in her eye, she pulled off her pajama top and put her arms through the straps of the suit. After fastening the back, she kicked off her pajama pants and pulled on the red bottom. She drew up the window shade. There was just enough light to see herself in the mirror. "Wow," she whispered. Her hand rubbed across her stomach. *It feels funny not to have this covered.* She adjusted the straps and ran a finger down the cleavage between her breasts. *I didn't realize I'd have so much skin showing. I know it's a bathing suit, but it feels…like underwear.*

Sarah turned to a sound coming from downstairs. Someone was in the kitchen. The fear of being caught…like this, spurred a quick change back into her pajamas. She flattened the paper wrapper as best she could, folded the suit into it and put the package in the bottom of the drawer.

Nora pulled her hands out of the sink and toweled dry as Sarah walked into the kitchen. "All done sleeping?"

"I can't get past five o'clock without my eyes popping open," she said. "Of course, now I have no reason to get up."

"My offer still stands. You're welcome to stick around and just enjoy the summer. No one says you have to work." Nora put a glass of orange juice on the counter. "Are you hungry?"

Sarah sat and swung around on the stool. "I might do that. There's a lot of the town I haven't seen. It'll also give me a chance to mend a few fences."

"With Griff?"

"For one. I'd also like to do what I can to defuse the rift between the town and the lakeshore."

"With Griff you've got a chance. With the rift, I don't know. You're dealing with knuckleheads and inflated egos. Ignore them. This will all blow over in a couple of days."

Sarah took a sip of juice. I also need to apologize to Ted down the street."

Nora spun on her heels. "For what? What did you two do?"

"We didn't do anything," Sarah said flatly. "But he could have gotten into trouble with Greystone for using their car to drive me to Middletown."

"To buy a bathing suit, right?" Nora pulled two slices of toast from the toaster, buttered them, added strawberry jelly, and slid the plate in front of Sarah. "Did you buy another like the one that got torn?"

Sarah's slight shake of the head and impish smile left Nora wondering. "Which one, the pink one?" Nora continued to name styles and colors of those Sarah had tried on. Each time, Sarah shook her head. Then, as if struck by lightning, Nora gasped. "You didn't?"

Sarah nodded as her smile broadened.

"The red one…the two-piece…the one in the window? Oh my gosh, did you try it on? How does it look?"

"I didn't have time in the store, but I put it on just before I came down."

Nora pulled off her apron. "Come, show me. I want to see how you look."

Nora sat on the bed as Sarah took the package from the drawer. "I'll be right back," she said and dashed off to the bathroom. When she returned, she was wrapped in a large towel.

"C'mon, let me see." Nora said, her voice full of excitement.

Sarah felt her face flush as she slowly opened the towel and let it fall to the floor. Turning, she posed in front of the mirror. Her face was as red as the suit. "It's revealing, isn't it?"

Nora came from behind and looked at the image in the glass. "Stunning, I'd say. It looks like that suit was made for you, and you for it. The question is, will you feel comfortable wearing it in public?"

Sarah ran her fingers and hands over every inch that was covered and what was not. "I guess it shouldn't be a problem, outside of my stomach, all the important parts are covered."

Nora picked the towel off the floor. "And the parts that are not create a thing of beauty."

"You gals up there?" The shout came from the bottom of the stairs.

"Duke," Nora gasped. She threw the towel in Sarah's direction and called out the door. "I'll be right down."

"Don't let him come up here," Sarah pleaded, as she hurriedly wrapped herself in the towel.

"That's okay," Duke yelled. "I'm leaving for work. I've got a few more boats to get ready for tomorrow."

Nora stood at the top of the stairs. "Do you want some breakfast? Did you make yourself a lunch?"

"I've got the jelly toast you left on the counter. I'll swing by the hospital at noon and spear some food off the kitchen help. Bye. See you then. Love ya."

Nora came back into the room. "He's always in a hurry. Sometimes I think he's got ants in his pants." She watched as Sarah opened the towel and took another look at herself in the mirror. "If you're uncomfortable with having Duke see you, you may be in trouble here, but, oh Lordy, you'd give Esther Williams a run for her money." Nora was about to leave when she turned and said, "I've been meaning to tell you. Some people opened a riding stable north of town. As much as you enjoy riding horses, it might be a fun thing to do."

"Really!" I'd love to. Will you take me sometime? We could ride together."

Nora's hand pushed the air. "Not me," she said. "I'll take you there, but you couldn't pay me enough to get on a horse." She shuddered. "The darn thing would probably run off and take me with it."

Sarah laughed. "You have to let the horse know whose boss and rein him in."

"The horse knows who's boss. It's him. No, thank you. I'll leave the riding to you." She stood in the doorway. "I'm going to the hospital. Duke and I should be back late this afternoon. Stay out of trouble, okay?"

Sarah chuckled. "I'll try." She took one more look at herself in the mirror and smiled. *I could probably get myself into a lot of trouble wearing this.*

CHAPTER THIRTY-NINE
A Day of Many Surprises

The first thing Sarah did after getting dressed and eating a light breakfast of milk and corn flakes, was step onto the front porch to see if the Greystone woody was parked in Ted's driveway. Her heart sank. It wasn't there. *I hope he didn't get fired. It would be my fault if he did.* Every ten to fifteen minutes she repeated the ritual, looking for the Black and tan Oldsmobile. She breathed a sigh of relief when she finally saw the car parked on his driveway. Hurrying down the steps, she half jogged, and half fast walked to his house. Ted answered on the second knock. "Hello," he said, opening the screen door. "I see you're still in one piece. He chuckled at his attempt at humor. "What's up?"

Sarah backed away. "I've been waiting. When I didn't see the Greystone Car, I thought you might have gotten fired."

He laughed. "They knew all about our little runaway. Gossip travels fast in this town." He pointed to the glider and waited for her to sit. The porch became his stage. Taking command, and with a bit of puffery, he began. "I told them it was an errand of mercy, you were being hassled, and I only did it to put a little space between you and the town. In the end, Mrs. Langdon was patting me on the back."

"Really?" Sarah let out a long stream of air. "That makes me feel better."

"Of course, she warned me to never do it again."

"Oh, of course."

Ted took a seat beside her. "I've got more big news. I took your advice and called Debbie…Debbie Morrison, the girl I told you about. We had this really long conversation. She asked why I never showed any interest in her before. I got the feeling she was happy I called. We're going to the corn roast and watch the fireworks on the fourth. I'll have to work until ten, but we'll have the whole rest of the night together."

"Were your folks upset about yesterday?" she asked. "They looked angry."

"Oh yeah, I'm supposed to stay away from you. They said you're a bad influence."

Sarah's head dropped. "I'm sorry, I didn't mean…"

"Don't worry about it, they're way over-protective of me…ever since Joey drowned."

"Still, I'm sorry they feel that way."

"They'll get over it. I told them I was old enough to choose my friends, and that you were a really good person."

Sarah smiled. "Thank you for saying that." The words barely left her mouth when she caught a glimpse of the black convertible coming up the street. She slunk in her seat.

Ted shot her a puzzled look. "What's up? What's the matter?"

She put her finger to her lips. "Sssssh," she said, and pointed to the car. "Watch where it goes."

That's Griff MacDonald," Ted said. "He comes to Greystone, a lot. Are you hiding from him?"

"It's a long story," she whispered.

"Well, he just pulled into your driveway," he said in an exaggerated whisper, "and I doubt he can hear us from there."

She punched Ted in the arm. "Just tell me when he's gone."

Each minute felt like a lifetime. Then, without warning Ted jumped to his feet and trotted down the steps. He gave a loud whistle and waved his arm.

Sarah lifted her head enough to see the black Ford pull to the curb. *What is Ted doing? Why did he flag him down? I swear to God, I'll kill him if he tells Griff I'm up here.*

"Sarah," Ted yelled, "there's someone here who'd like to talk to you."

She sat up. Her smile camouflaged her true feelings. *I'll kill that Ted the first chance I get.*

Sarah grudgingly got up and went down the stairs. She likened the long walk to the street to heading to the gallows. *Okay, sure, I want to make amends, but this is awkward.* She approached the car and, if looks could kill, Ted Dobrinski would be ready for a cold slab in the morgue. She stopped when she reached the sidewalk.

Ted no doubt felt the angry vibes and backed away from the vehicle. "I'll leave. You two probably have a lot to talk about." He headed for the house, looping in a wide circle, keeping a safe distance from Sarah.

Griff got out and came around the car. Clad in khaki pants and an oxford-cloth, button down shirt, she couldn't help but admire him. "How are you doing?" he asked.

"I'm fine. When did you get back?"

"About a half hour ago." Instead of going to her, he leaned against the passenger side door. "Mom told me about you losing your job. You must have been hurt."

"I'll survive." She turned and started walking towards Nora's place. "I'm glad you made it back."

"Wait," he said, pushing himself away from the car and running after her. "Won't you give me a chance?" He grabbed her hand. "You're all I've been thinking about. It's crazy, I'm at school, getting things setup, and I can't get you off my mind."

Sarah stopped and pulled her hand free. "So, what are you saying? This isn't some kind of proposal, is it?" Her lip curled. She meant it as a putdown.

"No…maybe…I don't know. Can't we just be friends, enjoy some time together and see where it takes us?"

"Your mom will never accept me."

"I'm sure she would, once she got to know you…and Dad thinks you were clever in how you got the boys to give themselves up."

"It didn't work out all that well for me. I was ready to leave and go back to Ely."

"I'm glad you didn't." He took her hand again. "Please, I know we've hit a rocky stretch here, but I really enjoyed being with you when we skied. You enjoyed it, didn't you?"

Sarah let her guard down. "I'd love to try it again."

"How about tomorrow? The lake will be busy but there's always room for a few more people."

She broke into a smile. "I got a new bathing suit." As soon as the words came out of her mouth, she realized she had basically committed to wearing it.

Griff looked at his watch. "It's almost noon. Would you like to get something to eat? I left Chicago at six and could use some nourishment."

"Where? I can't go to the Bay Side and don't care to go to Greystone."

"We could drive over to Middletown. They've opened an A & W Root Beer stand. You drive up and they serve you in your car. I hear they have good hot dogs."

"Okay," she said. "But first let me run to the house and leave a note for Nora. Pick me up there. She ran a few steps, stopped, and returned. Leaning over the door, she asked, "Do you know about a riding stable near here?"

"One opened last year. I've driven past it but never stopped."

"Could we go there? Maybe after we eat?"

He laughed. "I've never been on a horse, but I'm willing to give it a try."

"I'll change. Pick me up at the house." She dashed off before he could answer.

Sarah ran into the kitchen and scribbled a quick note for Nora, and then high-tailed it up the stairs. Rummaging through the meager selection of clothes in the armoire, she slammed the drawer in disgust. *I don't have long pants. Maybe I can borrow something of Nora's.* She hit every other step on the way down. She began to panic as she pushed aside hanger after hanger. "C'mon, you've got to have pants," she muttered. It wasn't until she reached the last few hangers on the bar, that she saw a pair of

Levi's and pulled them free. *I hope this is another piece from your thin period.* She took the pants, grabbed a red and blue plaid shirt, and hiked up the stairs. The jeans fit perfectly, as did the shirt. She grabbed a pair of gloves and a large red handkerchief from the armoire. Tying the scarf around her neck, she moved the knot to the side. A quick glance in the mirror made her giggle with delight. She grabbed her purse and skipped down the stairs.

Sarah finally took a normal breath as she stepped onto the porch. Griff jumped out of the car. "Wow! Look at you, a dyed-in-the-wool cowgirl and a true Dale Evans look-alike," he said, holding the car door open.

Sarah soaked up the compliment. "I can't believe I'm going riding," she said, sliding onto the seat.

CHAPTER FORTY

A Frosty Glass of Root Beer

The A & W was a small, black and orange, wood building sitting on the side of the road. Cars pulled up and parked haphazardly around it as girls came running to take the food and drink orders. The fifteen cent hot dogs and dime root beer floats in a frosted mug, came on a tray that hooked on the car window. The hot dog, smothered in mustard, was yummy, but Sarah truly enjoyed the root beer and ice cream concoction. "Thank you, that was really good," she said handing him her empty mug. She didn't want to create a scene, but she wished he'd hurry up and finish his drink so they could go to the riding stable. Her mind was bombarded with images of being on Jubilee, her hair flowing in the wind, as they galloped along the tree line behind the Johnson's ranch. "How far is it?" she asked.

"Six or seven miles." He laughed. "Are you sure you want to do this?"

"Yes. Yes." Her excitement bubbled out as she bounced about on her seat. "I can't wait to get back on a horse."

"As I remember, it's on County Trunk T, halfway between Middletown and Pine Lake." He waited for the carhop to remove the tray. The girl gave him an enthusiastic thank you when he told her to keep the change. "It should only take about fifteen minutes." He started the car.

Sarah didn't know what to expect and was a little disappointed when Griff turned into a farmyard consisting of a large barn, a rundown house and a collection of various sized buildings and sheds, all badly in need of paint. Near the barn, under a crudely made canopy, six horses, already saddled, stood tied to a rail. Their tails swooshed as they tried to keep the flies at bay. To most, the smell of manure, would be overpowering. For Sarah, it brought back fond memories of being at the Johnson ranch and being with Dee.

Griff brought the car to a stop and leaned her way. "Okay cowgirl, it's time to teach the ski instructor how to ride a horse."

Sarah giggled as she pulled the leather gloves from her back pocket. She looked around. "I wonder where we ride."

A lad of about fourteen, sitting on the fence, must have heard her. "The trail is through the woods, skirts the hay field, runs along the road and into the orchard. From there, it comes back through the woods. Don't worry, the horses know the way."

"See," Griff said. "We don't have to worry. The horses know the way."

Another youth, in the seventeen to eighteen-year range, untied a medium sized, brown mare and led her into the yard. "Need help getting up?" he asked, as he handed her the reins.

"Nope." She hung the reins over the horse's neck. "I've ridden before." She grabbed the horn, put her foot in the stirrup, threw her leg over, and settled in the saddle. The horse responded to her pulling on the reins and took a few steps sideways. Sarah brought the horse's head back. "Easy girl," she said, patting the animal's neck.

The older boy reached for the horse's bit. "Whoa girl, C'mon Nellie, settle down." He looked at Sarah. "Are you okay?"

"No problem." She leaned forward and continued patting the horse. "Nellie and I are going to get along fine."

The younger boy walked out of the corral leading a good-sized black stallion. Even having neither the size nor spirit of Samson, Sarah couldn't help but draw the comparison. She thought about asking the boys for a different mount but said nothing.

Griff immediately showed his lack of experience by approaching the horse from the right.

"Mount on the left," Sarah said.

Griff gave her a puzzled look but made a large circle around the back of the horse. "The horse knows his left from his right?" he asked in jest. Sarah held her tongue. Griff put his foot into the stirrup and grabbed the saddle horn. He made a couple of attempts to raise himself enough to swing his leg over the horse. Even with the older boy holding the bridle, the horse swung his rear away from Griff.

Sarah pointed. "Stand on the fence. It'll be easier to get on."

Griff climbed to the second rail. He glanced at Sarah sitting relaxed in the saddle. He didn't have to say a word, the frustration on his face spoke volumes. This was a man used to being in control and he clearly was not comfortable with the situation. To his credit, as soon as the horse was close enough, Griff swung his leg over and sat down hard in the saddle. The boy handed Griff the reins and led the horse around to the side of the barn. "Blackie knows the way from here, enjoy the ride." The horse walked up the well-worn path with Griff stiffly holding the reins in one hand, while the other held a death-grip on the saddle horn.

Sarah brought her heels into Nellie's ribs. The old girl's head came up and swung to the side in protest. It took a light slap of the reins on the horse's rump before Nellie understood the message. They soon caught up to Griff and Blackie. "These horses are so used to walking the path, they don't want to take direction."

Griff turned his head to the side. "Walking is fine with me."

Sarah laughed. The trail through the woods was narrow and the encroaching brush prohibited riding side by side. Although she had the itch to ride hard, she was content to sit back and enjoy being in the saddle. The sunlight braking through the trees in long dust filled streams, the sounds of hooves brushing through dead leaves, and the chatter of squirrels high above, added to the pleasantness of the moment. "Isn't this the most fun you've ever had?"

"You mean better than having a root canal…without Novocain?" He laid his head back and spoke into the air, as if the words would go up and come back down when they got to her.

"Do you have any flies back by you or do I have them all up here with me?"

Sarah choked on her reply. "It'll be a lot better once we're out of the woods." No sooner had she spoken when they broke free of the trees and into a hayfield that had been recently cut and baled. Blackie immediately turned and walked up a beaten down path that followed the fence line. Nellie followed in line. Sarah had another plan. She pulled the reins sharply to the side, kicked her heels into the horse's stomach, and slapped the leather straps across Nellie's rear flanks. Nellie reared in momentary defiance. Sarah push hands and reins into Nellie's mane. "Yah!" she yelled and repeatedly sent her heals hard into the horse's ribs. The horse dug her rear hooves into the stubble, leaped forward, and took off across the field in a full gallop. Sarah continued to urge the steed onward with an occasional slap of leather. Reaching the far end of the rolling field, she eased back on the reins. Nellie slowed to a loping gallop and then to a trot. She stopped abruptly when Sarah sharply pulled back the reins. "Good Girl," Sarah said, as she patted the horse between her ears and along the neck. On the way back she continued to test Nellie's ability to accept commands, making turns, and moving up from a walk, to a trot, to a full gallop.

Griff had managed to halt Blackie long enough to observe Sarah horsemanship. He clapped his hands as she came riding up. Blackie spooked and reared. Griff grabbed the horn with both hands leaving the reins to fall. Sarah kicked Nellie and blocked the black stallion before he had a chance to run. Then, leaning over she grabbed the loose reins and handed them to Griff. "I think you spooked him by clapping."

"Sorry, but you impressed the heck out of me. That was some real horseback riding."

Sarah ran her hand up and down Nellie's mane. "I think at one time she was a good working horse." Nellie shook her head and whinnied as if she understood the compliment.

Blackie on the other hand, decided it was time to go and began walking up the path. "Whoops," Griff said, grabbing the reins and horn. "I guess we're leaving."

Sarah pulled Nellie in behind.

At the end of the field, the path turned to the right, and ran alongside the road. Nellie seemed unaffected by the passing cars, but Sarah noticed Blackie flinched as each one passed. She was happy to see the orchard up and to the right.

It all happened in the blink of an eye. A car full of boys, laughing and shouting, screeched to a stop as a sparkling projectile came flying through the air. The string of firecrackers began exploding in Machine Gun fashion. Nellie reared, but Blackie took off like a shot with Griff trying desperately to stay in the saddle. "Pull back on the reins," Sarah yelled, as she gave Nellie a kick. "Pull hard."

Sarah was gaining but still far behind as Blackie made the turn and raced past the first apple tree. She saw the look of terror on Griff's face as he bobbed and weaved trying to avoid being hit by the low hanging branches. Sarah slapped both sides of Nellie's rump with the leather straps, as she ducked under branches. "Pull on the reins," she repeated."

Griff looked back. He appeared confused and afraid. He probably never saw the heavy limb when he turned back forward. It caught him across the forehead. His body crumbled and like a scene from a western movie where the bad guy is shot out of the saddle, Griff's limp body fell hard to the ground. Sarah reined up, hopped off Nellie and spun the reins around a tree branch. Diving to his side, she didn't know where to start. His eyes were closed, blood oozed from a large gash on his forehead and his right arm hung in an unnatural angle from his shoulder. "Griff, speak to me." She patted his cheek. "C'mon, please, speak to me." She felt his pulse. It was strong but he wasn't responding.

Sarah pulled the shirt tails out of her waistband, striped off the shirt, and began tearing it up the middle of the back. With the first piece she wrapped it around his head and tied it tight. *Got to stop the bleeding.* She used the second piece to cautiously sling his arm to his chest. "Hang in there," she pleaded. She dug in his pocket and pulled out his keys. "I'll be right back. I've got to get help." She jumped up, tore the reins from the branch, and was on Nellie in a matter of seconds. She looked down the row of apple trees, but the woods at the far end blocked any view of the farm. *Damn…which way? Can't take a chance…Gotta go back the way we came.* Nellie responded to Sarah's every command, and in a heartbeat, the two were going at full speed, back along the road and through the hay field. It got a little tricky going through the woods. Without a shirt, the tree branches and long reaching brush produced welts and scratches to her arms and chest. Racing into the barnyard, she leaped off the horse and threw the reins to the startled youngster. "Get your brother," she yelled. "My friend is hurt. We have to go get him." By the look on the lad's face, seeing a young woman running around in just her bra on top was not only unexpected, but a bonus in a rather, up-until-then, uneventful day.

All she could think about as she ran to the black convertible was the sequence of how to start it. Although she had never done it on her own, she felt confident of using the foot pedals and the shifting lever. She jumped behind the wheel and fumbled with the keys. *Which one is it? Why does he have to have so many?* She found the one with the Ford logo and stuck it into the ignition. *Push the clutch—shift into neutral—push the starter button.* The car fired. She ground the gears trying to put it in reverse. *Dammit, push the clutch all the way down.* Easing off the clutch, she pressed the accelerator and spun the wheel around to the left. The Ford swung backwards. *Brake, clutch, shift.* Sarah brought the car to the corral amid a cloud of dust and slammed on the brakes next to the boys. "Get in," she screamed. The older boy jumped in the front seat while the younger one dove over the side into the back. Although they tried to be inconspicuous, she felt their eyes glued to her chest.

"Which is the fastest way to the apple orchard?" Now was not the time to worry about what they could or couldn't see, nor what either might be thinking. She had to get Griff to a hospital.

The older boy pointed to the other side of the barn. "We have to go around back."

Sarah popped the clutch, turned the wheel, and pressed the accelerator to the floorboard. The rear of the car fish tailed as it made a swooping turn, spraying dust and gravel from the spinning tires.

"We have to stop and open one gate" the boy said, as they sped around the far side of the barn.

"C'mon, hurry," Sarah yelled, as the boy pushed the gate to the side. She stopped the car long enough for him to jump in.

He pointed. "At the end of this field, turn left. You'll be in the orchard."

Damn. It would have been shorter to come back this way. She misjudged her speed and in making the turn spun the car in a complete circle on the slick grass. The young boy screamed as they both hung on for dear life. The rear fender came to rest against a large boulder. The car barely came to rest, before she pulled it into first gear and spun back around. She slowed and drove between two rows of trees. Blackie stood off to the side. She slowed more. *For God's sake, I don't want to run over him.*

The boy stood. Holding onto the windshield, he pointed to the left. "There. He's over there."

Sarah spun the wheel, and drove along side, keeping a safe distance away. She turned the key, jumped out, and ran to Griff. Dropping to her knees, it appeared he hadn't moved. "Griff, can you hear me?" She grabbed his hand and felt his pulse. It didn't feel quite as strong. "We have to get him to a hospital." She pointed to the younger boy, "Go open the door on the passenger side and get in the back." She motioned for the other one. "I'll grab his feet. You go in front and take him under the arms. Be careful, the one is broken or dislocated." The boy did as she instructed and together, they lifted Griff and began carrying him to the car. "He's most likely got a concussion," she said. "It's better if he sits up. Your brother can hold him while we go."

Once they got him situated in the back, cradled in the boy's arms, she looked at the lad. "Are you going to be alright?" She placed his hand on the bandage. "Keep light pressure. We need to stop the bleeding.

The boy nodded, but she saw fear in his eyes. She hated putting him in that position but had no choice. She turned to the older brother. "Which way to the nearest hospital?"

"Pine Lake. Take a left out of the driveway and stay on "T." It'll take you right into town." He pointed to his brother. "Jerry knows the way."

Sarah jumped behind the wheel and started the car. She waited for the older boy to get in.

"You go," he said. I'll corral Blackie and ride him back to the barn."

Retracing her way back to the farmyard, Sarah kept an eye on where she was going but glanced numerous times in the rearview mirror to see how her passengers were doing. Once she made the left turn out of the driveway, she floored the gas pedal, easing enough to shift down to third. *Dear God, please don't let him die. I couldn't bear to lose another friend this way.*

CHAPTER FORTY-ONE

Trouble with the Law!

The road sign read, *Pine Lake 2 Miles*. Sarah adjusted the mirror above the windshield so she could see what was going on in the backseat. Griff's eyes were closed. "Is he still breathing?" she asked. The lad nodded. "We're almost there," she said, glancing down at the speedometer. The needle held steady on the number eighty.

She heard the siren before her eyes caught sight of the flashing red light in the mirror. Sarah debated whether to stop or to keep going. *Maybe he can help get us to the hospital faster.* Sarah put light pressure on the brakes and pulled to the side of the road. She didn't wait for the officer to get out of his vehicle. "I've got an injured person," she screamed, as she came running. "We have to get him to the hospital." She pounded her fist on the hood of the deputy sheriff's coupe

The officer jumped out and chased her back to the convertible. His eyes bounced from Griff, sitting unconscious, to the boy holding him in his arms, to Sarah, standing there in her white brassiere.

She covered her chest with her arm. "Please, we have to get him to the hospital."

The policeman could have asked a hundred questions, starting with, 'why was she was running around in her underwear.' Instead, realizing the seriousness of the situation, he yelled, "Follow me," as he hustled back to his car.

The officer sped ahead with his siren screaming and red lights flashing. Sarah dropped the car in low, stomped on the accelerator, and squealed the tires as she came onto the pavement. By the time she hit second and pulled it into third, they were doing seventy-five.

As they approached the outskirts of town the deputy eased off the throttle, but they were still going forty through the heart of town. People on the street stopped and gawked. Others scrambled out of shops and restaurants to see what the commotion was. Sarah kept her focus on the cruiser in front of her but managed a small wave to Blanche, as they passed the Bay Side. Her heart pounded with relief when she saw the word hospital on the building ahead. *Dear God, we made it.* The officer stuck his arm out the window and pointed to the emergency entrance. Sarah wheeled the car up the drive and under the canopy. Her hand shook as she reached for the key. She panted. It was like she couldn't catch her breath. Until now, her only thought was to get Griff to the hospital. Adrenaline spurred her on, but now a rush of emotion was taking over. She put her face against the back of her hands gripping the steering wheel and sobbed. "Please," she whispered. "Don't let him die."

Nora, pushing a gurney, was the first person through the hospital door and barked orders. Two men in white climbed into the back seat, lifted Griff's limp body out of the boy's arms, and maneuvered him onto the wheeled cart.

With Griff's head heavily bandaged, it took a minute for Nora to realize who she had on the gurney. She spun around as Sarah lifted her head from the steering wheel. "Oh, my God." She rushed around the front of the car. "Sarah, are you alright? Are you hurt?"

"I'm okay," she whispered. "But Griff is hurt bad."

"What happened to your shirt?" Sarah pointed to Griff. "Let's get you inside." Nora helped her sister out of the car and put an arm around her.

"Wait," Sarah said, as the young boy wobbled as he attempted to climb out of the back seat. "He could be in shock."

Nora put an arm around each of them and walked them to the building. "We'll have you both checked out."

As soon as they were inside, Nora pointed to a couch in the waiting area. "Sit over there. I'll have someone check on you." A nurse came running. "Keep an eye on them," Nora instructed. "Check them for shock. Get the girl a scrub to or something to cover up with. I want to see what's going on in ER." The nurse brought Sarah a top. "How do you feel?" she asked.

Sarah put the shirt on over her head. "I'm cold and my hands feel clammy," she said. "Could I have a blanket, and maybe one for him, too?" The wool cloth stopped her chattering teeth, but didn't help with the light-headedness, nor the urge to close her eyes and sleep.

The deputy who had given them the high-speed escort, stepped through the door. Sarah watched him approach. A slender man in his early thirties, lacking the body mass necessary to pull the wrinkles out of his uniform. He sat next to her on the couch and opened his pad. Pulling a pencil out of his shirt pocket, he touched the lead to his tongue. "I know this is a bad time, but there is the matter of going thirty miles per hour over the posted limit. Could I see your driver's license?"

Sarah pulled the blanket up to her chin. "I don't have one." Her response was barely audible.

The officer leaned forward, "What was that?"

She vexed her brow and looked directly at him. "I said, I don't have one."

The lead broke as he almost pressed the pencil through the pad. "Oh, my gosh, that's not good." He searched through the back pages of the citation notepad while mumbling, "Speeding, driving without a license," he paused and pointed to the door. "Whose car is that?"

She pointed to the Emergency Room.

"The guy that was hurt, did he give you permission to drive his car?"

"I couldn't ask. He was unconscious."

The deputy put his pencil back in his pocket. "I'll have to get back to you on this. I have to talk to Sheriff Durham. He stood and put the pad in his hip pocket. "I'll have to ask you not to leave town, and under no circumstances, are you to get behind the wheel of that car." He quickly added. "Or any other vehicle." He turned to leave.

"Wait," she said. "Check with the nurse. If it's alright, would you mind giving this boy a ride back to the riding stable? He didn't do anything wrong and has been a real trooper helping me get my friend here."

The officer muttered something about being a taxi as he walked to the nurse's station.

Nora came out of the OR. She pulled her face mask under her chin and smiled. "He's awake. A little mixed up but he should be fine. The shoulder was dislocated. You did well to put it in the sling. Sorry you had to tear apart your shirt."

Sarah giggled. "It wasn't mine. It was yours."

"I thought it looked familiar." She stared at Sarah's pants. "Mine, too?" Sarah nodded sheepishly.

The doctor came through the door, stripping off his gloves. He put them and his mask in his cap as he walked over. "Well, young lady, there's a fellow in there that should be thankful you got him here when you did. We sewed up the nasty gash in his head and taped his arm to his chest. He's weak, lost a lot of blood, but we're pumping a couple of fresh pints into him. We'll keep him overnight for observation, but he should feel a lot better by morning."

"Can I see him?" Sarah asked.

"Keep it short. He's still pretty groggy.

Sarah stood. The room started to spin. She wobbled and fell back onto the couch. "Whew, I'm a little dizzy."

All heads turned as an elderly couple rushed through the Emergency Room doorway. The woman was yelling, "Where is he? Where's my son?" Mrs. MacDonald was a member of the hospital board, a large contributor, and known to everyone on staff, so no one questioned when the woman behind the counter pointed to the Operating Room."

Mr. MacDonald jumped ahead to open the door for his wife. She frowned at seeing Sarah on the couch.

Sarah groaned. "Looks like I'll be blamed for this, too." She laid back and covered her face with the blanket.

"Stay here," Nora said. "Let me clock out and we can head home."

Sarah kept an eye on the OR door, expecting Griff's mom to come charging out any minute. "They'll probably want me to pay for the dented fender, and chip in for gas," she grumbled. Luckily, she and Nora were out the door and on their way home before Griff's parents emerged.

Sarah felt completely spent. It took all her strength to make it into the house and up to her room. She flopped on the bed. "I just need to crash for a while."

Nora pulled the spread out from under her and laid it across the girl's shoulders. "That's okay," she said, pulling off Sarah's shoes. "I'll keep an eye on you."

A muffled grunt was the response as Sarah drifted into dreamland.

Sarah woke and blinked her eyes into focus. Moonlight peeking around the shade cast an eerie outline of various objects. *Where...* Recognizing the armoire brought a sigh. She was safe in her own room. Rolling, she kicked off the covers and was surprised to find she was still fully dressed. *What time is it?* She sat up and leaned to see the clock. *Three.* She began processing the events that led to this point. *Oh my gosh, I hope he's alright.*

She walked to the window and raised the shade. The harvest moon hung like a giant saucer in the night sky. She cracked open the window. Strictly by feel, she loosened her belt and let her shorts fall to the floor. Stepping out, she kicked them aside. One by one, she pulled the fabric off each button as she gazed at the star-studded sky and recalled the things Ted's grandfather had told him, especially about moving on. Sarah took a deep breath as a soft, warm breeze moved through her hair and whisked her blouse away from her body. *It's you, isn't it?* One star seemed to twinkle brighter than the others. She closed her eyes. "What are we going to do?" she whispered. "This whole thing about college and working for the FBI was your dream. I'm sorry, but I don't think it's right for me."

She finished getting undressed and into her pajamas. "I'll always cherish our time together, the rides we took, and the thoughts and feelings we shared, but I think it's time for me to let go of the past and see where my destiny leads me." She climbed into bed. "As my special angel, I'd appreciate a little more help keeping me out of trouble." She smiled and closed her eyes.

Nora was on the phone and Duke had his nose in the newspaper when Sarah shuffled into the kitchen. "Good Morning."

Duke raised his head. "Well, little Miss Sleepyhead decided to get up. You missed the fireworks."

"Fireworks?" *Did I sleep for two days?* "What day is it."

Duke got off the stool. "It's the fourth of July, but the fireworks started last night."

"Yes," Nora said into the phone. "She just got up. I'll call you later."

Sarah plopped her butt on a stool.

Nora hung up. "That was Gladys. She thinks we should all go to the corn roast around noon, and maybe a swim after that. Her mom is making fried chicken and potato salad for supper, and later we can watch the fireworks at the farm. How does that sound?"

"Good by me," Duke said, as he folded the paper. "It should be fun. The Legion always does a great job with the corn."

Nora put a glass of orange juice in front of Sarah. "How do you feel?"

"Fine," Sarah said. "I woke at three and put on my pajamas. What fireworks did I miss?"

"To start with," Nora said. "The sheriff stopped by and wanted to talk to you. I told him to come back today." She put a couple pieces of bread in the toaster. "Then Mr. MacDonald called. They wanted to come over."

"Oh my gosh," Sarah crossed her arms on the counter and sank her face on them. "Did he sound mad?"

"Not that I could tell." Nora buttered the toast, spread some jelly, and slid the plate across the counter.

"What did you tell them?" Sarah bit into a slice of toast.

"I said fine."

FINE. They're probably mad that I talked him into going riding. Sarah threw down the bread and jumped off the stool. "I better get dressed. I don't want them to see me in my pajamas." She rushed out of the room.

Sarah had just finished combing her hair and was applying a bit of lipstick when she heard the doorbell. She held her breath until she recognized the sheriff's voice. *All he can do is put me in jail. Griff's folks are probably ready to kill me.*

She had already started down the stairs when Nora called for her. "The Sheriff is here to see you," she said as Sarah passed. "He's in the kitchen."

Sarah walked in and extended her arms.

The Sheriff stood. His one eyebrow arched.

"Aren't you going to cuff me?" she said. "You did come to arrest me, didn't you?"

The officer's belly shook from laughing. "And what, lose the next election?"

It was Sarah's turn to be confused.

"But you're right, young lady." He wagged his finger as he took a seat on one of the stools. "I came to put the fear of God in you. What are we looking at?" He counted on his fingers. "We've got speeding, driving without a license, and leaving the scene of a fender-bender. I could throw the book at you, but I don't think that would sit well with a lot of people in town. You're somewhat of a hero."

Hero? "Me? I don't understand."

"Your actions probably saved the young MacDonald's life. Ordinarily, you'd be facing some serious charges, but under the circumstances we're going to let this slide." He stood and pushed the stool under the counter. "A word of warning, I better not catch you driving around in my county until you're properly licensed, you hear?"

"Yes, sir!" Sarah said. "I won't. I promise."

"Well, then." He tipped his cap. "Y'all have a wonderful fourth of July.

"Thank you," Nora said, as she led the officer to the front door.

"Who taught you to drive?" Duke asked. "I was under the impression you didn't know how."

"Ted down the street showed me how to clutch and shift and Griff let me drive the boat. The rest, I picked up on my own."

Duke shook his head. "That's some mighty fast learning."

"Look who we have here," Nora said, as she walked back into the kitchen. Eleanor MacDonald shot forward as soon as Nora stepped aside. "They were coming up the steps as the sheriff was leaving."

Sarah moved back as the woman rushed to her. Eleanor wrapped her arms around Sarah. "Thank you," she whispered. "Thank you, for saving my son."

Mr. MacDonald waited for his wife to release her grip on Sarah. "The doctor who stitched Griff's forehead said your fast action in compressing the wound and getting him to the hospital no doubt saved his life."

Eleanor butted in. She looked squarely into Sarah's face. "Please, let me apologize. I'm just a silly old woman who thinks she has to protect her son, even though he's a grown man and perfectly capable of choosing who he wants in his life. He's certainly proven that by choosing you." She fumbled in her purse to find a hanky. "I told Terrance the night you left the restaurant, I said, 'I like that girl, she's got spunk.'"

I've got spunk? Sarah smiled. "How is Griff doing? What about his arm? I never got to see him."

"We're on our way to pick him up." Eleanor said. "The shoulder was dislocated. They taped it up. He should be fine. The doctor wants him to take it easy. He figures Griff had a concussion but should be okay in a few days."

Nora stepped forward. "May I offer you coffee or juice?"

"That's okay," John said. "We had breakfast at the Bay Side. We heard Sarah worked there and thought we might see her. The woman, Blanche, told us about the backlash she got from some lakeshore mothers."

"We have a Yacht Club Board meeting on the fifth," Eleanor said, "and I'll have a few words to say about that. Those kids were in the wrong, and I'm going to let people know that."

"Please, don't," Sarah said. "It's okay. I'm going back to Ely in a day or two. Just let things die down on their own."

Mrs. MacDonald was the first to react. "Does Griff know you're leaving?"

Sarah shook her head. "I just decided last night." *In the middle of the night, actually.* "I need to get ready for school. I have a scholarship and I think I would like to work with children. A lot of kids lost their dads in the war…"

"And they're going to need help." Eleanor said. "You'd be wonderful at that." She turned to her husband. "Come, John, let's go and pick up our son."

Mr. MacDonald leaned toward Sarah. "We won't tell him you're leaving. You can do that yourself."

Nora led the way to the front door. She, Duke, and Sarah stood on the porch and waved as the couple backed out of the driveway.

"You know, you don't have to go," Duke said, as they walked back into the kitchen.

"I already told her that," Nora said. Then turning to Sarah, "Are you sure we can't change your mind?"

Sarah shook her head. "I want to spend some time with Mom and Dad and to let them know how much I love them for taking me in and treating me like I was one of their own. I want to visit the Johnson's and share with them what a beautiful and loving daughter they had. But most important, I have to lay Dee to rest. I'm thankful for all the wonderful times we had together, but she's gone, and I have to move on with my life."

Nora hugged her sister. "I am so thankful for the day you came into my life."

Duke put his hand on Sarah's shoulder. "You know you're welcome here any time."

Sarah had to talk around the lump in her throat. "Maybe next summer."

CHAPTER FORTY-THREE
Maybe a Little Racy
for the Times

Sarah stood looking at the two bathing suits, laying side by side in the drawer. The plan was to go for a swim after the corn roast. *Do I dare.* She picked up the blue one with the torn strap that Nora had so nicely repaired but couldn't take her eyes off the bright red two-piece still sitting in the drawer.

"Are you ready?" Nora yelled from the bottom of the stairs. "We should be going."

Sarah turned and faced the opening. "Be down in a minute." She made her choice of suits and hustled off to the bathroom to change.

Nora was already by the car when Sarah came down the front steps. "Did you bring a suit?" she asked, as she got in behind the wheel.

"Got it on." Sarah opened the back door and jumped in.

Duke settled in the passenger seat. "This is going to be one, super fun day, and thanks to the Yacht Club we'll have a nice firework display to cap it off."

Lakeside Park was loaded with people, many of them hovering around the beer tent. Kids chased one another in a game of tag. Men stood two-deep along the rail of the turtle race stand, yelling encouragement for the slow-mover they bet on. Ladies of the Legion Auxiliary were busy selling chances on fine crafted blankets, crocheted scarfs, hats, and table doilies. A cloud of smoke hung over the barbeque pit. Men stalked both sides of the long narrow box made of loosely laid concrete blocks. Ears of corn, still in the husk, laid in rows on the metal grates as the legionnaires continuously turned them for an even roast.

On the Starlight Stage, a four-piece polka band kept things lively with their Oom-pa-pa music. People danced on the grass.

Nora pulled into a parking spot just two blocks from the park. "How lucky can I be? I thought for sure we'd be all the way out to fairgrounds."

Sarah stepped out of the car. "Listen, we can hear the music."

"Gladys said she would go a little early and save one of the picnic tables," Nora said, as she double stepped to keep up with Duke. "Keep an eye out for her."

"I'm having a beer," Duke said, as they reached the park entrance. "What would you girls like?"

"Get us each a coke," Nora said, "and see if you can spot Gladys and her mom. We'll get in the food line."

Sarah took a quick look around hoping to see Griff. *They probably don't come to these 'townie' events.* She kept her head down as they fought their way through the crowd, leery of how people felt about her. She was unaware the music had stopped.

A squawk of microphone feedback preceded the rich baritone voice. "Hey folks, could I have your attention for a minute?"

Sarah's head swung to the stage. She recognized the voice. There he stood, head bandaged and his right sleeve hanging empty. *What is he doing up there?*

Griff pulled the microphone from the stand and strolled across the stage. "I think most of you know me. I live on Chicago Avenue and have been coming to Pine Lake every summer since I was two years old." There was a smattering of applause."

"I'm sure you've all heard about the fight I picked with a tree limb." He waited for the laughter to subside. "The limb won." He moved to the other side of the stage amid a few chuckles. "But this isn't about me. It's about a young lady who came and took this town by surprise. Many of you know about her from the gossip that's been floating around, but please, reserve judgement until you've heard me out. I've gotten to know Sarah Jean Connolly first-hand. She is the strongest, brightest, bravest, most beautiful gal you'll ever meet." The crowd hushed. Everyone stopped to watch and listen. "If it wasn't for her, I probably wouldn't be standing here." His pause was well timed. "This girl went through hell getting me to the hospital. And at the expense of her own personal vanity." Those standing near Sarah turned and smiled. The lump in her throat felt the size of a grapefruit.

He used the microphone to point to his head. "They sewed up a three-inch gash in my noggin. I lost a lot of blood, and the doctor said, 'It's only because she got you here when she did that you are still alive.'" He took a moment to compose himself, then, looking at Sarah, he said, "I know she's about ready to kill me for doing this, but she's standing right over there in the navy blouse." Everyone turned to look where he pointed.

Sarah forced a smile and an abbreviated hand wave.

Griff put the microphone back on the stand. "I would like to publicly thank her for saving my life and I hope you will join me in giving her a big round of applause." He stepped back and began clapping. It was spontaneous. It was loud, and it was long. As the noise subsided, he waved and headed for the side steps. He stopped and returned to the microphone. "There's one more thing. I think she is one very, special lady." The applause rose to another level.

People shouted, wolf -whistled, and patted him on the back as he made his way toward Sarah.

Blanche got to her first and shouted over the noise. "Your job is still open. We'd love to have you back."

"I'm going back to Ely," Sarah shouted, "but hold a spot for me next summer. I'll be a struggling college student in need of a job."

"You got it," Blanche said, and gave her a thumbs up.

Griff finally reached Sarah. He whispered in her ear, "Let's get out of here." Then taking her hand, he led her in the direction of the boat dock as the crowd went back to enjoying the afternoon's festivities.

Sarah looked over her shoulder at Nora and got an approving nod. "Where are we going?"

"I had them gas up the boat. I thought we might go for a ride."

"Are you crazy? How are you going to drive the boat?"

He laughed. "I'm not. You are."

The boat was tied at the end pier. Griff held Sarah's hand as she stepped down into the boat and waited for her to get behind the wheel. "Just keep it under eighty, okay?"

She paused "Wait. Do I need a license to drive the boat?" Her face showed concern.

Griff Laughed. "Of course not. Why do you ask?"

"I promised the sheriff."

"I'm sure he was referring to driving a car…on the street."

Sarah rolled her eyes, embarrassed for asking. She waited for him to untie the boat and ease himself down on the seat before starting the engine. Once he was settled next to her, she pushed the shift lever forward, increased the throttle and began following the channel. "Where should we go?"

"I don't care, just put us in the middle of the lake. We can drift and talk."

"About what?"

"About us."

"I didn't know there was an "us."

"Dang it, Sarah can't you see I'm nuts about you."

They had just passed the last channel marker, so instead of an answer, she gave it the gas. The bow came up, then slowly leveled off and sped forward.

"You handle the boat well," he said, adjusting the bandage on his head.

"It's a lot easier than driving a car, there's not so much clutching and shifting."

"And dodging other cars."

"Right, and the roads are narrow."

"Maybe, I should be thankful I was out cold on the ride to the hospital."

Sarah laughed. "I probably would have scared you to death. I know I was."

They were well past the middle of the lake, and Sarah hadn't made a move to slow down. "This is good," Griff said, as he reached over and brought the engine to an idle. He turned off the key and let the boat drift to a stop. A breeze off the water felt wonderful, but the afternoon sun wasted little time heating up the dark varnished wood surfaces. "It's warm." Griff fumbled to unbutton his shirt with his left hand. "A swim would feel great. It's too bad I didn't let you know my plan. You could have brought a suit."

"I've got one on." She finished unbuttoning his shirt and helped him out of it.

"I'm sorry I can't join you, but you're welcome to dive in."

She looked over the side. "It's too deep here. Can't we go to the inlet, where it's shallow?"

He looked at the east end of the lake. "It's probably shoulder-to-shoulder with people down there. I've got a better idea. We'll go over by Sliding Rock. There's shade and we can tie off on one of the over-hanging tree branches. He waited for her to start the engine before pointing in the direction he wanted her to go.

Sliding Rock was one of the last pieces of shoreline undeveloped. It's sandstone bluffs and steep inclines limited access by land. Sarah eased back on the throttle as they approached shore. "How close do you want me to go?"

"Turn right and go along the shore." He worked the shifter between forward and reverse to come to a stop under a large branch. "If you climb up on the front deck, there's a rope in the hatch."

Sarah stepped around the windshield, knelt, and opened the hatch. She pulled out a length of rope. "What do I do with it?"

"Tie one end to the tree branch and the other to the eye hook in front of the hatch. Leave some slack so the boat can swing in any direction."

Sarah climbed back in the boat. It felt good to be in the shade. She lifted the wet hair off her neck. "Whew, I've worked up a sweat." A cool pine scented breeze brought some relief.

Griff picked up the ladder and hung it over the side. "It's about five feet deep." He lifted the backseat cushion, brought out a towel, and handed it to Sarah. He put the cushion down and took a seat. Hanging his arm over the side, he waved his hand around in the water. "It feels great."

Sarah refolded the towel, hesitant to begin disrobing.

"Is this the same suit that got torn?"

She shook her head. "It's new."

"Well, let's see the new suit."

"You have to close your eyes. I want it to be a surprise." *Why am I being so self-conscious. Half the town saw me driving by in my bra.* "C'mon, close your eyes."

Griff did as he was told. "Okay, let me know when you're ready."

Sarah kicked off her shoes while feverishly unbuttoning her blouse. She dropped her shorts, pulled off her socks, adjusted the straps on the bright red top and was ready to give him the word. In less than a heartbeat she lost her nerve, grabbed the towel, and wrapped it around herself. "Okay," she said.

Griff opened his eyes a little bit at a time. Then straightening, he laughed. "Is it made of terry cloth?"

She slowly let go of the towel and let it fall to the floor. His eyes flew open and he practically swallowed his Adam's apple. Her face flushed as red as the suit.

Griff covered his gaping mouth. "My God, Sarah, you're killing me."

She rubbed her hand across her bare stomach. "It's too revealing, isn't it?"

"Yes…no…I mean…Holy Cow…you look stunning." He struggled to get off the seat.

Before he could get to his feet, she giggled, climbed on the side, and dove into the water. When she surfaced, she wiped the hair from her face and wagged her finger. "You can't get me now."

He slumped back on the seat and watched her lithe body glide through the water. She dove under, came up beside the boat and spit a stream of water at him. She held onto the splash rail and smiled impishly.

He watched the water splash across the top of her breasts and pour in and out of the space between them. "You really know how to torture a guy, don't you?"

She threw a handful of water in his face.

He hurried to wipe the water off the bandage.

"I'm so sorry," she said, pulling herself up. "I didn't mean to get that wet. Is it okay?"

"It's fine. It actually feels good. It's pretty warm up here.

"Why don't you kick off your shoes and put your feet in the water? It'll cool you down." She dipped below the surface.

"It would probably take an ice-cold shower," he mumbled as he stretched to untie his shoes

"Did you say something?" she asked, as she bobbed up.

"Nothing." Using his big toe, he pushed off his socks. He moved to sit on the back deck, swung his legs around, and dangled them in as far as he could. The water came to mid-calf.

"See," she said, taking hold of his ankles. "Doesn't that feel good?"

"I'd like it better if I could be down there with you."

She cupped her hands and drizzled water on his knees and watched it trickle through the web of hair. His eyes darted between her hands and her breasts. It made her self-conscious. "Did you mean it?" she asked.

"Mean what?"

"About me being a very special lady."

"It all depends."

"On what?"

"On whether, if I asked you to marry me, you'd say yes."

There was a long silence. "I want to say yes, but not now, it's way too soon. You've got four years of medical school and your mother would kill me if I messed that up. And I...I haven't decided in which direction I want to go. How would it be if I gave you a firm maybe?"

Griff laughed. "Yes, Mom would definitely kill you. I also think it's important for you to get a degree. I think I'm good with a *firm maybe.*"

"Will you write to me?" she asked, as she pushed away and floated on her back

"Every chance I get."

She breast-stroked herself back to the boat. "There's one more thing."

"What's that?"

"Here we are, practically engaged, and you've never kissed me."

"It not for lack of wanting," he said. "I would have kissed you the night you danced around on the Starlight Stage if you had given me the chance. It seems like something is always getting in the way. Right now, I want to jump in the water and kiss you into tomorrow, but with this banged-up head and useless right wing you'd probably have to save me from drowning."

She laughed. "You stay right there. I'm getting in the boat." She swam to the ladder and pulled herself up. He brought his feet around and stood near the back of the boat. Sarah took two wobbly steps, caught her balance, and walked slowly towards him.

His eyes flashed to every curve and angle of her body. "My God, you're beautiful." He murmured

She put her arms around his neck and slowly brought her chin to meet his. Their lips touched. A tinge of heat and energy surged through her body. He put his arm around her back and drew her to him. He kissed every part of her mouth. His breath was warm and sweet. Spreading her lips, his tongue probed deep into her throat. Sarah's heart raced. She struggled to catch her breath. With her hands on either side of his face, she pushed his tongue and let hers follow it back deep into his mouth. Time stood still. Neither wanted the moment to end.

Beep. Beep. The horn blast and jeers of a passing excursion boat broke the spell. Sarah hid her face against his chest. As soon as the sound indicated the boat had passed, she lifted her head and felt his shirt. "Oh dear, I soaked it." She stepped back and patted the cloth. "Will it hurt the bandage?"

He drew her back. "The bandage is fine, but we probably should be thankful that boat came along, I don't know if I would have been able to control myself."

Sarah rested her head on his chest. She knew in her heart of hearts she would have let him go as far as he wanted. "Me neither," she whispered.

"I think we should go back and join the festivities in the park."

She stepped back and picked up the towel. "I am a little bit hungry." It wasn't a lie, but deep down all she wanted was to kiss him, feel his hands on her breasts, and satisfy the wanting she felt between her legs. She continued to dry herself.

"I don't think you should wear that suit in public."

She giggled. "I'll keep it just for you." She put on her blouse and stepped into her shorts. Once she had socks and shoes on, she climbed to the front deck and untied the boat.

"You're becoming quite a sailor."

"Just one of my many talents." she shot him a sly smile and got behind the wheel.

CHAPTER FORTY-FOUR

A Candlelight Dinner for Two

It was close to five by the time Sarah and Griff got the boat put away and were back to the park. There was only a smattering of people hanging around. One legionnaire poured water on the smoldering charcoal as another stacked the few remaining ears of corn. Others were busy tearing down the food stand. A few of the men helped the ladies take down their booth. On stage, the accordion player wrapped his instrument in a cloth and placed it in its case. The other musicians worked packing up the equipment.

"It looks like we missed everything," Griff said.

Sarah looked at the fire pit. "Do you think they'll let us have one of those ears of corn?"

"Let's ask."

Not only were the men happy to share the leftovers, they striped back the husks, dipped the ears in the melted butter, and sent them off with a handful of napkins.

"Let's sit over there," Griff said, pointing to a picnic table by the water.

Sarah chomped down through two rows of kernels on the way. "I'm starving and this is so good."

Griff laughed and used his napkin to wipe the stream of butter from her chin.

"I've never had corn cooked this way," she said.

"The corn around here is only knee high. They have to bring these up from southern Illinois." He swallowed a mouthful. "Are you planning on leaving?"

The question caught her by surprise. "What makes you ask?"

"The way you asked if I would write to you."

Sarah studied the rows of yellow kernels. "I've been trying to find a way to tell you."

"When?"

"I'm not sure, maybe in a couple of days."

"Why? I thought we'd have more time."

"To get into trouble?" Sarah took a few more bites and threw the rest of her cob in the garbage can. "I need to get back to Ely, spend time with friends and family and get ready for school. You'll be starting in a couple of weeks and I'd have to leave sooner or later. I think it's best to leave now before we get any more involved."

He acknowledged her meaning. "If that's the case, I want to take you to dinner at Greystone…just the two of us. You can wear the black dress. What do you say?"

She lowered her head. "I think that would be wonderful," she said in a low tone.

Griff threw the rest of his corn in the can as they headed for the street. "I'll make a reservation for six-thirty."

Sarah chuckled.

"What's so funny?"

"I was wondering how we were going to manage this, you're in no shape to drive and I promised the sheriff."

He put his finger on her nose. "Don't you worry your pretty little head about that, I have it all figured out. Can you be ready at six-fifteen?"

She looked at the clock in the liquor store window. "Maybe make the reservation for seven. I'll be ready at six-forty-five."

Griff turned and looked around. "Wait, I don't have a car. I'll have to call my folks to give us a ride."

"That's okay," Sarah said. "You go in the store and call. It'll only take me fifteen minutes to walk to Nora's. I'll probably be home before your folks get here."

He bent and gave her a kiss, not a real kiss, like the one on the boat. This was more of a peck. "I'll see you at a quarter to seven."

Once she passed Ted's house, she ran the rest of the way and was out of breath when she reached Nora's front porch. Nora met her as she came through the door.

"Griff is taking me to dinner at Greystone," Sarah said before Nora could hit her with a slew of questions. "I have to be ready by six-forty-five." She unbuttoned her blouse and stormed up the stairs with Nora on her heels.

"Where did you guys go when you left the park?" Nora picked the girl's blouse off the floor and hung it on a hanger.

"For a boat ride." Sarah kicked her shorts to the side.

Nora picked them up. "And?"

"We just rode around and talked." Sarah stopped to admire her bathing suit in the mirror. "I did get to go for a swim."

"So, what did he think of the suit."

The girl flashed her impish smile. "He said I was killing him."

"You didn't…"

"We were kissing when a boat came by tooting it's horn. We decided to come back before things got out of hand."

The air came out of Nora's lungs in a long slow breath. "Smart girl."

Sarah didn't dare tell her sister how little resistance she would have mustered if he had wanted to take things further. "I've got to shower and put some rollers in my hair." She pulled the black dress from the armoire and held it up. "And, I get to wear this again." She took fresh underwear and headed across the hall.

Nora stood outside the bathroom door. "Duke and I are leaving in a few minutes to go to Gladys's. We'll see you later, okay? Don't forget about the big fireworks show."

"I won't." Her reply could be heard over the sound of water hitting the shower walls.

Sarah enjoyed having the time to herself. She put a fresh coat of polish on her nails and waited for the row of curlers along the bottom of her hair to dry. Checking the clock, she was down to the last five minutes of putting the package together. She eased the dress over her head, making sure not to yank on the curlers and slipped into the black flats. She zipped up and looked at herself in the mirror. *It's not a Cinderella gown, but I feel like a princess.*

A horn tooted as she took out the last curler. *Darn, how did he... He couldn't have driven here by himself.* She hastily made a few passes through her hair with the comb. The ends flipped up giving her a striking Lauren Bacall pageboy. The horn tooted a second time. "Hold your horses, I'm coming." She smacked her lips and added a layer of bright red lipstick.

Griff was on the front porch when she came out the door. He was nattily dressed wearing a white dress shirt with the top button open, and navy slacks. A light blue blazer with an empty right sleeve camouflaged the arm taped to his chest. His hair was combed, and a small patch bandage had replaced the hospital head-wrap. Griff's face came alive and his smile stretched from ear to ear. "You get more beautiful every time I see you." He offered his left arm.

The Greystone station wagon stood parked on the drive with Ted holding the back door. "How did you wrangle that?" she asked.

"A big smile for Mrs. Langdon and a big tip for Teddy."

"You're looking lovely tonight," Ted said as Griff helped Sarah in. She giggled at all the attention. Griff slid in beside her. His after-shave was intoxicating. She put her arm around his. *This is what it must feel like to be a movie star.*

Ted wheeled the car under the Greystone porte-cochere. People stood in groups by the front door. Teddy raced around to open the door. Griff stepped out, turned, and offered his hand to Sarah.

"Welcome to Greystone," Ted announced, as Sarah stepped out of the vehicle.

Men stared and the women whispered as they shot curious glances at the couple. Griff ushered Sarah into the restaurant.

The lobby was packed, people hovered around the hostess's stand. Waitstaff dressed in formal attire scurried about the dining room, pouring water, setting down platters of food, and taking orders. Griff raised on his toes and smiled at the hostess.

"I have your table, Mr. MacDonald." She picked up a couple of menus. "Right this way."

Griff nudged Sarah to follow the woman. Sarah felt her cheeks flush. She heard the murmuring and saw the disgruntled faces as they made their way passed the others. A tuxedo-clad waiter stepped aside to let them pass. All the tables were full except for a small candle-lit table in the far corner. "Will this be alright?" The lady asked.

Griff held Sarah's chair. "It's perfect. Thank you." The woman waited for Griff to sit before handing Sarah a menu. "Welcome to Greystone, we hope you enjoy your dinner."

"I'm sure we will," Griff said, accepting his menu.

Sarah pretended not to see the stares and attention they were getting from others in the dining room. She peeked around her menu. "How did you get a reservation?" she whispered. "I'm sure they had to have been booked for weeks."

Griff coughed his reply under his breath. "Eleanor MacDonald wields a lot power."

"Your mother…"

He put his finger to his lips. "It's her way of saying thank you."

He opened his menu. "I believe we were at this point the last time, so may I suggest we start by sharing a shrimp cocktail. We'll skip the Caesar salad, and each have a small Filet Mignon and baked potato. Is medium okay?" He saw her puzzled look. "Do you like your steak with a hot pink center?" That she understood. "This way we can save lots of room for their Chocolate Delight dessert. It's a fudge brownie, with two big scoops of vanilla ice cream, covered with hot fudge, and topped with whipped cream and a maraschino cherry." He closed the menu. "Does that sound alright to you?"

Sarah nodded. "The dessert sounds delicious." She was surprised how much she enjoyed the large prawns dunked in red horseradish sauce. Griff had to order a second serving to get a couple of shrimps for himself. Eyes in the room watched their every move.

"Are you sure you want to leave," he asked. "There is so much more we could do."

"And more time to get in trouble." Catching Griff's raised eyebrows, she realized how that sounded. "I didn't mean you and me." Her face turned red. "I was thinking of the liquor store business and the townspeople."

Griff studied his glass of water. "I suppose with this arm we'd be limited with what we can do. We couldn't water ski."

"Or ride horses."

He looked down his nose at her. "*That* would definitely be off the list."

The waiter pushed his cart to the table and set a platter with a sizzling steak in front of her. "Be careful the plate is very hot." He served Griff with the same admonishment. He looked at Sarah "What would you like on your baked potato?"

She shrugged and looked to Griff.

"We'll play it safe, butter only for both of us," Griff said.

The waiter pinched the potatoes and heaped mounds of the yellowy cream on top. "Enjoy," he said, setting a steaming potato by each of them. He backed away, taking his cart with him.

Sarah had never eaten a piece of beef as tender or tasted as wonderful as this. She even enjoyed the Bearnaise sauce that came with it.

"I hope you left room for dessert," the waiter said, as he gathered their empty plates.

Griff moved his water glass aside. "We're going to tackle the Chocolate Delight."

"Good choice. One Death by Chocolate coming up." The man shouldered the tray of dirty dishes and left.

"It's hard to believe you've only been here a little more than a week," Griff said. "I've forgotten what life was like before meeting you. Do me a favor, don't ever get rid of that dress." He leaned closer. "Or that bathing suit," he whispered. "You look stunning in both." He looked into her eyes. Seeing you right now is the way I want to remember you when you're gone."

Sarah covered her eyes. "You shouldn't say things like that. You make me feel bad. It won't be forever; I'll be back next summer."

He groaned and fell back in the chair. "That's a whole year from now." He bolted forward. "What are you doing for Christmas? Would you mind if I came and visited you in Ely? I could meet your parents. See where you live."

Sarah squeezed his hand. "That…that would be wonderful."

"It's still a long way off," he said, "but I'm sure I'll need a break from school by then."

I'm sure I will too. She let go of his hand when the waiter set down the mountain of chocolate. "That's sinful," she said, as she picked up a spoon. "We'll never be able to eat all of that."

"We can die trying." He spooned the cherry out of the whipped cream. "Open up," he said, before popping the candied fruit into her mouth.

She savored the taste. "Thank you. I've never had one of those before."

They alternated scooping out mouthfuls of cake and ice cream. Sarah was surprised when it came to the bottom of the bowl, they playfully fought over the last spoonful.

A loud bang accompanied Griff putting his spoon in the empty dish. "They're starting the fireworks."

"Where can we watch them?"

He motioned for the waiter, signed the check, and held Sarah's chair. "We watch from the patio."

Unfortunately, everyone had the same idea and all of the chairs were filled. "I guess we should have thought of this sooner," he said.

"That's alright." Sarah tugged on his hand. "Let's just walk down by the water." A loud report overhead sent a shower of red and green particles of fire across the sky.

Sarah leaned against the trunk of a large oak tree and pulled Griff to her. "Do you have any more of those kisses left?" she whispered.

He put his hand above her head and pressed his lips to hers as another cannon shot exploded. His tongue probing the inside her mouth and his chest heaving against her breasts sent another kind of fireworks deep to her core. She visualized herself lying naked next to him, enjoying every kiss, every touch. She pulled back. "I really have to go."

He pushed away from the tree. "Now?"

"Tomorrow," she said, "I think it would be best if I head back to Ely, tomorrow." She didn't dare tell him of her thoughts, her wanting and desires. Another shell burst overhead. She put her head against his chest. "I love you, but this is just so hard."

"You're right. I don't know how much longer I can keep my hands off you." He looked up at lights from the restaurant. "We've had a good time, a wonderful dinner, but we better not let our emotions get the better of us. Would you like to go home?"

They walked up the hill. "I guess I'm not much into fireworks tonight," she said, "at least not the ones in the sky."

Ted opened the car door. "Going home early?"

"Pooped," Griff said, waiting for Sarah to get in. "It's been a long day. She's ready to go home."

Ted closed the door and got behind the wheel. "Ain't much of a show, anyway, shooting one off every three to four minutes is really dragging things out. I about fell asleep."

Sarah nestled in Griff's arms. "Will you come and see me off?"

"What time is the bus?"

"Around noon."

"Teddy," Griff said. "Stop here." He turned to Sarah. "Let's get out and walk. It's such a beautiful night and I'm afraid it's ending too soon."

Ted pulled to the curb. He stuck his head out of the opened window. "Should I leave? How are you going to get home?"

"Just turn off your headlights and follow us. It's only a few more blocks."

Sarah giggled. "The gossip ladies are going to be burning up the telephone wires when this gets out."

"Let them." He took her hand. "I'm glad you came to Pine Lake. I've always thought of the place as being a little dull, but you breathed life into it."

"I'm glad I came."

"It's like we were destined to meet.

"Meeting you is a big part of it, but I've learned so much about myself…and about life." She looked up at the stars. "It's been less than a month since my friend died. I was crushed. I wondered if I could survive, but I've come to realize that no one is born to lose in life. We each have to travel our own path and see where destiny takes us."

"What about us? You did give me a firm maybe."

"Time apart will tell whether this is real or just a summer fling." Standing on the curb in front of Nora's place, she put her hands on his chest, adjusted his jacket, and straightened his shirt over his bandaged arm. "Maybe we should say good night here." He moved close to kiss her. "Make it nice," she whispered. "Remember, Ted's over there watching."

The kiss was short, but he held onto her for the longest time. Letting go, he backed off. "That'll have to hold me until Christmas." He stepped off the curb. "I'll see you tomorrow at the bus stop." He stared at her as he walked backwards as if creating an image of her in his mind. She watched until he got in the car. Both he and Ted waved as they drove off.

CHAPTER FORTY-FIVE

A Ticket to Ely

Sarah was showered, dressed, and putting the last of her things in the suitcase when Nora appeared in the doorway. "How was your dinner?" she asked. "You were already asleep when Duke and I got back from Gladys's. Didn't you watch the fireworks?"

"The dinner was wonderful, and we did watch a little of the fireworks, but we were both tired and decided to call it a night. I hope you don't mind; I'd like to wear these Levi's on the bus, it gets cold going through the mountains."

"Be my guest. You did pack the black dress, didn't you?"

"I did, thank you."

"So, is Griff okay with you leaving?"

"He'd like me to stay, but we both have school to get ready for. It's probably best to leave now." *For everyone.* "I left the red bathing suit in the armoire. I won't need it in Ely, and it will save a lot of explaining to Mom."

"That's for sure," Nora said, as she closed the cabinet door. "Maybe it will be at the height of fashion next year?"

"Or, I'll work up the courage to wear it anyway." They laughed.

There was a long moment of silence. Nora put her arms around her sister. "I'm so happy you came, even if it was just for this little while. Promise me you'll come back next summer."

"I promise." *That's a long way off, but that is the plan.* She closed the suitcase. "I'm going to run to the drugstore and buy my ticket and make sure of the time the bus comes through town."

"Do you need money? I can drive you?"

"I still have a little bit of graduation money and I'd prefer to walk off a bunch of nervous energy."

"How about something to eat before you go? Duke left early. He's got all those boats to service and put back in their stalls."

Sarah shook her head and patted her stomach. "Butterflies. I'll eat something when I get back."

Sarah strolled down the sidewalk. The air was light, filled with the scent of lilacs. Unlike the previous few days when the town was loaded with tourists, there were only a few cars on the street. She gazed at the houses and yards along the way, painting a mental picture to take with her to. Downtown showed little sign of life. She counted less than a dozen people on the main street.

The lady behind the counter at the drugstore was very efficient in writing out the ticket. She handed it to Sarah along with a bus schedule. Looking back at the large clock on the wall, she said, "Southbound hits town about noon. I suggest being here by eleven-thirty in case he's early."

Sarah smiled and handed the woman a twenty-dollar bill.

"A one-way to Salt Lake is seventeen dollars," the woman said, as she handed Sarah the ticket. "You'll have to pick up the Pony Express to get to Ely."

Sarah chuckled and took the ticket. "I know, I've made the trip before."

"Then you know it's a small intrastate bus company and you don't have to ride horseback all the way to Ely." She made eye contact with Sarah. "But from what I hear, you could probably handle doing that too. That was a good thing you did for that young Mister MacDonald."

"Thank you. I'll make sure I'm here in plenty of time to catch the bus."

Ted Dobriski rush out as Sarah walked by his house. "Wait up," he yelled.

Sarah waited, not knowing if he had something to say about last night, or about Griff.

"Debbie and I are going steady," he said.

She touched his arm. "That's great."

"After dropping off you and Griff, I drove to her place and picked her up. We caught the last of the fireworks show and took a moonlight swim at the inlet." He flashed a broad smile. "If it wasn't for you, we may never have gotten together."

"I'm happy things are working out," Sarah said. *I hope I'm making the right decision about leaving.*

Nora was busy at the counter when Sarah walked into the kitchen and flopped down on one of the stools.

"I'm fixing a lunch and some munchies to take with you on the bus." She set a glass of juice and some sliced fruit in front of Sarah. "You need to put a little something in your stomach."

"I know, but I'm really not hungry." She popped a strawberry into her mouth.

"Gladys called. She and her mom are coming to see you off."

"That's good, I feel bad. I never got to spend time with them."

"They're fine. We joked about you being in love."

They turned to the noise of the slamming screen door. Duke entered the kitchen and hung his cap on the rack. "It's all over town. Mrs. MacDonald went to the yacht club meeting this morning and raised holy hell. She told those mothers they needed to do a better job of teaching their boys the difference between right and wrong and that it was totally unfair the way you were treated."

"She did?" Sarah came off the stool.

"You came all the way home to tell us that?" Nora said. "I thought you were buried in work."

"Yeah, I've got to get back, but I wanted a chance to say goodbye to Sarah, and to give her this." He handed her a small gift-wrapped box.

"What is it?" Her fingers tore at the paper.

"A little something, I think you might like."

Nora edged closer to see what was in the box.

Sarah lifted the cover and pulled out the silver charm bracelet with the canoe and seahorse She held it up. "Oh look, there's a water skier, too. I love it."

"I had them put that on. It will remind you of your summer…or at least part of it, here in Pine Lake," he said.

Nora helped Sarah put it on her wrist. "He told me you mentioned seeing it in Warner's window, but he did this all on his own."

Sarah came around the counter and gave Duke a big hug. "I had forgotten all about it. Thank you for getting it for me."

"Have a safe trip," he said. "And if you promise to come back next summer, I'll teach you how to drive the Harley."

Nora swatted him on the back. "You'll do no such thing."

"I would love that," Sarah said. "You've got a deal."

Nora threw her hands up. "Dear God, what next?"

Duke gave Sarah a kiss on the forehead and pecked one on Nora's cheek. "I've got to get back to the dock." He grabbed his cap. "Say hi to the Jensen's for me," he yelled, as he ran out the back door.

Nora shook her head. "That man is going to have a heart attack someday if he doesn't slow down."

Sarah stood holding her suitcase as Nora searched her purse for the car keys. "Damn, they have to be here some place." She squinted and scrunched her nose, determine not to let the tears flow. "I know I'm going to cry," Nora said, as she yanked out the keys. "I just hope I don't make a spectacle of myself."

"I haven't heard from Griff. He said he'd be there."

"I'm sure he'll be there." Nora led the way out the door.

When Nora turned the corner onto the main drag, they were surprise to see a crowd of about two dozen milling about in front of the drugstore. Nora applied light pressure to the brake petal. "What do you suppose that's all about?" The crowd spread apart as she pulled to the curb.

Blanche opened Sarah's door. "Did you think you could just sneak out of town?" she said. "Word flew through town that you had bought a ticket on the noon bus. We all want to give you a nice send-off."

Sarah stepped out of the car. She saw Gladys and her mom standing in the background and gave them a wave of her hand. She looked at Nora. "I don't believe this."

Nora brushed back a tear. "That's one thing about small towns, people can be cruel, but they are also some of the most caring folks in the world."

Sarah stretched her neck to find Griff, without success. A woman ushered three boys to the front of the group. "These young men have something to say to you." It was the boys from the break-in. One by one they apologized for any trouble they may have caused her. Sarah found it hard to swallow and simply smiled and nodded her approval.

A horn blast from the bus had people scurrying onto the sidewalk.

"I'm holding a spot open for you next summer," Blanche shouted, before being pushed aside.

Sarah gave a quick nod before swinging around to look for Griff. Nora handed the suitcase to the driver and the sack lunch to her sister. They hugged one more time. "Call when you get home."

The driver pushed his way to the opened door. "Alright, who's getting on? Let's move it. I've got a schedule to keep."

"Just one more minute," Sarah said, as she saw Griff fighting his way through the crowd.

"I'm sorry," he said as he made it to her side. He pointed to the arm taped to his chest. "I had to wait for Mom to get home from her meeting." He put his good arm around Sarah. "I love you and I'm going to miss you." They kissed like there was no tomorrow. The crowd whistled and clapped.

"C'mon. C'mon, let's go," barked the driver.

"Write me," she said, as she broke free and boarded the bus.

"I'll see you at Christmas," he yelled, as the door swung shut.

Sarah sat by the window and waved to everyone. She made eye contact with Nora and then with Griff. "I love you," she mouthed, as the bus pulled away. As much as she tried, she couldn't hold back the tears. She leaned forward, buried her face in her hands, and cried as the memories of the last few days streamed through her mind. Christmas seemed so far off.

She finally sat up and leaned back against the seat. She pulled an apple out of the sack and took a bite as the green Wisconsin countryside roll past her window. "This is it, Dee," she said softly. "It's time for me to let you rest in peace and find my own way in life. Hopefully, I can count on you to be my special angel and watch over me along the way." She chuckled. "It's hard to believe it's only been thirty days since you've been gone, but you have to admit, it's been one wild and crazy month." She held up her arm and watched the skier charm dangle from the bracelet.

*****

About the Author

Joe grew up in Green Lake, Wisconsin. In school, he divided his time between sports and carrying the lead in a number of plays. He also did some directing. He uses his theatrical background in his writing to build memorable characters, strong dialogue, and compelling story lines.

"Born to Lose" follows "Born Yesterday" and "Battle Born" in the series that follow the experiences of a lovable cast against the backdrop of small, resort town living, in what Joe calls "true to life" stories.

Joe has a total of five books currently available on Amazon.com. He's also authored many short stories, with many chosen for publication in the last five Henderson Writers Group's Writer's Bloc anthologies.

Visit Joe's website, www.joevanrhyn.com for the latest information on upcoming projects. You can also contact him at jjvanrhyn@cox.ne

Check out the first two books in the series

BORN YESTERDAY

Finding love while searching for the past

It's the spring of 1964. The people of Pine Lake, Wisconsin are skittish when a stranger is found unconscious in the park.

His wounds suggest he'd been severely beaten. He subsequently slips into a coma.

With nothing in his pockets, and no one coming forward, his identity remains a mystery.

Waking only complicates matters, when the man has no recollection of who he is or what happened to him.

ALL JOE'S BOOKS ARE AVAILABLE ON AMAZON.COM

BATTLE BORN

It's 1945. The war is over. Army nurse Nora Jensen just wants is an uneventful life free of military regulations.

A chance meeting with a fifteen year old girl could once again put Nora in a life and death situation.

journey with her as she tries to stay one step ahead of the law and those who would tear her life apart. A lover from the past may be her only ally.

For the latest news on upcoming projects go to: www.joevanrhyn.com

Check out two of Joe's other books!

The Kid's Last Fight

Delivers a Punch and a Tender Love Story

Johnny "The Kid" Whalen blew his chance to fight for a championship and is now fighting for peanuts in small out-of-the-way towns.

When a boxer, in a highly touted bout is injured, Johnny hopes it's his chance to get back into big-time boxing.

Instead, faced with life threatening decisions and his manager's sinister plan, Johnny's boxing career might end abruptly. An old acquaintance with a shocking revelation further complicates Johnny's life and could jeopardize the lives of those he holds dear.

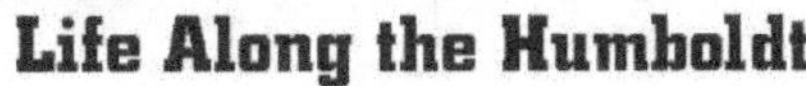

JOE'S BOOKS ARE AVAILABLE ON AMAZON.COM

A Novella Depicting Early Life in the Battle Born State.

Life Along the Humboldt

In April of 1862, newly-weds, John and Sara Graham left St. Joe, Missouri as part of a wagon train heading for California.

For five months, these determined pioneers trudged across verdant prairies, snaked through narrow canyons, and made their way over treacherous mountains.

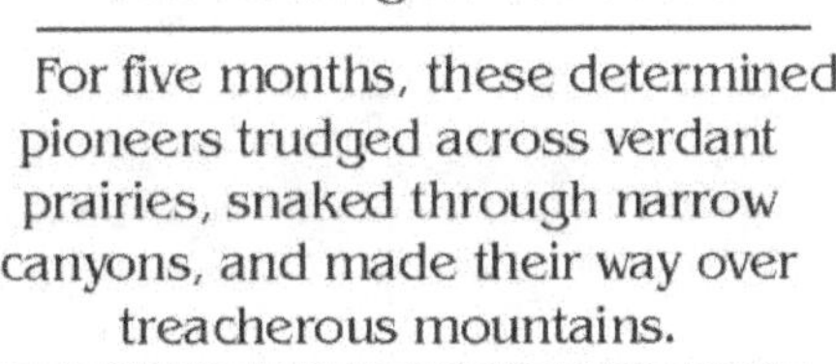

They sloshed through mud, baked under scorching sun and endured whatever Mother Nature threw at them. They Settled in Northern Nevada. Their struggles didn't end there, they had only just begun.

For the latest news on upcoming projects go to: www.joevanrhyn.com